Cover design by Ashley Ruggirello

Edited by Kisa Whipkey

Book design by Ashley Ruggirello

Electronic ISBN: 978-1-942111-56-6

Paperback ISBN: 978-1-942111-58-0

This is a work of fiction. Names, characters, places and incidents are either the product of the author's imagination or are used fictitiously, and any resemblance to actual persons, living or dead, business establishments, events or locals is entirely coincidental.

❀ Created with Vellum

ALSO BY J.M. FREY

The Accidental Turn Series

Touch the
Sky!

THE SKYLARK'S SONG

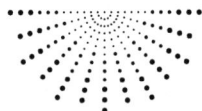

J.M. FREY

REUTS PUBLICATIONS

"This book soars with action, adventure and clever world building. The details are perfect, the characters are snappy, clever and real. Strap on your seatbelts, it's quite the ride!"
—Arthur Slade, bestselling author of the *Mission Clockwork* series.

"A romantic, action-packed and just plain fun adventure, *The Skylark's Song* is a classic superhero origins story that also manages to subvert tropes and expectations. I give it five fabulous jet packs."
—Adrienne Kress, *The Friday Society* & *The Explorers* series

"Some adventures soar more than others, *The Skylark's Song* takes to the sky and never looks back. Full of aerial battles, potential betrayals, political and philosophical chess matches, all combined with romance, humor, and, best of all, heart."
—Peter Soloman, *Henry Franks*

"If you're looking for a rollicking steampunk adventure, *The Skylark's Song* has it all—action! Intrigue! Romance! Cool contraptions! The Skylark is my new favourite [sic] heroine!"
—Rob St. Martin, *Sunset Val*

"I'm a big fan of J.M. Frey's *Accidental Turn* series

that I was stoked to pick up this title. Though steampunk dystopia isn't my go-to flavour [sic] of book, I enjoyed how thorough the world was. I am always happy to see diversity in characters, and women being badass is a win for me, so that made me want to read more. The relationships got steamy (pun intended) and the dynamic of how that came about was a hard read, but I liked that it wasn't a formulaic approach to fantasy romance; it got me mad and sympathetic and a whole mess of emotions while reading it. I'm looking forward to the next installment as I need to know what happens next!"

—Adrianna Prosser, *Stories Like Crazy* podcast

"*The Skylark's Song* is both a fantastic adventure story and a sensitive look at the interplay between power and attraction in a relationship. Can't wait for book two!"

—Liv Rancourt, *Vespers*

For Poppa—
who told us it didn't matter if we were ditch-diggers, as long as we were
the best damn ditch-diggers we could be.

AND THE BEES SHALL FOLLOW ME HOME

(Traditional Sealie Folk Ballad)

My house is all around me
And no matter where I roam
As long as there is field and sky
The bees shall follow me home.

Oh Gods, how you do smile
On the man who treads on foam
Of sea shore bright, and forest crisp,
Where bees do follow me home.

The hive is on my wagon,
And honey's on my tongue
There's mead within my flagon
And buzzing my ears rung.

So Gods, I need no cities,
No wealth from bankers who loan,
All that I need is my family and my wagon,
And bees who follow me home.

And the Gods are our Queens
And we the Sealies her drones
And we do as they bid
And we follow them home.

CHAPTER ONE

ROBIN THUMPED HER TRAY DOWN ON THE TABLETOP, SLOSHING HOT tea down the side of Al's arm.

"Robin," he moaned, dabbing at his sleeve. Al had hair like a chimney brush and a face like a brick wall—all square bones and reddish-brown skin. But Robin had known him long enough to see the playful smirk behind the theatrical frown he leveled at her.

She snorted at his mock distress. "What? It's not like you've washed it in the past month."

"But now I'll *have* to." He punched the top of her arm hard enough to leave a small bruise. His stature had intimidated her the day they met—their first day, when the new group of Sealie kids had been sorted and handed off to instructors like livestock. But now, at seventeen, her arms were just as corded with muscle as his, though she'd never really achieved the sheer width of shoulder that he had, nor his expanse of height. Grinning, Robin punched back.

Then she elbowed Al to the side and wriggled into the gutter of space between him and the snotty blond kid whose name she never bothered to remember. She set her oversized canvas

1

satchel and its precious cargo under the bench with more care than she had shown her meal tray, bracketing it between her knees.

Child apprentices started young in the shipyards. Fourteen if they could afford to stay in school. Eleven if they needed the money. Robin had needed the money, so she'd had six years to develop the whippet musculature of a mid-flight engineer. And since she was smaller, shorter, and lighter than most of her colleagues, Robin's pilot, Wade, could bring up two more cases of ammunition than his cohorts. Robin was not-so-secretly grateful that he liked that advantage, too. It meant that she didn't have to work in a laundry, cleaning stained shirts like Al's with her mother.

Al made a dramatic, twisting face of agony, clutching his arm where her elbow had landed.

Robin snorted at him. "Oh, shut up, you baby."

Al offered a lopsided grin before they both turned their attention to the small breakfast of rationed fruit, meager portions of sausage made with a filling Robin tried not to think too much about, and dry bread. She sipped her tea. It was bitter, strong-brewed and twice-strained, with only the faintest ghost of honey to coat her tongue. Perfect. She wrapped her hands around the battered tin cup, reveling in the way the warmth spread throughout her stomach and chest. It dispelled the last of the early morning chill and the exhaustion that still clung to her.

She'd spent the earliest hours of the morning picking her way carefully through the ore-dawn fog and brick-dust haze kicked up by the enemy aeroships that had bombed part of the factory fields outside of town. Most people dove beneath their beds when the warning bells started to clang in the middle of the night. Robin threw on her working leathers, shoved her feet in her boots, snatched up a large canvas satchel, and went a-picking.

"Hey, you awake?" Al asked, his voice low and tender even as he tugged on the length of her dark brown braid. It made her far shoulder knock into the blond kid, who sneered in return and shuffled a bit further down the crowded bench.

"Barely," Robin said, turning back to Al. "Tea helps."

"Gift from the gods," Al agreed. "Been home yet?"

Robin glanced at the room around her before she answered. "This isn't home? There are bees enough for me."

The cavernous hangar that served as the Air Patrol's canteen rang with the clink of metal utensils. The air hung heavy with the scent of baking bread, fruit just this side of being too ripe, burnt fat, engine grease, and the slightly sour tang of too many people wearing yesterday's undershirts. She had eaten in this very room, at this very table, nearly every breakfast of every day since she was old enough to apprentice with the Air Patrol. She only ever spent time in her parents' crumbling row house when there was a holiday to observe, or an on-the-job injury from which to recover (those had been blessedly rare, seeing as the Air Patrol docked pay for days missed). To her, this room smelled and sounded more familiar and welcoming than the place her parents called home. That was just a building to sleep in. This was where her heart lived.

"Buncha bees crowded around one flower don't make it a hive," Al said, but he had siblings to go home to, and parents who approved of his choice of apprenticeship.

"Close enough for honey," Robin said flippantly. "Doesn't matter, anyway. We're not due to go up until day after tomorrow."

Al wrinkled his nose at her. "I thought your gearbox was busted, and your glider was out of the running for this mission?"

"Don't *invite* the ill-luck. Omens," Robin said, crossing the fingers of her free hand and brushing the luck off her shoulder. No point in letting it settle. Beside her, the snotty kid stiffened and shot a heated glare her way. "Oh, what?" she snapped at him. "It's not like your All-Mother gives a toss."

The kid sniffed, far too officious for someone in the striped coveralls of an apprentice, and went back to his conversation with the person on his other side. Both of them were Benne, the upper-class who worshipped only one goddess and, in Robin's Sealie mind, called bad luck down upon themselves by ignoring the rest.

Not that Robin really cared who worshipped whom. Or didn't.

She'd rather be here, hemmed in with other Saskwyans who shared her sense of patriotic purpose, than anywhere else she could fathom. She was comfortable here, surrounded by chattering boys and girls in their striped coveralls, by the burly corporal smiths, by the whippet-strong mid-flight sergeants and the set-jawed pilots, the grim officers and the dedicated serving staff.

This was a place where she knew her place.

This was where Robin had meaning and motivation, and she felt grateful every day that at the end of her morning walk, the shipyards waited for her. Robin cared about her pilot, her glider, her missions. She cared about the war in a general sort of way, but only in that she cared about doing everything in her meager power to make it end. She cared more about the feel of the air as it skimmed her ears when she opened the bomb doors while they were flying, about the way it caressed her skin under her leathers where it blew in through the seams. She cared about the only freedom she had; she cared that, when it was just her and her pilot up there, nobody cared who she worshipped, or kept her on a rigorous base schedule, or chased her down if she was out past her people's curfew.

She cared about the freedom that lived between the clouds.

Robin nudged Al's leg with her own, then looked down meaningfully and tapped the canvas satchel with the toe of her boot.

"Oh, yeah?" Al said, eyebrows climbing.

"Yeah."

The warehouses that stored the components for the

Saskwyan aircraft known as gliders were the new target of the near nightly bombing runs, and mid-flights had to get resourceful if they wanted to keep their charges in the sky. Even if that meant illegal scavenging among the debris in the factory fields.

Wade knew it. The officers knew it. In fact, the only people who didn't seem to know it were the ones who had the power to sign the requisitions orders. The general of this particular base kept refusing parts requests. Whether it was because he knew that the mid-flights had taken to scavenging and approved (despite its legal ambiguity), or because the Saskwyans had been on the losing side of the war for the better part of ten years and there was nothing *left* to requisition, Robin didn't know. What she did know was that it made her and her cohorts more resourceful on the ground, which taught them a desperate creativity that served them well in the air.

Despite that, Al raised his right hand and waggled his thumb at her, the meaning clear.

"I'm fine. There was a close one—had to climb a tree, thought the dog was gonna give me away. But I'm fine. See? Still attached." She held out her hand in demonstration, only a little surprised when Al took it in one of his own, as if he needed to check. His forge-rough skin looked all the redder beside hers, which was brown as her mama's best honey and tanned gold from her time up in the sunlight. "Besides," she went on gently, "what's worse? Having no thumbs? Or falling out of the sky in the middle of no-man's-land?"

"You couldn't work without thumbs," Al said, forcing lightness. "Could get married, though." His finger started to trace a line down her palm, and Robin snatched her hand back.

"Ugh. Papa would love that," Robin complained, scrubbing her palm on her leather trousers, unsettled by the open gentleness of Al's suggestion. "He's been trying to talk me around to it, wants me to leave the heavy lifting to the boys. Has been ever since I got my woman's blood. As if suddenly being mature means that I'm too stupid and weak to continue doing what we've been doing since we were eleven."

Al wrinkled his flat nose. Robin shoved him, grinning, desperate to yank them back into the playful banter from earlier.

"You're so easy to gross out," she laughed.

"You're in a good mood," Al lobbed back with a smirk.

"Don't I have a right to be?"

"Sure, but keep it down. You're being an ass."

"You're both asses," the snotty blond kid muttered.

Al farted in agreement, and Robin shoved him again, hiding her grin behind her teacup. "Al," she chided. She wasn't offended, though. Boys were stupid. It didn't matter if they were Benne or Sealie; it was a universal ailment. A fact of nature and the will of the gods. There was nothing that Robin could do about it, even if she'd cared to.

Shoving back, Al said, "It's not my ass that's his problem, is it, Fron?"

The blond kid's eyes dropped to Robin's behind. His ears turned bright red, and he yanked his gaze away. He pivoted on the bench, putting his shoulder to them, and concentrated on his plate. Robin, who worked just as long and hard as every other mid-flight sergeant in the yard, had a rear no fatter than any of the other folks who did her job. Fat bottoms meant too much weight in the rear of the glider, and that meant getting left on the ground.

"My ass is not fat," Robin hissed at Al, choosing not to dignify Al's dig with the much deserved slap to the back of the head that it called for.

"Sure it is," Al said, leaning in to match her whisper for whisper. He held his hands apart an insulting length. "It's gone like this, all wide and jiggly."

"Those are hips," Robin snapped. "Ladies have them."

Al grinned. "You ain't no lady, Robin Arianhod."

"Fine. *Women*, then." Robin sniffed and took another sip of tea. "I still don't see what his rudding problem is."

"Your ass . . . I said so." Al gave her a look like she'd had fallen out of a glider one too many times. "He stares at it."

Robin straightened, aghast. "Why in the name of the gods would anyone stare at my ass?"

"I know," Al said. "These are much prettier." He made a reach for her breasts. Robin smacked the back of his hand with her metal cup. Al laughed and pulled it back.

"Omens!" he said, shaking his hand and blowing theatrically on his knuckles. "Thank the goddess of the hearth for delicate, demure women."

Robin smirked at him. "Thank the god of the woods for men built like gliders."

Al's blocky face screwed up, puzzled. "Gliders?"

"Yeah—grab their control stick the right way, and you can lead them anywhere you want." Robin reached down to show him, but he grabbed her wrist before her hand could connect, braying with laughter.

"Oh, keep it down!" Fron snapped.

"Peace, Fron," Robin said back, trying to keep her light mood. "No one asked you."

"*Undignified*," Fron sneered.

Robin laughed harder. "Prig," she volleyed in return.

Fron grumbled something else and deliberately ignored her, as if this was supposed to be some sort of horrible slight. Ridiculous.

Al, bored with Fron's airs, flipped back the flap of the satchel, trying to be subtle—which wasn't easy for him. "What shape is it in?"

"Needs some work," she said quietly, letting the general noise of the people around them hide their conversation. No point in discussing stolen goods out loud in the open, after all.

The gearbox was only slightly mangled from the factory that

had dropped on top of it. It was the kind used in the pulleys that operated the aircraft's yoke. It was dappled with rust and not so bent out of shape that she couldn't bang it back into serviceable condition at the forge. The intake was crushed, though, a mangled bit of chain dangling forlornly from the mouth. She'd have to reshape that. But only one lever was missing, and she could make a replacement easily.

Taking a thoughtful bite of his bread, Al looked back up. "Better'n I figured. I'll ready a forge after breakkie, then," he said, a spray of crumbs sprinkling the table between them. Robin got her hand over her cup just in time to keep her tea from getting contaminated. Robin shot him a look. "I wish you'd be more careful, though," Al said gently. His dark eyes got wide and sincere, and Robin looked away, swallowing heavily.

She hated when Al looked at her like that, like he was looking for something in her gaze, something she didn't know how to give him. Or if she even wanted to.

She shoved a wrinkly apple chip in her mouth. "I always am."

"I just don't like thinking about you, and the dogs, and the night-guard's knife—"

"Oh, gods, now you sound like Papa!" She tickled at his ribs, knowing it would make him squirm. "I scavenge. I have scavenged. I will continue to scavenge. Conjugate it any which way you want. It doesn't change the fact that I'm gonna do what I gotta do to keep me and Wade in the air."

Fron's spine got, if possible, even stiffer. "Captain Perwink, if you please."

"I don't please," Robin bit off.

"You speak about that scrubbed-up pilot as if he's your friend," Al pointed out.

"He invited me to use his name."

Fron made a sound of shocked disgust, even as Al said, "You should still use his rank in public, Robin—"

"You should respect his rank at all times, you—"

"Hey, shut it!" Al barked, jabbing one blunt finger in Fron's face. "She wasn't talking to you."

"Al, I don't need you to fight my battles."

"This ain't no hardship—"

"No."

Fron scowled and deflated. His fingernail picked furiously at a scuff in his tray, his jaw working hard.

Al glowered at Robin, and then apparently decided to try a different tack. "Scuttlebutt's already started today. Yesterday, the Coyote—" He stopped, clicked his teeth shut, screwed his eyes closed, and then went on: "How many?"

Robin shook her head sharply, back and forth, just once. "Four. Two pilots, two mid-flights. Same as always. No bodies."

"That could have been you, Robin," Al said. "He's ruthless. They say he steals the corpses."

Robin sucked in an annoyed breath and rolled her eyes, even as she brushed the invitation to ill-luck off her shoulders. "They also say that he eats them to gain mystical powers. And that he's a spirit from the aether, or a hobgob from the bottom of the world. It's all just fairy tales."

"I'm being serious, Robin."

"So am I."

"You could have been shot down. And we would have been left with nothing to bury. Come work with me. Be a forge-drone. Be safe, on the ground."

"Nobody is safe," Robin sighed wearily. "Even on the ground."

"Robin, every time you go up there, you could—"

"But I wasn't."

"You could have—"

"So what?" Robin hissed. "Wade needs me."

Robin crossed her arms over her chest and frowned.

This crack in her armor was already sore from his repeated attempts to wriggle through it. All the same, Al added: "He's not

9

your friend, you know. You know what people like him think of us."

Robin laughed again, but it was low and mirthless. "At least the Benne think us Sealie deserve to live. That's more than what the Klonn think." She gestured southward violently, jabbing at the invisible boundary between them and their enemies.

Fron scoffed bitterly.

"What was that?" Robin asked him archly, temper flaring, sick to the teeth of everyone attacking her this morning. She stood, pushing the satchel further under the table, just in case. "Have something you'd like to add, you docile *cow*?"

Across the table, two Sealie forge-drones gasped at the slur.

Fron shot to his feet, pale face flushing a mottled, ugly red. "You're a *thief*, you stupid, self-important *leech*."

More voices rose in gasps around them, heads whipping up, eyes darting around. There were some things you just didn't say out loud—not to people's faces, anyway. Not when they were all Saskwyans in the Air Patrol together. Not when they were all supposed to be on the same side.

Al loomed up behind her, like the hobgob she had just compared their most storied enemy to, and Robin shoved back her annoyance. She didn't need Al's help.

"At least I'm not afraid to see what's happening out there for what it really is! Your nose is so high in the air, I don't think even a glider could get your scrubbed-up ass to catch up with it," Robin shot back with a snarl.

She should have seen it coming, but honestly, Robin hadn't thought the skinny little apprentice had the stones to hit a mid-flight sergeant. Fron's fist smashed into one high cheekbone, knuckles popping against the upswept corner of her eye. Robin grunted, staggering back a step. Al's chest stopped her from falling all the way, his hands around her shoulders, a roar already building in his throat.

But before he could say anything, Robin replied to Fron's

punch with one of her own. There was a satisfying snapping sound and a spurt of blood as her fist connected with the bridge of Fron's nose. The boy dropped like a Klonn aeroship out of fuel, clutching at his face and howling.

His friends immediately descended on him, grabbing him by the shirtsleeves and tugging him to the door on the far side of the canteen as the crowd parted around them. Most of the Benne in the room looked shocked. Most of the Sealies looked bored.

"What? Not going to finish your breakkie?" Al taunted as they retreated, and everyone around them went back to their meals. Best to pretend it had never happened, after all.

"Waste of food," Al muttered as he sat back down to his own meal.

He didn't need to say that the kid was on the fast track to pilot, that he would be an officer in no time, that his father was probably an officer and that *he'd* never gone to bed knowing what an empty, gnawing stomach felt like. It hung in the air between them like a well-known—and unwelcome—imaginary friend, all the same.

Al reached out and snagged Fron's left-behind bread and cheese, popping the first into his pocket, and the latter into his mouth. Robin scooped up the last of the blond kid's apple chips and shoved them into her own pocket.

The Air Patrol was fed as best as they could be on the rations available. Can't win a war on an empty stomach, or so they said. But Robin still made a point to put aside some of her food to pay the Wise Women for good luck charms. She could put up with a bit of hunger at night in return for the assurance that her glider and her pilot were in the prayers of the Wise Women and the sights of the gods. Fron's sudden departure was a welcome opportunity—she didn't have to sacrifice part of her own ration now.

Robin dropped back onto the bench, probing her cheek and wincing.

"It's not bad," Al said, peering down at her.

"Just grazed me," Robin said. "Smarts, though."

"You should find some ice."

"I'm fine," Robin said. "Pull out that burlap on the top of my bag. I want to show you what else I got."

Al pulled the gearbox out, hiding it behind his thick legs, and Robin bent down to grab the satchel, face throbbing as the blood rushed into her head. She felt heady, alive, triumphant in a way she usually only felt when she and Wade were the last aircraft still in the air after a dance with the enemy.

That is, until one of the security officers clapped his palm down on her shoulder, jerked her off the bench with his fist in her shirt, and hauled her toward the back door. Around her, the Sealies burst into raucous applause. Robin threw the room a dazzling smile, though it made her cheek pull and burn. Laughing, Al snatched up her canvas satchel and tossed it to her as she was dragged down the hall to the discipline officer's door. He was careful, Robin noticed, to keep the gearbox hidden.

CHAPTER TWO

LAST MONTH, THE WINDOWS AT THE FRONT OF ROBIN'S HOUSE HAD been blown out by a bomb. It had been dropped right onto the cobblestone street, with no regard for the dilapidated row homes on either side. It was by no means the first bomb to go off in a residential area, but it was the first in Robin's neighborhood, close as they were to the factory fields at the edge of the city. The Klonn usually saved their ammunition for the bigger targets if they were this far out. Not that night, though. The brittle crunch of brick under metal had given her about a second's warning before the flat *crack* of the explosion itself, followed by the reverberating *whump* of the shock wave, had sent her window flying inward in fragments so small she would have been blinded by glass dust if she had been standing nearby.

She tried not to think about what had happened to the neighbors who'd been stupid enough to watch the sky that night. Didn't mean the nightmares didn't still come when she had no work to distract her, though. Terrible visions of burned hands, or stumps where those hands should have been, haunted her in the darkness. Images of blood running from eyes, of mangled faces and limbs, danced in the shadows of sleep, and under it all, the horror of being rendered useless, of being unable to work, of becoming a ground-bound *burden.*

She'd been asleep when it fell, time-eaten curtains drawn tight across the pane, held in place with clothespins in the event this very thing happened. The glass that had smashed inward had been mostly caught by the fabric. The pieces that were big enough to break free had fallen in a waterfall, radiating out across the floor. Robin had been curled up on her lumpy old mattress in the closet. She hadn't slept in the room's actual bed in years. It was too dangerous.

Luckily, Robin's boots were in the closet with her, and she hadn't needed to navigate the floors barefoot. By the time Robin had gotten home from work that day, her mother had swept up the dust and shards, and had set them aside to sell back to the glassmaker. Anything that could be reused, or remade, was kept. Her father had scavenged a thin sheet of splintering wood to nail across the frame. He'd scrounged some rags from the fallen houses nearby and had stuffed wads of fabric into the gaping holes in the board.

Robin could see the ragged ends of those fabric wads fluttering in the early autumn breeze as she hovered under the guttering streetlamp a block away, peering through the haze. Her stomach unwound at the familiarity of it. It was the same sense of relief she felt each time a skirmish ended, and Wade turned their glider back toward the safety of the hangar. While she hadn't lied to Al when she said the shipyards were more home to her now than the building before her was, it didn't mean she wasn't still happy to see it standing at the end of each workday, and the finish of each nightly strafing.

She stalled, working the toe of her right boot into the ashy debris on the cobblestones, her satchel slung over her shoulder and her face smarting. The sun was weak and watery today, lost in the haze of brick dust and the smoke that blew in off the factory fields. The fires from last night's bombs must still have been going, to turn the late-morning sky so sooty-dark. The lamplighter hadn't even bothered to make his rounds that day. If he'd even survived the bombing at all, that is.

The smoke stung her eyes, but Robin's goggles, hung around her neck while she was on the ground, wouldn't be much use down here. They were reflective, amber-tinted, meant for intense sunlight. They would leave her blind under the cover of so much ash. And the roads had heaved again—she didn't trust that her muscle memory would lead her home safe. Around her, the close houses leaned against each other in the shadows. They looked like weary soldiers who'd just returned from the front. Square-toothed maws gaped from partially collapsed walls. Lightning-bolt cracks zigzagged from roof to foundation. But despite that, the familiar scents of her childhood neighborhood reached out to envelop her, to welcome her back—brick dust, wet stone, boiled vegetables, honey, and gunpowder.

Robin tried to remember the last time her house had looked welcoming. She had vague memories of the small, walled back garden brimming with wildflowers and her mama's hive. And she still heard echoes of her papa's tales—growing up on his parent's wagon, feast days filled with bright bunting streamers and visits from the Wise Women. Now, everything was hard, and scrabbly, and dark.

Her family was lucky, though. The homes of their relatives still stood. No extra families needed to crowd into their space—yet. Robin's father was still employed as a postal carrier. News and letters still had to bandy to and from the front lines. Her mother still found work as a seamstress, patching and repairing clothing and uniforms. And, together with Robin's pay from the Air Patrol, they brought in three separate incomes. Three incomes kept them afloat, and fed, though it still couldn't replace the street-facing windows—which would have been a spectacularly dumb idea, anyway, as the next bomb would likely do to the new glass what it had done to the old. Their income was enough to keep them all clothed, and bought enough coal to keep the skinny, spindly house warm. It even allowed them to help their neighbors do the same, when there was little enough to spare.

She didn't mind coming back here. But to be doing so before lunchtime was humiliating.

Sent home without pay, suspended for the rest of the day. And for what? For walloping a kid who'd hit her first? Unfair. If Fron had been a Sealie, they wouldn't have even bothered to run her in and mark up her files. They would have just let them beat each other, and then get on with their work, bloody and bruised and okay.

No point delaying the inevitable, Robin thought morosely as she fished her key out of her shirt, pulling it from where it was tied to a button with a piece of string. Her stomach gurgled at her. *Not if I have any hope of lunch, anyway.*

She unlocked the door, and pressed down on the knob as she opened it to keep the hinges from squealing. She placed the satchel beside the wall, and then closed the door with the same caution. She locked it, threw the deadbolts, and turned, hardly daring to breathe.

The hall was empty.

Thank the gods for that, too, then. She sagged against the wall for a moment, rubbing her aching shoulder. Honestly, after the early morning scavenge and the brawl in the canteen, it would be nice to get an afternoon off. It would be almost like a vacation, even if it was without pay.

Maybe I'll be lucky and Papa will be out on a special mission of his own. Surely someone has to schlep the maps of that new front from base to base. The thought lightened her mood, and she swung down to retrieve her satchel and head into the parlor.

The parlor that, it turned out, was *not* so empty.

Papa stood by the fireplace, arms folded across his thin chest. His bushy black moustache quivered with anger, and his brown skin was flushed along his cheeks. Frozen in the doorway, Robin straightened, gave up all pretense of being quiet, and marched inside. Her mother stood by the good sofa, the one reserved for the clients who came for her expert needle. Once, it had been for the height of Benne fashion. Now, it was for invisible patches and subtle repairs on uniforms.

Or it had been, until her loom broke. It had been shattered so badly by the bomb that had taken the windows that it had barely been useful as kindling. Without a loom, Mama couldn't pull apart and reweave old curtains and torn garments into trimmings, patches, and smart little coats for the children of her clientele. Mama watched warily, gaze on Robin's rapidly blackening eye, as Robin stopped to withdraw her second prize from the satchel. Playing the footpad had paid off.

Mama was thin and gray, her skin far paler than the average sienna of most Sealies because so much of her work kept her indoors and out of the sun. Her curled shoulders sagged with cold, and were worn round from a lifetime over the needle. Her limpid hair was doing its best to mimic ivy, curling around its braid and escaping in reaching tendrils, and her eyes were puffed with the need to sleep. But in Robin's mind, Mama was still the fresh, straight-backed, pretty young woman with a ready smile, a bronze complexion, and curling brown hair that she saw in the single precious tintype on the mantle.

Robin didn't dare look at Papa as she held the wrapped item aloft and carefully removed the fabric that kept it from view. She had wrapped the tabletop, factory-issue loom in yards and yards of the burlap that had been abandoned beside it, protecting it like a precious treasure until she could bestow it upon its new mistress. She'd found both in the cinders of what had once been a textile mill. The roof and upper floors had been gone, but the walls had been intact, and the locks on the doors were still solid. She'd had to pick them just to get inside a place that was still half on fire, irony be damned. The fabric reeked of stale smoke, but Robin knew that that would wash out.

"What do you think, Mama?" she asked, pride filling the spaces that had been left behind by her scanty breakfast. Mama carefully took the loom from her grasp. "It's just like your old one. When I pulled it out—ha, the embers were still hot! The whole thing must have gone up like a Gods' Day rocket! Lucky it was still in one piece, eh? And the burlap—I bet you could fetch a good price at market."

Mama plunked down on the sofa, stroking the frame of the loom she cradled timidly. "Oh, little birdie, you shouldn't have. This was a bad idea."

Joy turned cold, shattered against the sharp edges of her ribcage. "Shouldn't have?" Robin spluttered, taking a step away. "*Birdie*? I contribute to this household. Don't call me a baby."

Papa made a disgusted sound. He stepped forward, ran his fingers over the embossed seal on the foot of the loom, the one that marked the factory it had come from. "They'll be able to trace that."

"So don't show it to anybody. Sand it off! Cover the loom when you have clients over," Robin snapped. "You're welcome, by the way!"

"For going out into the night and risking arrest? You could have been maimed for theft," Mama snapped back, setting aside the loom and rising to her feet, her hands fisting in the sides of her threadbare skirts. Robin rocked back on her heels. For a brief, silent second, she was dumbstruck. Mama was almost never angry, and hardly ever raised her voice. Then the bitterness surged back.

"For bringing you what you need to start working again! I suppose I shouldn't have bothered, though, should I?" She whipped off her cap and threw it against the wall. A long, sparrow-brown braid tumbled down her back. "Maybe I should just go put on a skirt and bat my eyelashes at the next unmarried slob who stumbles by. Maybe I should get hitched, and pop out a few screaming brats I won't be able to afford to feed."

"It would be a gods-damned sight better than never knowing where you are, never knowing whether or not you're even alive!" Papa bellowed.

Caught flat-footed by his volume, Robin's retort jammed up behind her tongue. She blinked hard, twice, and turned her back on her parents, clutching at her sleeves.

"Robin, darling," Mama called, but Robin didn't uncurl. "It's just that . . . you're still just a child. You're still *our* child. We can't help but worry about you."

"I thought I was old enough to be sold off to the next man Papa approves of," Robin sneered.

"Oh, my birdie," she breathed. "You know—" She stopped herself, swallowing tremulously, her work-worn hands trembling in her skirts.

"I can burn it if you don't want it," Robin muttered, petulant.

"No!" Her mother's hands shot up, her eyes, the dark rich amber of fresh honey—same as Robin's—widening. "No, that would be . . . there's no point, now that the crime is done." She brushed the ill-luck off her shoulders, even as she said it.

"Robin," Papa said. "Why are you home early? And what happened to your face?"

"I gave better than I got," she grunted at him.

"A Benne?"

"So?"

Papa rubbed the middle of his forehead with his thumb. He only had the one. He'd been a more desperate man before he'd married Mama and settled down, before he'd gotten the job running letters.

"You can't pick fights with them, Robin. You don't know what it was like—"

"—when you were a boy and they took us in off the wagons for nothing because the sickness was killing everyone, and then there was a *war*, and our people were trapped in brick houses with beehives on the roofs, and it's nice to have security and predictability, and *I've heard* it, Papa."

"Then why don't you listen to it?" he snapped.

Sick to the teeth, Robin snarled to herself. She was hungry. She was angry. She was ashamed to have been sent home. And she was just so *tired* all the time. She just wanted the war to stop long enough for her to *sleep*.

Instead of answering, Robin pulled a jackknife from the lip of her boot and cut a strip about a hand's span wide off the end of the burlap sheet; it wasn't much, but perhaps the gods of luck would appreciate her offering up something of value. That was the point of a sacrifice, after all. Robin considered, and then cut a second strip for the gods of fools, as well, just to be sure. She stuffed the knife back into her boot sheath and the fabric into her pocket. Only then did she turn to face Papa.

Refusing to be intimidated into guilt, Robin crossed her own tired arms across her own chest, mimicking Papa's stance. The kind of anger that pulled at his mouth had once inspired awe and fear in little Robin. But now, she was nearly as tall as he was and, like Al, her arms were just as corded with muscle as his. She deliberately turned her back to him and headed toward the door.

"We're not through here—!" Papa began, butting in in front of her, but Robin held out a hand and stopped him. This wasn't a fight that was going to be won today, so she'd rather not continue it.

"Is there any lunch left?" She brushed past him, returning to the hallway and crossing through into the kitchen.

There was a cloth bundle on the table, and when Robin untied the knot, she found a small slice of cheese, a crusty bun, and a bit of stew in a clay pot. It smelled wonderful, especially after the chill of the autumn air and the acrid stench of soot and machine oil that filled the streets outside.

She sat on the stool by the hearth and lifted the pot to her lips. The stew was cold, filled with pepper and the sharp, bright tang of fish. She set it down as close to the waning embers in the hearth as she could, and turned her attention to the bread.

The thick knot of discomfort that had cramped her stomach eased with each nibble of cheese she took; she went slowly to make it last.

"You didn't even come home before you went to the yard!" Papa barked, following her into the kitchen and trying to pull her attention away from the food.

"Can't you just be happy that I went out for Mama?" Robin said, careful not to slam the pot against the scratched wooden table, no matter how frustrated she was.

"Just me, birdie?" Mama asked, following them into the kitchen. She was folding the burlap as she walked, carefully measuring out the yardage.

"And some stuff for Wade's glider," Robin admitted.

"Surely there must be another way," Papa insisted.

She looked up and deliberately stuffed the last of the bun into her mouth, puffing out her cheeks in a show to prove that she couldn't answer. She stood and brushed the crumbs off her pants. Papa was still in the doorway, as if uncertain whether or not he wished to block it and try to force her to listen to commands they both knew she was just going to ignore, or whether he wished to step aside and save them both the headache.

Apparently having chosen to err on the side of paternal consternation, he raised his right hand and waggled his remaining thumb at her meaningfully.

"There's nothing left in Pyria to requisition," Robin snarled with all the defiance she could muster. Papa blinked, swallowing back the rest of whatever he'd planned to say. Sometimes, he was so subservient that the right tone of haughty indifference could shut him up. It made Robin's gorge rise and twist with anger. Papa was just such a damn Sealie.

"So, I do the same gods-damned thing that every other rudding mid-flight sergeant does in the dead of night to get their glider in the air, and somehow, I'm in the wrong? It's as easy as that. I just damn well do it."

"Robin, birdie," Mama tried. She'd pulled a cool bottle of milk from the pantry and was laying the glass against the side of Robin's bruised temple. Robin brushed her away with a frustrated gesture. "We just don't like—"

"So don't like it!" Robin didn't deny the urge to roll her eyes this time, nor to throw up her hands in frustration. "It won't stop me from going!"

Papa glowered, and then, apparently decided to try a different tack. "I read in the newspaper today that the Coyote —" Papa stopped, clicked his teeth shut, screwed his eyes closed. It was the same expression Al had made; the same expression all Sealies made whenever the Coyote was mentioned.

"So, what?" Robin hollered. "You want me to quit the Air Patrol because I might die? Maybe you should stop carrying the post because a rock might fall from a cloud and crack your skull. Papa, I am needed. Why do I have to keep proving this to everyone? Why does no one *believe* me?"

"Birdie, you're still our child—"

Robin pulled herself upright. "Either I am a child who must be kept home, or I am a woman old enough to marry, which means old enough to make her own choices," Robin challenged. "Which is it?"

"Not old enough to tell the difference between stealing and—" her father began, but Robin cut him off with a growling sound of indignation.

"Stealing!" she echoed. "And what the hells does that Benne proprietor care? He's probably insured the whole building, and is getting paid right now for his losses—probably for the people who died there, too!" For there had been horrors in that rubble. Things that Robin had refused to look at, to go near, to acknowledge. "I needed the gearbox to keep Wade's glider in the air. And

Mama needs a loom to work. That Benne *cow* would have used it for kindling!"

"We raised you better than this," Papa snapped. "What's happened to you?"

Robin scowled at him, summoning her most fearsome frown. It made all those junior to Robin in the shipyards cower. It just made Papa match it, and he'd had several decades more experience with the expression than she.

"War," she snarled, when she realized she wouldn't be able to out-glower him today. She turned on her heel to go up to her room and to bed.

Funny how hauling glider pieces and ammunition around never tired her out, but this argument, day after day, always did.

She was exhausted. And it had very little to do with how much sleep she'd gotten.

Why did nobody *believe* in her?

❁

Captain Wade Perwink was tall, broad across the shoulders, narrow in the hips, and had a fanciful little moustache that was sparse and slightly paler than his sandy-colored hair. Like most of the pilots—Benne to the last of them—he treated his Sealie mid-flight sergeant with respect and courtesy while in the air. But would never be caught eating at the same table, or engaging in any sort of social niceties outside of the workplace.

Which is why it was quite remarkable when, the next morning, as Robin produced the stolen gearbox from her satchel, Wade threw his arms around her shoulders and kissed her square on the temple, right over her bruise—more green than purple today, thank the gods. Robin laughed and pushed back to keep him from strangling her with his hug, but he squeezed tighter and cried, "No, no, no. I'm never letting you go, you marvelous, resourceful genius, you."

Then he contradicted himself by stepping her back far enough to get a good look at the gearbox squashed between their stomachs. It wasn't in tip-top shape. But the gears themselves were intact, and that was what mattered. The rest could either be fixed or replaced.

Wade's face glowed with the sort of shining pride that was usually reserved for the fathers of newborns. "It's a bit of a mess," he said teasingly, running his callused fingers over the rust patches that marred the dented outer casing.

"Omens, Wade," Robin said. "You know me better than that."

Wade wrinkled his nose at the expletive—the Benne didn't believe in omens; their goddess never gave away hints—but his smile remained in place. "So, you'll have it done in time for the general to come inspect our glider at noon?"

Instead of answering, Robin just rolled her eyes at him. "They'll pick you, Wade. If this mission is as important as the scuttlebutt suggests, then they'll want their best on it. We have the best glider, and you're the best pilot. They'll pick you."

"And I have the best mid-flight," he said, thumping her once on the shoulder with a scarred, meaty hand. Wade's palms were a spider's web of puffed scar tissue from the time he'd spent in the air, hands wrapped around the nodal grips on the glider's control stick. Robin accepted the compliment and the gesture for what they were—conciliatory. "Though, I nearly didn't. This is nice, by the way," he said, tapping the side of his thumb against her temple, right over the bruise.

"I'm here now, aren't I?"

"You need to watch yourself," Wade said softly. "Fron's father is high in the chain of command."

"He *started* it," Robin protested.

"And you finished it, I know, but Robin . . ." He hesitated, licked his lips, and then plunged on. "This mission means too much to me—to *us*—to both our careers to lose it over a . . . a fist fight and a bit of . . ."

"Rough language?" Robin bit off.

"Exactly so," Wade said. "It's even more risky than how you get these." He tapped the tip of one finger against the gearbox. "Are you even well enough to go up tomorrow?"

"I can see out of it just fine," Robin protested. "And it'll be even better by then."

"I never said I didn't think you couldn't fly the mission," he assured her, ducking down to inspect the damage. Robin was never quite sure if he knew how flirtatious he sounded when he complimented her, or if he knew the way his eyes twinkled when he looked at her so seriously. Robin tried to swallow her heart, which had tried to crawl up out of her throat, the traitorous thing. "Just think about me, will you, when you're slinging your fists around the next time?"

"Sure," Robin said, with an affected shrug. *People worry I do nothing but give you too much thought—or more. Nosy prigs.*

"Thanks," he said, and with a final pat on her shoulder, and a hungry look at the gearbox, he returned to his pre-flight check of the glider.

Dismissed, Robin made her way to the repair bay. Al had promised to get a fire going strong inside the smithy, and to have a hammer ready for the long morning of banging it would take to get the intake back in shape. There was one advantage to having a master corporal as her best friend—he could get all the little forge-drones to swarm in exactly the right way to make her life easier.

Mind on the bellowing heat and the morning of sweat that awaited her, Robin looked to the sky and lifted her hands. She held her palms up so the gods could hear her, and thought: *The things I do to fly! Might just be easier to spend all my energy on trying to sprout some wings.*

Al was good to his word, as usual, and there was a forge ready and red with heat waiting for her when she got to the smithy. Al was glaring off a few of the other mid-flights, who were trying to sweet-talk him into letting them at the prepared anvil and tongs. "Nope, nope. This is for Sergeant Arianhod," she heard him say as she got close.

"Omens, Al!" one of the boys snarled—he was a skinny, muscled thing that Robin vaguely remembered from primary school. He stuck his chin out at Al. "Why don't you just give her some flowers like a regular guy? C'mon, man, she's out there with her captain. Who knows how long they might be at that. It'll be ages before she arrives. The rest of us have repairs to do!"

"Don't you tell lies about Sergeant Arianhod," Al snapped at him. "She ain't that kinda girl."

"True," Robin agreed as she came up beside the other mid-flight and spoke directly in his ear. He jumped and whirled to face her, dark eyes comically huge in his wide-boned face. "And it ain't like that between me and Al, neither. Besides—a ready forge is a better thing for a master corporal to give a mid-flight sergeant any day. Thanks, Al."

She grinned at him and patted his shoulder as she walked by, setting the satchel with the gearbox down beside the anvil. She waved to an apprentice, who immediately scampered over with a bucket of cool water, scattering the other mid-flights who had crowded around the no longer free workspace.

"Hey, anything for you, Robin," Al said, and patted her shoulder back.

"How about a sheet of steel, then, if you're offering *anything*," Robin asked, hands occupied with laying out chain to cut.

"Sure thing," he said, and turned to fetch just that.

Wiping away the sweat that had already begun to accumulate on her forehead, Robin picked up the heated tongs and got to work.

CHAPTER THREE

"SO, I'M NOT ALLOWED TO KNOW? WHY?" ROBIN WHISPERED. THEY always whispered, though there was no way anyone on the ground would ever be able to hear them. Superstition or not, neither Benne nor Sealie raised their voices in flight unless they were in the pitch of battle. There was something sacrosanct about the silence, the thoughtful whisper of air against canvas.

Robin sat directly behind Wade, the back of her seat to his, strategically positioned to keep the balance of the glider as far to the rear as possible. Nose-heavy aircraft didn't tend to make it into the air, and two people side by side at the front could dangerously outweigh a tail section filled with tools and ammunition—especially when the ammunition started to run out. A wide leather strap was bolted to the floor beside her left leg. The other end was clipped to the harness that hugged her hips. The heavy press of the steel clasp was annoying, and tugged uncomfortably between her thighs. She would have loved to fly without it, but she had heard the boot camp horror stories of mid-flight sergeants being thrown from their gliders midair. As much as she loved the sky, she didn't much relish the idea of dying in it.

Robin sat up and craned her head around, trying to read

Wade's expression in the reflection off the windscreen. His eyes were inscrutable behind his amber-lensed goggles.

"I don't know," Wade admitted. "Those were my orders. Only I'm allowed to look at the map. But now that we're up, I can tell you that the target's in the middle of the forest, the one that skirts Lylon. We're dropping the bomb there. They think there might be an outpost or . . . some sort of private runway in the woods."

Robin's heart slammed up against the roof of her mouth. She swallowed hard, trying to get it back to where it belonged, and feared she might have sucked some teeth down with it. "That's really far into enemy territory. I mean, isn't that—?"

"The Coyote's territory?" Wade nodded, his cap throwing long shadows through the interior. "Yes."

Robin discreetly made the gesture to ward off bad luck. Unlike some of the other Benne, Wade tolerated her Sealie idiosyncrasies. But Robin tried not to make the gestures in his presence, all the same. She respected Wade, and she didn't like the thought that he might be judging her for something other than her skills.

"The ones two days ago . . . the ones he . . . who was it?"

"Benjamin Lue and Earl Geen," he said.

"John Wodin and Adam Res," Robin filled in, offering up the names of the mid-flights who had gone down with their pilots.

She let the silence hang for a moment, offering up a small prayer for the afterlives of her fellow mid-flights. She cupped her palms to the sky, ready to take whatever blessing the gods may offer as the glider filled with ceremonial silence. That would have to do. There could be no funeral for Wodin and Res. Not without remains.

"I know he's not, but I can see why people think he's a . . . you know . . . a hobgob," Robin said at last.

Wade laughed. "There's no such thing as luck personified, and if there was, I don't think it would pick the Klonn side."

"I know that," Robin protested. "I just mean . . . it's creepy.

Have you ever seen him? You flew for two years before I was your mid-flight."

"Robin," Wade said, voice dropping to a near inaudible whisper. It was as if he dared not say what he was about to say out loud, lest an ill-spirited demon happen by and mistake it for a wish. *How very un-Benne of him, she thought.* "Anyone who's been on the receiving end of courtship from the Coyote has not lived to tell of it."

Robin snorted. When Wade didn't laugh, his seriousness, and the intimate imagery of dancing in the sky with the scourge of the Air Patrol, gave her chills. "Then where do the stories come from?" she asked, her voice so strangled with horror that she wasn't sure Wade would hear it.

"Ground support," he whispered. "They've seen him through the spyglass—his tail is painted like a wolf's mouth."

Robin frowned. "But his nickname is 'Coyote.'"

Wade made a sound deep in his throat: half chuckle, half snort of disgust. "*We* gave him that name. He acts like a coyote—picks off the weak and the crippled. He never shoots at a healthy glider, Robin. He will always go for the pilots who are trying to retreat. He scavenges near the ground. He isn't . . . honorable."

"It's a war, Wade," Robin said. "There's a lot that isn't honorable in what we do."

"Still, you don't shoot at a retreating glider. It's simply not done. You meet face-to-face on the battlefield and you dance proper. Or not at all."

Robin flopped back into her seat and stared at the ceiling to avoid looking at the drop hatch at the rear of the glider, at what was lashed to the floor directly on top of it. Sometimes, the Benne's view of combat was just as exhausting as Papa's nagging —it was unrealistic. Like they had no idea of what real war was, and thought they were just a pack of school boys meeting on the dueling field with the old-fashioned swords of generations past. Not . . . well, that *not* was the war that Robin knew. Bombs, and theft, starvation and desperation. They didn't see the real war. Not the way the Sealie did.

"He must be a special kind of bastard, then," Robin said.

Wade made the chuckling-snort noise again. "His aeroship is repaired so quick and so often, they reckon he's got to be some sort of nobility—and for me, Klonn nobility is about the most special kind of bastard you can get. They're the ones who started all of this." He made a gesture with his hand, indicating the glider, the sky, Robin, the bomb—everything.

This.

Robin grunted. "That, at least, is something we can agree on."

Wade looked down at the topographical map at his feet, the one Robin wasn't supposed to look at, and tugged at the yoke a little. It bit into his scarred hands. The sound of creaking wood echoed back from the cockpit. Robin sucked in a breath as the glider turned slightly to the left.

It took tremendous strength to be able to wrench the steering columns that made the sleek canvas darts dance so poetically among the clouds, and tremendous nerve to face off with the forces of gravity, relying on instinct, on training, on the scent and feel of the air as the aircraft navigated through updrafts and breezes like a meadow bird. If the pilot missed even one updraft, the glider would plummet.

Pilots were easy to pick out of a group; they had arms like iron hammers and palms like ground beef. The hand grips on the glider's control stick were intentionally designed to cut into the pilot's fingers to ensure a better purchase on the yoke. But the steering column could also jerk in the pilot's hand, cutting into the skin hard enough to draw blood. Scarred palms were a badge of honor, and Benne pilots wore their white palms with pride.

Robin looked back at the bomb, the sight of it pulling at her like gravity. She had no idea what could be so important about this particular target, why the Air Patrol command would protect its location with threat of a court martial for even looking at a map. Why they would have been sent to the heart of the Coyote's territory with only one case of ammunition, and a bomb that weighed so much they could carry little else.

Outside, the cloud cover was frighteningly thin, but the setting sun was bright enough to out-glare the stark, light wooden frame and unbleached canvas of the glider's body and keep them hidden—at least for now. Robin wondered if it would be enough when it came time to glide lower, to brush the tops of the trees with their glider's belly and let the bomb fly.

The wind hissed and whispered down the canvas, and Robin pretended that she didn't hear the dire warnings and ill omens in it. Robin stared at the bomb, flicking the clasp of her harness with her thumb so it made a steady, soft click. The bomb, no more than a collection of metal, chemicals, and fabric covered in painted code words, seemed to stare back. Even without having eyes, it seemed to cut through Robin's skin and peer deep inside her spirit.

What makes your mission so special that I had to commit theft to get us up in the air? She thought at it. *Where are we going, that you're worth what I did?* With last night's anger dissipated, and this morning's good humor spent, Robin felt tired, guilt surging up to mingle with exhausted resignation.

Very rarely did she let herself think about the things she did for the Air Patrol command. She had killed people. She had killed them by making sure that Wade stayed in the air, which was surely as good as if she had thrust a knife under a Klonn pilot's ribs herself. She had stolen. She had disobeyed her parents. She had disappointed the gods. Sometimes, she wondered if the war was enough of an excuse to get away with what she'd done. Or if punishment was waiting in reserve for after.

The worst part of a stealth mission was always the waiting, and the overthinking that inevitably accompanied it. Trying not to bite her nails or jitter her leg, Robin counted backwards from one hundred to calm her nerves. There was nothing else she could do. Prepping the guns would front-load the glider and make it harder for Wade to keep the nose up. There was nothing to repair, because nothing was broken, and nothing to tinker with for fear of making too much noise. The biggest advantage the Benne gliders had was their silence, that they were able to hear the Klonn aeroships with their self-propelling engines as they approached, and she couldn't afford to distract Wade while he focused on keeping them alive. All she could do was sit, and wait, in infuriatingly ignorant silence.

"We're in Klonn," Wade whispered when Robin had counted down to thirty-eight. "Twelve minutes to target."

The first time she had crossed enemy lines, Robin had expected the landscape to look fundamentally different somehow. The Klonn worshiped technology instead of gods, so she had expected to see one single, sprawling metal city with soot-streaked glass where trees and fields ought to have been—or rows of metal monsters guarding the boundary line. Instead, there was just more forest.

As the fighting had moved farther north, skirmishing soldiers had been forced to shoot through the trees. The forest had developed bald patches where bombing runs or bullet strafes had cut through the canopy, sometimes taking down the venerable old trees entirely. Robin closed her eyes and said a small, heartfelt prayer for the wood nymphs who must be suffering the loss of their trees, victims of a war that had nothing to do with them.

Or perhaps it had everything to do with them. The Klonn had gone to war over this very belief. They had demanded that the world accept that there were no gods at all, and were hells-bent on subjugating everyone to their own system of belief—in themselves. *Arrogant and barbaric*, Robin thought. The Klonn burned the Benne's churches to the All-Mother whenever they took a town. They tore down the Sealie temples built high in the branches of the trees, and kicked over the altars placed at crossroads. Robin had been told all her life that such blasphemies angered the gods.

So why, she wondered, were the Klonn still winning?

Maybe the rumors were true, after all. Maybe the stories about the Coyote were true and he *was* a hobgob. Maybe it wasn't just a base rumor used to haze new apprentices.

It was a horrendous, treacherous thought, and the moment it entered her head, Robin ducked instinctively, as if the meaty hand of a drill sergeant might be aiming a swat at the back of her neck for having dared to think it. There was no drill sergeant to punish her up here, though, and Wade couldn't read her mind.

A passing god might have heard, however, so Robin closed her eyes and lifted her palms. *Sorry. I'm sorry. I have no place questioning the luck I've bargained for. Although, if there was anyone nearby who would see fit to make sure this mission runs smooth, then I would be more than happy to offer up some of tonight's rations.*

A swift, high ripping sound whistled through the cabin, and Robin snapped to attention. The sound of bullets tearing canvas was a prominent theme in Robin's nightmares, and she recognized it readily.

"Guess you didn't want that dinner, then." Robin muttered, and then swore, yanking her own goggles down over her eyes. Ignoring the sting of the leather strap as it cut into her bruise, she dove for her toolbox. "Nuh-huh!" she said, and threw herself immediately upon the tear.

Her body blocked most of the howling wind that threatened to blow their gear around the interior of the glider. The patch kit was at the top of her toolbox—Robin had learned long ago to keep what she used most at the top—and within seconds, she had pressed a hastily glued swatch of canvas over the gaping hole. The glue dried quickly with the air blasting against it, but it wouldn't stay in place forever.

Before Robin could close her toolbox and secure the lid, Wade threw them into a series of twisting turns that had even Robin losing her sense of direction. Luckily, the strong magnets in the bottom of the toolbox held, and while the interior of the glider was suddenly filled with paste patches that fluttered around like feathers, the heavier tools stayed in place. Adrenaline and fear surging, Robin clutched hard at the series of handles bolted into the frame, tucking her knees to her chest to keep her feet from swinging and kicking a hole through the siding—or worse, hitting her pilot in the head. The sky spun crazily beyond the windscreen. She let out her breath, closed her eyes, and hung on, wincing each time an abrupt change in direction tugged them away from the pull of the horizon. Her stomach crawled up into her throat, and she swallowed hard, happy that she had skipped lunch to install the gearbox.

"Dammit, dammit," Wade muttered. Robin saw his lips moving in the windscreen reflection more than she heard the words over the howl of the wind. "Glorious Mother, give me an updraft, just one updraft."

The glider swung around hard, lurched through a drop, and then suddenly, Robin's feet were on the floor again. The smell of damp puffed in through the walls, and the world vanished into mist as Wade dove into a cloud for cover.

"How close are we?" she shouted. The echoing rattle of another burst of bullet fire drowned out her words, and she had to scuttle over to repeat herself in Wade's ear.

"Almost there!" he shouted back, jaw clenching with the effort to keep the glider level and out of sight of whatever—or whoever —was shooting at them. "Get back to the lever and wait for my signal! We have to get back into the open sky."

"They'll shoot us down before it even deploys!" Robin said.

"We'll be fine," he shouted back.

"Wade! We need to abort."

"That's an order, Sergeant!"

Robin wanted to argue, but Wade rarely pulled rank without

good reason. "Understood, sir!" she snarled. She made her way back to the center of the glider and the bomb.

They don't expect us to come back, Robin realized as she got her feet planted and wrapped her fingers around the lever that would deploy the bomb. That's why she wasn't allowed to look at the map. *If we go down, and somehow survive . . . if I'm captured, they don't want me to have any kind of intel . . . they don't want me to lead them back to—*

The whole glider jolted as they dove out of the cloud cover, the wooden frame shrieking in protest.

"Did they just godsdamn *ram* us?" Robin yelled as the aircraft spun sideways like a tossed playing card.

"Skimmed us with the leading edge of his wing—Robin, watch out!"

The screaming tear as a massive swath of canvas came away from the side of the glider pulled her attention from both horrified revelations. The suck of the atmosphere tore her hands off the handle. Her feet were ripped out from under her, and she had just enough time to grab on to the leather strap connected to her harness before she was yanked out into the open sky.

Fear surged against the roof of her mouth. Then her tether snapped taut, the straps of her harness digging into the joints of her hips, inertia swinging her limbs wide.

"*Hells!*" she screamed, giving voice to the sudden, grinding pain. She grabbed on to the tether and held on—her carabineer shivered with strain, but held. She wasn't going to drop.

She closed her eyes for half a second, thanking the workmanship of her fellow Sealies, and then spared a glance at the bomb. It was still strapped down, trembling in the change of air pressure. It wasn't going to fly out and smack her in the head. That was the important part.

Twisting in the air currents, Robin managed to brace one foot against the trailing edge of the glider's wingtip. She hauled herself back toward relative safety, hand over hand, the tether cutting into her gloves. Her braid was flying out behind her like a pennant, pulling painfully in the wind.

Something silver flashed past Robin's feet, and she looked down along her body. An aeroship pulled up beside them, so close the wingtip nearly brushed Robin's foot. Goosebumps plunged up Robin's arms and across her neck. Her tongue felt hot and thick in the back of her mouth. The world fell silent, like it had been wrapped in batting.

The Klonn pilot turned his face up to her. He wore a silver helmet, the nose elongated to resemble the snarling snout of a lupine creature. She could see his eyes, the irises almost as gray as his mask. They narrowed at her. The skin of his lower face was pale, and his upper lip and chin were hidden behind a goatee that was scruffier than she had thought a Klonn officer would be allowed to get away with. Underneath the facial hair, his teeth flashed white in a vicious, triumphant smile.

It's him! It's the Coyote! Gods protect us, Robin prayed.

The aeroship drifted closer, its closest wing dipping below the glider's. Under its belly, a pair of automatic guns turned in their mounts to aim directly at Robin.

"Not if I can help it!" Robin snarled. She kicked out. The flat of her boot connected with the areoship's wing,the jolt just enough to upset the aircraft's balance. The Coyote's head whipped back to his controls. Suddenly, the aeroship was tumbling and flashing through the twilight, careening toward the ground.

"Crash. Go on, crash!" Robin snarled, the words torn out of her mouth by the wind, only mildly surprised at her own bloodlust.

Except the aeroship didn't crash. It pulled up at the last minute, belly brushing the trees, sending a flurry autumn leaves billowing up in its wake. The aircraft stabilized, and Robin scrambled back inside the glider. Ears still filled with the rush of white noise from the wind, Robin flung herself at the bomb lever and awaited Wade's signal, hoping she hadn't missed it.

Wade pushed them down into a nosedive, until they were practically on top of the aeroship. Gravity yanked at Robin's legs, filled her guts with blood and dread. The only thing that kept her from slamming into the rear of Wade's seat was her grip on the lever.

"Omens," Robin whispered, staring at it as her emergency repair tools were shaken loose from her box—she'd twice failed to latch the lid properly in her haste—clanging and bouncing off the wooden floor, falling out into the twilight.

"Now!" Wade shouted, and hauled them upright.

Robin got her feet under her and *yanked.*

For a terrifyingly brief second, the bomb seemed to hover of its own accord in the open space the drop doors had vacated. And then the straps released, and it was gone, whistling into the air.

Below them, the Coyote's aeroship twisted out from under it and circled back, aiming another strafe of bullets at the glider. Wade yelped and jerked them to the side, tilting his whole body to the left to put more weight behind the turn. Robin obligingly sprang over to the left of the glider to lend her own bodyweight, feet planted on a wall strut, hands clinging to the rungs set inside the frame ribs.

The aeroship stopped shooting at them and dove after the bomb instead. It fired a single shot, and then a roaring flare of fire erupted, sizzling down from the sky in streams. A cocktail of chemicals fell like rain onto the trees below, and the aeroship twisted again, avoiding the shower of flames. Robin had never seen a bomb like that before, never seen fire fall like water. It would have consumed the entire enemy compound—if it had gotten there.

Instead, they had wasted it. It had been shot down too far up in the air—not even the trees were burning, the streams of fire snuffing out in the high breeze before they could even touch the forest.

"Hells!" Robin snarled again, slamming her palm against the frame in frustration. She threw herself into the task of covering up the hole she had fallen through. It took several of the largest patches, which she had to retrieve from all over the cabin, but they held.

Her heart thundering with adrenaline, Robin closed the drop hatch and looked around. The glider was listing sideways on an updraft, and slowly sinking.

"Wade? Pull up, man," she panted, trying to catch her breath. She turned to him, but stopped when she caught sight of the Coyote's aeroship as it retreated over the dark of the ancient forest. She stared, and for a brief second, it seemed as if the whole world had paused.

The aeroship's tail vanished into the thin cloud bank. Just as Wade had described, it was painted with a stylized canine face: yellow eyes over the exhaust ports created snarling teeth in the pipes that coughed out great dark clouds of smoke.

And then she heard it turn around.

"Captain Perwink," Robin said. Her voice felt like it was trapped in her larynx; only the smallest whisper of sound could escape. "Wade? Wade! Move. C'mon, Wade, move! It's the gods-hating Coyote!"

Wade didn't answer.

He was slumped sideways in his seat, eyes closed and mouth slack, blood bubbling from a raw, rough bullet hole in his shoulder.

CHAPTER FOUR

ROBIN DIDN'T KNOW WHAT TO DO. SHE *DIDN'T KNOW WHAT TO DO.*

Remember the training, she thought as she grabbed the side of Wade's chair, feet skidding out from under her as the glider tilted at an alarming angle. *What first? What first? Safe gliding altitude. Do that first.*

"Safe! Ha," Robin scoffed to herself, even as she reached around Wade's slumped torso and yanked the yoke back hard, pulling the nose of the aircraft level with the horizon. A draft caught the tail and shook the glider like a unexpected wave on the ocean. Jamming at the pedals with her hands as she scrambled over Wade's lap,she got the flaps on the wings opened enough to catch it, propelling them up in a dizzying vertical ascent.

That should buy her some time and, if she was lucky, hide her from the Coyote long enough for her to . . .

First aid, she scolded herself firmly. "Step one, check for signs of . . . of . . ." She squirmed around in the cramped space, yanking off her right glove with her teeth and setting her fingers against Wade's neck. There was a pulse, but it was thready and stuttered.

"Step two, stop the bleeding," she said. "Medical kit is . . .

rudding *hells*." The spot where it was usually secured on the slim shelving built into the ribs of the glider was empty, the straps torn and frayed. It must have gone out the side of the glider when Robin did. "Improvise, Sergeant!" she scolded herself when the wash of despair threatened to rob her of motivation.

Oiled canvas patches weren't designed to be absorbent. In fact, they were pre-pasted to be almost the exact opposite, ready to slap on a tear, not a person. Still, they would have to do. Yanking her scarf from around her neck, and keeping her ears open for the buzz of an aeroship, Robin scuffled around the cabin, the floor juddering and shuddering beneath her feet as the glider drifted, rudderless. She scooped up two patches that hadn't been sucked into the sky and, working quickly, folded her scarf into a pad big enough to cover a bullet wound. Then she jammed it down hard on Wade's shoulder, making sure it really got in there. She didn't have time to be disgusted by the way she could see right through to the bone, or by the smell of the raw meat and blood of him.

The medics could worry about how clean the scarf was and the possibility of putrid wounds *after* she got their asses back to Saskwya and down on the ground. Wiping the blood from the edges of the wound with the tail of her shirt, Robin slapped the two patches over her scarf, using their hastily applied adhesive to hold it in place. Wade grunted, head rolling, eyes open long enough for her to see just the whites.

"I'm sorry, Wade. I'm so sorry," she said, and then she unclipped him from his seat and heaved him around the back of it into hers. He made a rough, groan-scream sort of sound, but didn't wake up. Robin was no medic, but she didn't think that was good. Her hands were shaking too badly to get him clipped in right, so she just slung the safety belts around him, tucking his ruined arm in close to his chest, and tied him into place.

Then she threw herself down into the pilot's seat.

Home, she thought desperately. *Just get us home. You can do it, Sergeant. You can. Just . . . don't panic. Deep breaths.*

If it was there at all, the buzz of the Coyote's aeroship was lost in the whistle of wind against canvas. She couldn't hear him, but neither had they heard his first approach, either. "He wouldn't have given up. Don't get complacent," Robin warned herself. "Go. Get away."

Slowly, tentatively, Robin raised her arms. It felt like she was pushing through thick sand, and not just air. Her arms shook—hells, her whole body shook with the intense, screaming desire to *run, run, run away.*

Robin forced each finger to curl around the steering column, the nubs biting into her bare hands. *Faster, faster!* her mind screamed, but her body wouldn't comply. The world was quiet, slow, almost . . . almost *calm.*

"One foot here, one foot there," she said, placing them with deliberate care on the pedals. The crackle of paper drew her gaze downward, to the topographic map pinned to the floor with thumbtacks. A pair of red circles marked the target. And home, home was . . .

"That way," Robin said. She jammed the yoke to the side and shouldered into the turn.

The glider swooped and dove, careening to the right, cutting through the cloud cover in a steep bank that left her stomach far behind. She didn't dare get too close to the tree line, not without knowing where the Coyote was now, and not without the guarantee of an updraft to propel them back high enough to keep them on to the front lines. Wade would always rise in gentle circles on a breeze if he was able. Robin had no time for a slow ascent, hopping from gust to gust, watching the birds and leaves for signs of an upswell, like a small boat on a choppy lake.

She was concentrating so fiercely on staying aloft that the rip of a bullet through the wooden floor behind her made her scream. Wood splinters flew, and she was glad she had her goggles on still as they pinged off the windscreen and into her face. She pushed hard, slammed the glider in the other direction, ducking and weaving. The Coyote was directly below her. He had to be. She couldn't see him.

Get behind his tail, she thought, reminded of the dogs she'd evaded in the factory fields. *He can't shoot you if you're not upwind of him. His guns are under his cockpit, and on his nose.*

Another hard jerk, and she was diving again, belly skimming the treetops, head craned up to catch the shadow of his aeroship against the sunset. Gliders were, by nature, slower than the Klonn aeroship,s so he should pass over her in—*there!*

A flock of small brown birds burst out of the canopy in front of her, and she followed them up, rising behind the Coyote, and just too high for his belly gun to hit without first slicing through his own wings. She offered a sneer of her own at the tailpipes. The aeroplane swerved and looped, the silver helmet in the cockpit craned around to glare at Robin. She watched his hands, reflected through his own windscreen, and copied the motions, staying on his tail, using the heat from his exhaust to keep her aloft.

Dipping, diving, careening in tight circles, the glider's greater maneuverability and lightness of frame kept them dancing close. The yoke fought her, hard, her mid-flight-gained muscles just barely strong enough to keep it on her leash. Her palms burned, and a jagged tear opened on the underside of her thumb. But the longer Robin rode the controls, the more the intuition, the *feel* of the air around her, began to coalesce. She could work with it, instead of against the natural dip and sway. Just like she had guessed what Wade would do next, she began to anticipate the Coyote's moves, and then—oh, and then . . . then the clever, stubborn, horrible bastard *ran out of gas.*

His machine started to whine and sputter, coughing puffs of black smoke into the air. The sky was dark, the skinny moon and glittering stars reflecting like mercury off the aeroship's hull. It was enough for Robin to see by, though, and she watched as the Coyote turned tail and ran. Evening had cooled the forest, and the mist rising from the trees obscured his flight path, but Robin dabbed a fingerprint of blood on the map to indicate where he'd disappeared.

Fear and adrenaline washed away, and relief dropped like an icy stone in Robin's gut. Exhausted, aching, bleeding, and praying that her fancy flying hadn't taken so long that Wade was past the point of help, Robin wrenched the glider north.

#

They hit the hard-packed dirt of the runway with a juddering jerk. Robin barely had enough presence of mind to remember to yank the handbrake sharply. The glider stopped just short of its nose crumpling against the side of the hangar. Her hands, already blistered severely, protested sharply, splitting open and dripping blood onto her thighs when she finally prised her rigid fingers from the yoke.

Before the glider had even settled, someone from the ground crew had untied the door flaps, reaching in. The crewman paused, staring in horror at the interior of the glider. The few remaining pieces of Robin's tools were strewn across the floor, still skittering as the craft settled in place. The canvas on the other side of the body was entirely absent. Wade was slumped in Robin's seat. Sticky, ominous red puddled on the floor by his limply curled fingers, running into his palm from beneath his shirt cuff like a benediction.

"The captain's hurt!" Robin snarled from the front seat, and that was enough to startle the crewman into action. He called for a medical porter, and then hopped into the glider to detangle Wade's limp body from Robin's hasty spiderweb of crisscrossing safety straps. The crewman had to saw through the leather straps with his boot knife. Robin unclipped herself from the pilot's seat, and tried not to stare at the streaks of blood her own touch had left behind on the buckle.

Porters surged into the small interior, pushing Robin back when she tried to help them, barking at her to stay out of the way as they got Wade slumped out the door and loaded onto a stretcher. Once they had, another medic yanked her from the glider and shoved her up against its side, preventing her from following after the group who'd huddled around her pilot. The medic examined her hands, but Robin's eyes were for Wade only. Two solidly built porters knelt at the foot and head of the too-white stretcher, and hefted the whole thing onto their shoulders.

Wade's head lolled to the side, his lips bloodless. Robin's heart slammed against the hollow of her throat.

A third medic was already beside them, cutting off Wade's uniform jacket, pulling at the sticky glue on the canvas patches, revealing the injury that Robin had spent the whole flight back trying not to think about. There wasn't much of his shoulder left. She wasn't sure the medics would even be able to save his arm. He would definitely never be able to fly a glider again.

Then Wade was whisked away. Robin shoved aside the medic fussing over her hands and followed in Wade's wake like a tattered kite. The medic clicked his tongue in annoyance and rushed after her. They were forcefully separated again in the medical center's hallway. Wade was rushed toward the surgery theatre; she was chivvied into a private room.

"Up on the edge of the bed, Sergeant. Sit and don't move, hands out," the medic ordered. Robin obeyed. The medic shoved gauze into her palms and doused it with the yellow sting of iodine. Robin winced, but didn't let go.

"Do not move," the medic repeated, wagging a finger in her face. Then he rushed out with a clipboard and a harried gait to no doubt report in on Robin's health to some scrubbed-up Benne desk-pilot.

It was only then that Robin realized how dark it seemed in

the room. Though the gas lamps were apparently lit, going by the smell, she could hardly see anything past the bridge of her own nose.

She was still wearing her goggles.

Robin reached up with one hand and tried to undo the large buckle at the back of the wide strap, but her palms hurt too much. Using her knuckle, she shoved at the rim of the goggles until they rode up on her forehead. She was sure she looked a fright—blood streaking her cheek, hair shoved into bizarre tufts, braid loosened from her impromptu stroll along the glider's wing —but she didn't care. She returned her hand to the iodine-soaked gauze and told herself that the renewed sting was punishment for disobeying.

How can I pray now, she thought suddenly, *when the gods will be able to see the state of my hands? Will they mistake me for a Benne? Will they listen?*

The medic returned before Robin could think any further down that path, and she was grateful for the distraction. He looked serious and was trailing an administration officer in his wake; the woman was clearly freshly commissioned. Her uniform was too fresh, her expression too eager, too serious. She had a tight black bun, her dark brown skin scrubbed clean, and had a probing, eager gaze. Her uniform buttons still held their factory shine. The medic removed the gauze from Robin's hands and began the careful process of cleaning and wrapping them.

Robin ignored him and turned her attention to the officer. "How's Wa—Captain Perwink?" Robin asked.

"He'll live," the officer replied, and Robin slumped with heart-thumping relief.

He'll live. He'll probably find a pretty, rich wife after this and be done with the Air Patrol altogether, but I did it. I saved him, Robin thought. Handsome Benne men didn't need to find jobs after they got an honorable discharge, their pension, and the esteem bestowed upon them was usually enough to provide them with a comfortable existence among their fellow civilians.

"I'm not here to discuss Perwink," the officer said, tone abrupt. "Give me your report, Sergeant."

Robin was startled by the terseness, but she supposed the Air Patrol must be pretty desperate to know why one of their best officers was lying in the infirmary, half bled dry and shoulder a wreck. "The flight was normal and on schedule, as per our orders, until we neared the drop point," Robin said, forcing her tone to be neutral, her face to betray none of the pain she felt from her hands or the residual shock of the midair dance. "Just as we were about to release the . . ." She cut her eyes to the medic.

"Package," the officer supplied, not looking up from the careful notes she was taking. Her clipboard was also factory fresh.

"The package," Robin repeated. "When we were about to release the package, we were suddenly fired upon."

The officer still didn't look up. "You didn't hear the other aircraft approach?" For all her newness in her position, it was clear why she'd been promoted. She was serious, direct, and her tone betrayed absolutely no emotion. A chill went up Robin's spine, and she shook her shoulders to dispel the urge to ward against ill-luck with crossed fingers.

"No, we didn't hear it, ma'am," Robin replied.

"So, it wasn't a Klonn aircraft."

"I didn't say that."

"Then you did hear it approach?"

"I didn't," Robin insisted. She looked to the medic for confirmation that she had already answered this question. But he was focused on her hands and his job, professionally deaf. "And neither did Wade—er, Captain Perwink. Neither of us heard it, as far as I know. There was just gunfire. I assume it came up from below us—possibly took off as it watched us go overhead."

"Very well," the officer allowed, tone carefully blank and clearly unconvinced. "If you're certain."

"I know what it sounds like, ma'am," Robin harrumphed, slumping her shoulders. "But we didn't hear him approach."

It was possible that they had missed the faint sound of the engines coming closer while they'd been talking, but more likely, it was because the aeroship had been too far below or above them —at that distance, it was hard to hear anything over the soft rush of the glider cutting through the upper atmosphere. The officer looked up at the medic, and then jerked her chin at the door. He finished tying off the bandages, wiped his hands on a towel, and left with his trolley cart of supplies, without saying a word. Robin watched him go, feeling strangely like a baby bird left to the mercy of a vicious street cat.

Oh, gods. Did she know that Robin was holding back, that she hadn't spoken about her walk along the wing? Or how she'd meet the other pilot's gray, cold eyes through the windscreen? Or that she wasn't ready to share the uncanny experience that had shaken her to here core? She shook her shoulders again and squared them, ready to meet the officer blow for blow if she had to. The woman was full of the sort of high-minded Benne superiority that drove her crazy.

"And then?" the officer prompted, and Robin watched as one perfectly sculpted eyebrow rose above the edge of the clipboard.

"And then we fought," Robin said. "Captain Perwink had the situation under control, and I made repairs due to bullet holes. Once that was complete, I readied to drop the package, and did so at Captain Perwink's instruction."

"Were you on target?"

"Captain Perwink said that we were in position and told me to release the package."

"But were you on target?" the officer insisted.

"As per our orders, I have no way of knowing, ma'am," Robin admitted, gritting her teeth together and forcing a bland smile to hide her irritation. How dare they deny Robin the means to know, to *help*, and then grill her like this? "Even if we were, the other pilot shot it out of the air before it got too low—it exploded far above the tree line. The, ah . . . the effects smoldered out in the sky."

"Did any of it meet the target?"

"Not that I could see."

The officer took time to make notes, head bobbing to herself. Robin had no idea what that meant. The scratch of the pen on paper grated on Robin's nerves, but she remained at parade rest to keep from fidgeting—or as close to parade rest as possible while sitting on a cot. "But you did *know* there was a topographic map?" she asked at length.

"I found it spread out on the floor by the tail pedals when I took his seat."

The officer made a noise low in her throat, and Robin couldn't tell if it was meant to be encouraging or not. It sure didn't sound like it. "And have you had much flight training, Sergeant?"

"Just the standard emergency preparedness courses, ma'am," Robin admitted, getting antsy. "I don't have the . . ." *Money*, she thought uncharitably, but said, "time to do anything more than the basics."

"And how did you find flying the glider? Was it difficult?"

Robin frowned, uncertain as to why anyone would care. "No," she said, and then amended, "well, no more difficult that I thought it would be. It was a bit harder to wrestle the stick around with a deadweight in the cabin, but I watch the captain when he flies. I'm pretty familiar with the dash."

"Did the captain ever allow you to fly when you were on any other flights?"

"*What?*" Robin asked, startled. "No, of course not! That would have been completely irresponsible. Look, I'm sorry, Officer . . ."

"Vender."

"—Officer Vender, but I'm very confused by this line of questioning. Wade has never done anything that would require a formal reprimand while in the air, and neither have I. I told you, we were shot at. I only flew the glider because Wade was unconscious. What is this really about?"

Officer Vender finally lifted her gaze, but the look she sent Robin was cold and closed, impossible to interpret.

"What *is* this really about?" she asked again.

"Our scouts in the air said that there was some spectacular flying going on, and when the general realized that it was you flying on the way home . . ." Vender's expression softened, something akin to pride flickering in her gaze.

Robin shook her head, even more confused. "I'm sorry, are you saying that they were *happy* to hear it had been me dancing with the Coyote?"

"Captain Perwink is off the roster. Permanently," Officer Vender said, her face shutting down again, her tone clipped and impersonal once more, the very picture of Benne restraint. "We have a spare glider and nobody with the in-flight hours or expertise to fly it. The next pilot in line for a promotion is . . . well, unfit." She raised her eyebrows meaningfully. "They're young. Far too young."

Robin felt realization strike like lightning. "Surely you're not suggesting that I . . ." She trailed off, uncertain how to finish that sentence.

"*I* am not suggesting anything," Vender said, but she said it with a note of whimsy. She was lying, and on purpose.

"Omens," Robin said, slouching into the cot.

"Get yourself in order, Sergeant, and report to the general's office as soon as you're able." Officer Vender nodded curtly and tucked her clipboard under one arm. She offered Robin a smile so genuine and confident that it knocked the breath out of her as solidly as any punch to her stomach might have. Officer Vender then turned to exit the room. Just before she left, she paused in the doorway and looked back over her shoulder. "Congratulations, Captain Arianhod. Show those boys how we girls give the enemy hell."

Then she was gone. Robin was alone, dizzy and confused. Her heart fluttered against her ribs, her pulse beating in the hollow of her throat with such speed that, for a moment, Robin wondered if she would be sick. She reached up and pinched her own cheek, hard. It hurt. She assumed that meant she was awake.

There's no way they're serious, she thought. *Captain Arianhod?*

She brushed her shoulder with crossed fingers, just to be safe. *Mid-flight to pilot in one night, and an encounter with the . . .* "Oh, omens!" she cursed. She pushed off the bed and ran down the hall after Vender.

"Officer!" she cried when she caught up to the other woman, who was just turning to go into one of a long string of offices.

Vender paused and turned, her stern mask back in place and a frown playing at the sides of her mouth. "Arianhod," she replied, clearly not willing to spread the news of Robin's new title before it was made official. "Was there something you wanted to add?"

"Yes," Robin said. "The aircraft we danced with, the pilot—it was the Coyote."

Underneath her grave expression, Officer Vender turned clammy pale. "Are you sure?"

Robin nodded. "I saw the tailpipes. Clearly."

For a long second, Vender seemed to have completely lost the ability to speak. Her mouth worked, and she inhaled, but no sound came out. Finally, right as Robin was starting to wonder if she would have to pound her superior officer on the back to get her to stop turning blue, Vender coughed and sucked in a lungful of air. She patted Robin's arm once, as if laying down a blessing, and then said, "Very well. I will make certain that gets into the report."

CHAPTER FIVE

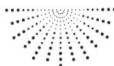

A<small>L WAS LEANING AGAINST THE WALL BESIDE THE GATES WHEN</small> Robin left the base. He didn't blend into the shadows at all—stealth had never been his strong suit. Robin stopped, not surprised, but not sure how to tell him what had happened, either.

"Omens, Robin! Are you in one piece? They said it was the Coyote, that rudding coal-bag, and I was scared stupid!" he said, shoving into the light to wrap his meaty arms around her shoulders. He squeezed so hard Robin's feet left the ground.

"How could you tell if you were scared stupid? Can you get any dumber?" Robin teased, but she leaned her head against his neck, grateful for his warmth and his concern.

"Har, har," Al replied, and set her down. He stepped back, cataloging her at arm's length. "Is everything where it should be?"

Not on Wade, Robin thought, but she couldn't bring herself to say it out loud.

Robin knew the kind of picture she must have made. Her new goggles were perched high on her forehead, keeping her hair back, if not contained. The escaping hairs around her face had been tickling at her eyebrows and cheeks since they landed, and the adrenaline and shock had worn off enough for her to notice. They were annoying, and too short to do anything about without the full use of her hands, which were swathed now in fresh white bandages.

The general had said nothing when she used her new captain's goggles as a substitute hair band, and Robin was grateful for that. She had removed her equally new capelet as soon as she was outside the general's office, and had folded it carefully to keep it from creasing. Now, it was bundled up under her arm, buttons shining in the lamplight. She curled her body around it, trying to hide it from view.

Al saw it, anyway, and for a second, Robin hoped he wouldn't recognize it. It was a stupid hope.

"Is that yours?" he asked, eyes wide and mouth slack with shock. "Holy omens, Robin. Did they promote you?"

"No!" Robin denied, and then rolled her eyes at her own vehement lie. "Yes." Al took another step back, and Robin kept herself from pushing forward, into his embrace, into the warmth and surety of support and friendship that she so needed right now. "Al, please, don't be mad."

"I'm not mad!" Al spat. "I just . . . don't understand. One of us? A pilot?"

"I couldn't say no," Robin said. "The pay increase. The station. Al, I'll be an officer."

Al's nose scrunched up.

"No," Robin insisted before he could say it. Now she did take a step forward. She got up in Al's face and bared her teeth at him. "You know me better than that, Alistair Brigid. I will not turn into a scrubbed-up snob just because they asked me to sit in a different part of the glider. Don't be an ass."

"I'm not being an ass!" Al snarled back, but he still turned his back to her, his whole posture slumped. Wounded.

"Don't make me feel bad about this! I'm scared, too, all right? But I'm proud that I've proved myself worthy of promotion, proud to be a Sealie good enough to rise above the restrictions they push on us, and proud that I have skills the Air Patrol wants. Can't you just be happy for me? Please?" Robin leaned her forehead against his back, headbutting his shoulder blade lightly. "C'mon, Al. Don't do this to me. Not now. Not when I need someone on my side."

He turned, and one of his thick arms wrapped around her shoulders. "Let's go get drunk."

"On what?" Robin snorted.

Al held up a clay bottle of what had to be his brother's horrific mead. The cork dangled by a string tied to the handle, and the bottle had been hanging from his belt. Al had been partaking of it already, then. No wonder he was being prickly.

"Absolutely not," she said.

"Then, how 'bout we spend that bonus pay you must have gotten."

"Al," Robin said, slowly, twisting her capelet into a tighter ball. "I have to report to the officers' breakfast tomorrow. I can't show up hungover."

"Fine. We don't have to celebrate," he grunted, mulish and hurt.

"I didn't mean—"

"I'll just walk you home, then," he interrupted.

The thought of walking through the slums alone, in Benne garb, made her uncomfortable. Grateful for the offer, she said, "Yeah, thanks. That's fine." Al pushed her forward, churlish. Robin took a step, and then stopped abruptly, driving a sharp elbow into his midsection.

"Oof," he said, just like she knew he would. She jabbed again, but he wouldn't rise to the bait and play, so she let him alone to his brooding. As they walked, she did a little brooding of her own.

Like water seeping into a dishcloth, Robin had the sudden foreboding sense that the gods had planned something for her, that they were positioning her on a playing board without Robin even knowing she was a part of the game. She had believed in gods her whole life, but she had never seen one. To feel, suddenly, as if she was holding the attention of so many, to see the evidence that they really were influencing her destiny, that they really did have their spindly fingers on the cards that determined her life, was unnerving in a way that Robin couldn't quite spell out.

Al walked her all the way to her front door, and then stopped, staring up at her from the bottom step. "You could turn it down, you know," he said softly.

Robin sighed. "And do what, Al? Drop out of the Air Patrol altogether? Because that's the only way to keep them from ordering me into the pilot's seat."

"Could do," he said, sniffing once and rubbing at his flat nose with the back of his grease-stained hand.

"Oh, sure, and then what? Get married, and have kids, and be content to wait for the next bomb to fall on my house? No, thanks."

Al lowered his eyes, mumbled a goodbye, and was lost to the shadows beyond the streetlamps so quickly, Robin wondered if he'd learned some woodland god's vanishing trick. She had no doubts that the pot of mead would be empty before he got home. Sighing, Robin turned and let herself inside.

Once there, Robin unrolled the fawn-brown leather capelet, with its gold braid trim and highly polished brass buttons, and hung it from the tree in the hall. Then she joined her parents in the parlor. She'd decided to simply say nothing, to let her appearance speak for itself. It was the coward's way, sure, but this was not the sky—Robin could be a coward here, in the safety of her own home. Papa looked up from his newspaper, which was so scraggly and creased that he had clearly brought it home from work after many other people had already read it.

Robin handed Mama the bonus pay packet. She took it, caught sight of Robin's bandaged hands, and started crying, soft and silent, tears falling into the mending she held cradled in her lap. When Papa realized why, he didn't shout, or rage—he just took Mama's hands between his own, comforting, and kissed her on the forehead. Then her lips. Then he raised her left hand to his mouth and kissed the thin, diagonal scar that ran across her palm —her Marriage Line. Papa had an identical one on his own left hand, where they had been bound together by the Wise Women on their wedding day.

Robin ran her fingers over the bandages that crisscrossed her hands. Pilot's scars would get in the way of anyone being able to see Robin's Marriage Line when it was ever her turn. *If* it was ever her turn.

Nerves churned in her empty stomach as Robin reported to the officers' mess in the morning. She paused just long enough in the hallway to slip her goggles on, letting them hang around her neck, and to shake out and then swing the capelet over her shoulders, covering the shirt her mother had spent the night scrubbing back into a semblance of its original cream color. Mama had also scrubbed Robin's hair clean, and had plaited it tightly into a rigid braid that reached nearly to the small of her back. Beeswax from the hive in the garden had been smoothed across her scalp to keep the flyaways regimented into a semblance of control. Robin's scalp still ached from Mama's vigorous fingers, and her ears hurt from the tightness of her hair. She had spent the whole walk to the base wiggling her eyebrows in an attempt to loosen the pull without destroying Mama's hard work.

Tugging the capelet into position one last time, Robin took a deep, centering breath, and, without knocking, went inside. The room was maybe half the size of the canteen hangar, close and as cozy as it could be made on a base. It was filled with small round tables and scuffed, mismatched chairs that were nonetheless more comfortable-looking than the wide, dented copper benches Robin had sat on every morning for the last six years. There were maybe a dozen tables pressed in around the long credenza on the back wall, and three times as many officers as that mingling around, arranging their breakfasts and curling over wrinkled, well-marked topographical maps.

She was greeted with the halloos of a room full of Benne officers who all stood when she came in. The wall of noise was startling and unexpected. Robin froze in the doorway, as if a night watchman at a factory had caught her thieving, knife ready in his hand.

Then a brawny lieutenant colonel wearing the most ridiculous of fanciful moustaches crowded up beside her, grabbed her elbow, and pulled her into the center of the cozy lounge that made up the mess. All her blood seemed to rush into her head, abandoning her feet as they stumbled along the high pile of thick rugs. Her boots—polished to as high a shine as possible, but still scuffed and cracked with age—snagged on the plush carpet.

Everything inside of her went shivery when a fellow captain clapped her on the shoulders and boomed: "Well done, well done. Gave that monster what for, you did! About time one of us sent him off with his tailpipes between his legs."

"I . . . uh, well, it was W-Wa—er, Captain Perwink who—"

"You saved his life!" another captain cried, raising a cup of tea as though it was a beer stein.

Robin twisted out from under the lieutenant colonel's scarred paw and took a step back from the claustrophobic press of the officers who had decided to welcome her. There was a distinct divide between them and the rest of the Benne who lined the walls with narrowed eyes and crossed arms. Robin stood her ground firmly in the no-man's-land between them.

Not a three-way war, my arse, Robin thought. She and Wade had often argued over the class divide that turned the two-sided conflict with the Klonn into a three-sided conflict no one acknowledged. A pang of worry stabbed through her, and she wondered how Wade fared. Had his wound become infected? Was he out of danger or still fighting?

"Captain," the lieutenant colonel said, gathering her attention. He held up something small, and round, and green. A medal of valor. The frontispiece was stamped with the dual outstretched wings of the Air Patrol, the Benne symbol for courage—the hollow circle that represented the All-Mother's all-encompassing embrace—nestled in between.

"What?" Robin said, flummoxed and confused. She watched the lieutenant colonel pin it over her heart on the capelet, crunching her chin down even as her eyebrows rose. "No, wait. I didn't do anything special—"

"Nonsense!" he blustered as he fixed the button in place with fingers thick like sausages.

Frustration curled in Robin's guts—there was little more annoying than a superior officer who *talked over you*.

One of the displeased officers along the wall strode forward to slap something into the lieutenant colonel's hand when he held it out, palm up, pilot's scars on proud display. He deftly flipped the little objects in his grip, and then pinned them in place, as well. Two brass rank pins were now secured to the front of Robin's capelet, on either side of the stiff, short collar. They were a pair of stylized, opened wings that spread across her collarbone, announcing her to the world as the captain of a glider. She breathed heavily through her nose and thought of the sky, and the breeze, and of not *falling over in a dead faint*.

Half the room burst into uproarious—and perhaps a bit too *forced*—applause. The rest tapped their palms on their thighs politely, and then went back to the their tea and their plans. The cheers rang off the metal walls of the room and clanged discordently in Robin's ears.

Pomp and faff done, the lieutenant colonel tugged an envelope from his breast pocket, under his own battered and wear-soft capelet, and handed it over. Then he saluted the room and strode out the door, his stride long and his gait confident. Feeling foolish, and still standing in the middle of everything like an awkward cat, Robin opened the envelope. Inside was another pair of wings for her leather waistcoat, so her rank would be clear even when she wasn't wearing the capelet, and her commissioning papers.

This is really happening, she thought. *That's my name, and that's the seal of King Auden. They must be completely daft. Or very, very desperate. They really want to reward me for sheer stupid good luck.*

Then suddenly, someone smacked her shoulder. Robin stumbled and whirled around, jaw and fists clenched, ready for a fight, only to realize that it hadn't been a blow. It'd been a congratulations. Someone else patted her shoulder, and then another, and Robin stood still and let them rain down soft blows on her back and shoulders.

"Normally, we shake hands," one of the pilots who'd decided not to hate Robin—at least, not openly—said, cozying up beside her. The woman had her hair pulled up in a severe, glossy red bun, smooth and honestly a bit intimidating. But her face bore the ruddy marks the fair-skinned among the pilots all got on their cheeks, where the pale line of their goggles ended and the sunburn began. Wade had them, too. "But not until your calluses come in." She handed Robin a small jar of salve with such grave solemnity that Robin might have been concerned, had not the pilots around her burst into raucous laughter the minute it was in her bandaged hand. Some sort of hazing ritual, Robin guessed. "Now, breakfast?"

She gestured flippantly at the overburdened credenza against the wall. There was more food on those platters than Robin had seen at home in two months. And now that her attention was on it, Robin could *smell* it. Roasted meats, fresh fruit, and fresh-baked bread. *Gods.* Her stomach yowled, and the pilot beside her laughed and nudged her gently toward the spread.

Torn between the superior offerings of the officers' breakfast and her desire to be with Al in someplace more familiar, Robin found herself stuck, unable to take a step. What would the rest of the Sealies say, she wondered, if she walked into the common canteen with her pilot's uniform, and sat down with them? She was going to have to find out sooner or later.

Eventually, she called herself a coward, and sucked up the courage to approach the small, terrifyingly civil breakfast buffet. She had survived a dance with the Coyote. She could damn well survive going over to that table and talking to her fellow captains, Benne or not.

They had congratulated her in front of their commanding officer, but now that the lieutenant colonel had left, presumably to take his breakfast with officers of his own rank, would she find her reception sedated? Robin swallowed hard. She hadn't spoken to many Benne besides Wade, and she had no idea if they would accept a Sealie among their ranks.

The woman who had given Robin the jar of salve jumped into the line behind her, and Robin offered her a strained smile. She returned it with one of her own, lighter and more free, and Robin felt something in her chest unclench.

"I'm Captain Renge, by the way," the woman said. "Catherine Renge."

"Robin Arianhod."

"Yes. I know."

"Oh. Right. Of course." Awkward silence descended as they each picked up their utensils and a plate. The line moved forward slightly, and Robin clutched at the heavy knife and fork, unwilling to reach forward to snag the first of the food from the serving trays and baskets, as she would have in the common canteen. *Patience*, she told herself. Robin was nothing if not good at being patient.

"Tea?" Renge asked as she poured some without waiting for Robin's answer. She used a china cup, far too delicate for service in the common canteen, and Robin suddenly felt homesick for the dented, cheap metal dishes she had known most of her life. Without asking, the woman dolloped sugar into the tea, and then handed it to Robin.

"Uh, thanks." Robin balanced it on her plate and stared into its grainy depths, trying not to pull a face.

"Something wrong?" Renge asked. Clearly, Robin hadn't succeeded.

"Uh," she said, and shook her head. Then she nodded. She could do this. "No honey?"

Captain Renge blinked. The warmth of her expression evaporated, leaving tawny eyebrows that rose upward and light eyes that narrowed underneath. "You'd actually prefer honey to sugar?"

"Yes," Robin said, and stood up straighter, refusing to be cowed, because dammit, everyone bloody well knew that Sealies couldn't afford to buy refined sugar. "I'm used to it, is all."

"Hm," Renge said. She took the tea from Robin's plate and placed it on her own, then deftly poured a second cup, which she then placed, less carefully, back into Robin's hand. Tea sloshed over the side and scalded Robin's knuckle, seeped into the backs of her bandages, but she didn't drop the cup. Mostly because she refused to be intimidated, but also because she didn't want the cost of the pricey china coming off her next pay.

With a lazy, dismissive gesture, Renge sent a boy in a server's uniform running to the kitchen for some honey. "Guess we'll have to keep honey in here from now on. I suppose you can remove the tick from the fur, but you can't . . . well." She said it with a sneer, and the man standing directly behind her chuckled. A few other sniggers were heard around the room, but they were thankfully among a minority of people, and mostly muffled against hands or cups.

Robin's shoulders ratcheted up again, and she bit down hard on her tongue. The line moved forward, and Robin forced herself to smile and say, "Thank you, that's very kind of you," to the woman before she turned her back and advanced. Robin filled her plate with all sorts of things she'd never had before—flaky breakfast pastries, sweet peanut preserves, something she highly suspected was creamed chocolate—and so much fresh fruit she wondered if she could actually eat it all. Just as she reached the end of the table, the serving boy returned with the honey. The little tarnished pot was freshly opened, with a delicate silver spoon perched beside it. The fine china dish and ridiculous paper doily it sat upon made it look even more dented, overused, and silly.

Robin suddenly felt very much like that honey pot.

She stopped deliberately, and in plain view of the others, to spoon a little honey into her tea, and the boy, his back to the Benne pilots in line, grinned at her, his dark eyes sparkling in his flushed face.

"Thank you, Mr. . . ." she said to the boy, and he was so surprised and pleased to be thanked that he nearly shouted his reply:

"Seti, Captain! Bill Seti!" He lifted his palm up to the gods to thank her for asking, and she repeated the gesture to thank him for giving it to her.

"Thank you, Mr. Seti," Robin said out loud, slowly and clearly and *deliberately*. She hadn't heard any of other officers thank the boy. "Is it possible to be sure there's honey every morning?"

"Absolutely, *Captain*," Bill said and grinned a grin fit to split open his face. Then he composed his features, ducked his head slightly, and returned to his place behind the table, servile and proper once more. Demonstratively, he set the pot of honey down between the tea carafes and the sugar dish.

Somebody in the rear of the line grumbled, but Robin lifted her chin and turned away. She found an unoccupied table in a corner and proceeded to pack half her bounty away in her cloth napkin. She also wrapped a choice piece of chocolate in an old waybill she found in her pocket. It would be good for buying charms. Then she set to the remainder with gusto. The bacon was still warm, and the tea was a bit weak for Robin's liking, but otherwise, the meal was fantastic. The pastry left buttery smears on her hands and, having no napkin anymore, Robin had to wipe them discreetly on the shirt under her leather vest, where nobody would see the stains.

No one came to sit beside her, but Robin didn't give a god's good ass. She wasn't here to make friends. She was here to pilot a glider, and to shoot down Klonn aeroships. She was here because she owed the Coyote for Wade's shoulder. And if the Benne prigs in pilots' uniforms had a problem with that, they could go hang. She had been promoted, so somebody in command thought her worth investing time and extra training in, felt she was worth trusting a glider to, and in the end, it was only their opinion that mattered.

Still, when she had finished eating, Robin lifted her bandaged palms to the sky, closed her eyes, and whispered her prayer of thanks for the meal as quietly as she could.

✺

Wade was still asleep when Robin stopped by the infirmary later. The medic pulled her aside before she went into his room and said, with a dour face: "I want you to be warned, Sarg—uh, Captain. His shoulder was . . . well, it was bad. About as bad as it could be. They couldn't save his arm."

"His whole arm?" Robin gasped. "By the gods."

The Benne medic sniffed at her oath, but let her in the room, all the same. Robin left one of the pastries she'd pilfered by the water glass on his bedside table, then forced herself to look at her former pilot and friend. His chest and shoulder were swathed with thick pads and crisp white bandages. But there was nothing past that lump of fabric. She touched the bandages over his shoulder briefly, lightly, and tried not to stare at the miserable line of his mouth, at the dark shadows under his eyes. The medic, who had been silently studying a stack of papers in the corner of the room, shook his head sadly when Robin asked if Wade had awakened yet.

"Thank you," Robin said, when what she really wanted to howl was: *It's not fair! The two of us survived a dance with the Coyote, and this is how the gods repay that valor?* Instead, she bobbed a polite nod to the medic and ducked out. Her stomach was in knots, her breakfast sitting too high in her sternum, and the backs of her eyes burned as she left the room.

Her next stop was the canteen, the napkin of treats clutched in nervous fingers. Robin hesitated in the open door, scanning the crowd for Al, fidgeting with the bottom hem of the capelet. She'd considered not wearing it, going back and forth with herself over whether that would look like she was trying to hide something that everyone else on base already knew, or whether it would look like she was gloating. In the end, she'd decided to just leave it on—like ripping off a bandage stuck to the skin with blood, the pain would be more intense, but over quicker.

She found Al seated at the very end of the back row, staring at the dingy metal wall, rolling his metal teacup between his hands. Needing time to firm up her resolve, Robin crossed the room in the opposite direction, going for the breakfast line. She wanted tea—wanted the faint, familiar metallic taste of the cup in her mouth, the honey-thick, bitter brew on her tongue when she spoke to Al. Though she felt kind of bad, going to breakfast tea again, after she'd had as much as she wanted in the officers' mess.

The line parted before her. The mid-flights that had been sneering at her just yesterday did a double-take, and then, with wide eyes, they stepped back and let Robin prepare herself a cup. Robin tried to gesture for them to go first, but they just shook their heads and refused to move until she had.

Mortified, she prepared her cup quickly, tongue like a shriveled grape behind her teeth, and slouched along the outer wall. She felt eyes boring into her back like needles and hated the stupid goggles perched on her forehead the way the pilots did, hated the ostentatious capelet. She hated that something that was good, something that she was supposed to be proud of, made her little more than an outsider no matter where she was.

A tarnished pot of cheap honey on a china saucer and paper doily.

When she reached Al's table, Robin hesitated, standing across from him with her steaming tea in one hand and the bundled napkin in the other. Al had to know she was there, had to have at least glanced up when the whispers around the room had started, but he just sat there. Just stared at the wall and kept rolling the cup between his whole, forge-calloused palms. Robin put the napkin down in front of him as a peace offering.

Al sniffed once, no doubt catching the rising scent from the warm butter pastries, and slid his eyes to the napkin. Then he lifted them higher, pausing at the capelet, tracing the fall of each gold braid, the curve of each round brass button, the cream-colored trim, the small moss green medal, the stretch of the brass rank pins. Finally, he looked up at Robin, his brown gaze jumping briefly up to the sparkling amber lenses of her freshly polished goggles, then back down to her face.

"Omens," he said, and reached out to tug apart the knot that held the napkin closed. "You didn't turn it down, eh? Now, how am I supposed to stare at your boobs?"

Robin threw back her head and laughed. It felt absurdly good, and it made every pair of eyes in the room turn to stare—trying, of course, to look like they weren't. It would be rude to stare openly at a superior officer.

Robin didn't care, though. She really didn't. Wade was alive, even if he hadn't woken up yet, even if he didn't yet know all that he had lost. She had been promoted, and her best friend wasn't angry at her anymore. Everyone else, Benne and Sealie alike, could go throw themselves in a frozen lake.

She sat down across from Al and sipped her tea. She trod affectionately on his toes with the hard heel of her boot.

"So, a captain, eh," Al said, mouth full of butter pastry and a blissful expression on his brick-wall face.

"They must be desperate to be promoting, you know, one of us."

Al let an amused snort rip. "Or maybe you're just that good, Robin."

Robin felt her cheeks get hot, the flush flagging across her nose. "Maybe," she said, but it wasn't really an agreement. "I have to spend all afternoon learning to shoot, and later, there'll be flight training and stuff. She fished the envelope out of the capelet's inner pocket, and showed Al the letters.

"You didn't crash the glider," Al said, setting aside the pastry to rifle through her commissioning papers. "That's a big bonus for them."

Robin smacked his shoulder half-heartedly. It felt good to be doing something familiar, to see the usual theatrical grimace on Al's face, and to feel the surge of friendly annoyance. Al raised a hand to shove her shoulder, but stopped when his palm touched the smooth, fresh doe-brown leather. He patted once with his fingers, and then pulled them away, awkwardly jamming his hands between his thighs under the table. His touch left behind a dull patina of ash and soot and engine grease, the signature that forge-drones left on everything. He cut his eyes to the stain, and then down again to his trapped hands.

Robin sighed. Right, well, maybe not *exactly* the way things were.

CHAPTER SIX

As all good Sealie parents did, Robin's had paid the traditional call to the Wise Woman before her birth. The old woman had smiled into her cup of glass beads, and then rolled her eyes heavenward as if to ask, "Goodness, why send me all of these ones today?"

"You had better name her after some sort of bird," the woman had said at length, "for she'll spend more time with her head in the clouds than any other girl I've yet had the pleasure of knowing."

So, when Robin was four, and she looked up into the sky and pointed to the sleek silver pleasure-zeppelin floating across the dappled blue and said, "Up, up, up, Papa!" her parents were only mildly surprised. They shared a look across the top of their daughter's head.

"Wasn't at all what I was expecting, but that, I s'pose, is a better choice than her wasting her time being a dreamer," Papa replied.

"Quite," Robin's mother had agreed, and they'd continued their afternoon walk into the walled Saskwyan city of Pyria. After purchasing the provisions they had come for—things that couldn't be foraged in the forest, like flour and bolts of cloth—they carefully counted their remaining coins and bought little Robin a small, sturdy book about zeppelins and aeroships. It was brightly decorated with primary-color infused cross-section illustrations of how the engines worked, how the balloons were inflated and the gasses inside mixed and heated gently to attain lift, what levers the captains had to haul on and when, to make the ornery things go in the proper directions.

Robin had spent all evening staring in rapt wonder at that book, seated on her papa's lap in the back garden of the brick house her family had lived in since the Great Sickness had driven the happily nomadic Sealies from their wagon homes. Back then, their house was on the outskirts of the town. Sealies weren't yet allowed inside Pyria's walls overnight. But Robin didn't mind—their neighborhood was bordered by the forests and roads their people had called home for generations.

Then, when Robin turned seven, the Klonn declared war.

The trees behind their house were sacrificed to make way for fields of factories, and Robin's neighborhood became part of Pyria itself, the border walls torn down to make smokestacks.

Soon after, the Saskwyan king introduced an edict drafting all able-bodied children ages fourteen and up (less, if certain economic hardships were met) into apprenticeships with one of the nation's vital public services—the armed forces, the factories, or the administrative sector. No one was surprised that Robin chose the Air Patrol. By thirteen, she was an engineering private, moved up swiftly to a forge corporal, and by sixteen, she was a mid-flight sergeant studying aeroship engineering on her days off. By seventeen, she was one of the few women who remained in service to the Air Patrol, the others having opted to drop out after the conclusion of their mandatory service, having left to become wives and mothers and raise the next generation of Saskwyan cannon fodder.

Now, just eight months after her seventeenth birthday, Robin

Arianhod had come home a pilot. Robin knew how fast gossip carried on the base, and she had no illusions about how quickly it would have traveled off of it. She wore her uniform home that night in its entirety, and let the few remaining neighbors stare.

Papa wasn't home yet, so Robin stripped off the capelet and goggles and left them hanging on the hall tree before she went to the kitchen to help Mama finish dinner. There wasn't much she could do, though, with her hands the way they were. The bandages were fresh, but only because gunnery training that afternoon had torn up her palms again.

Humming—like the soft, welcoming drone of bees—floated from the kitchen as her mother sang in snatches of words and a tumble of sighs. *"My home is all around me,"* she sang, the soft lullaby that Robin remembered well from her childhood and loved even better. *"And no matter where I roam—"*

Robin threw her arms around Mama's shoulders, buried her nose in her neck, and sang, *"As long as I have field and sky, and bees who follow me home!"*

"Ah, it's my daughter, buzz buzz," Mama said. "Hello, you." She turned into the hug.

Robin set another napkin-bundle on the cutting board, this time filled with a small wealth of savory rolls that she had snatched off the officers' mess buffet after her lunch. She wasn't sure how long she could get away with redistributing food without being reprimanded, but she was willing to do it until that happened. She would just have to remember to bring the cloth napkins back, so no one noticed a dent in the pile.

Mama opened the bundle, and nodded in appreciation. Then she pushed Robin down into the chair by the hearth and pressed a cup of very thin, very watered wine into her hand. "Your treat for being the Sealie everyone in this neighborhood is proud of."

"I don't know," Robin said. She sipped the honey-sweetened liquor. The rest of the bottle sat on the butcher block in the center of the room, and Robin guessed that Mama had traded the whole of the burlap Robin had stolen for it. "You didn't see the way the other mid-flights looked at me."

"Did Al look at you that way?" Mama asked, brushing her silvering curls off her forehead and turning her attention back to the meager vegetables on the cutting board.

"No."

"Then that is all that matters." Mama pressed the knife into the carrots. The rhythmic sound of her chopping was at once soothing and familiar. Robin sank back into the chair and enjoyed the sweetness of the wine, the warmth of the fire, the smell of hard work and home. For the first time in months, she felt full, and satisfied.

"That Al," Mama said, glancing at Robin slyly, mischief sparkling in her amber-brown eyes, "he's a good boy, and a good friend."

"Oh, Mama, no! Not you, too," Robin groaned, but she was smiling. "Do we have to do this? Now?"

"You're twice the catch now."

"And I've just been promoted. I can't leave."

Robin's mother stopped and frowned, and Robin couldn't help but echo the expression. It was true. If Robin were to leave now, the Air Patrol would be furious. They might even deny her resignation. They had the power to keep married women on staff, if their role was vital—and Robin didn't even want to think of the agony a husband might go through, wondering if his wife would make it back to the ground safely, especially if there was the possibility that she was carrying his child.

Robin slumped, all her good feeling suddenly overcome with the misery of knowing that, in accepting this promotion, she had also accepted the Air Patrol's complete control of her life. There was no longer any room for romance.

Mama left the carrots and knelt beside Robin, arms going around her shoulders, cheek pressed to Robin's neck. "If Al is happy for you, why can't you be happy, too?"

Robin knew Mama had a point, but she just couldn't get the nagging worry out of her head that something had gone wrong. Maybe they had made a mistake in picking her, and any second, an administrative officer would come to the door and politely ask Robin to return the commissioning papers and capelet. Perhaps, despite the assurances of her superiors and her fellow pilots, being at the helm of her own glider just wasn't what was meant for her. Or maybe it was the fear that, in taking this promotion, she had lost what it meant to be Sealie.

Robin pulled back and met Mama's eyes. "I just don't know if this is supposed to be my place in the world. What if this isn't what the gods intended for me? How can I be certain, Mama?"

"By believing in the words the Wise Woman told us when you were born," her mother said, turning Robin's hands palm up to display the blood-spotted bandages. "You were meant for the sky, little birdie. I cannot say that I'm not scared for you. And I wish that you did not have to fight. But if you must, then I would prefer you do it in the sky, with your head in those clouds you love so much."

❁

When Robin reported to the officers' mess for breakfast the next day, little Bill Seti's miserable expression told her she was in for a spot of trouble.

"What is it?" she asked as he tugged at the hem of her capelet. He had accosted her as soon as she'd gotten near the long breakfast table.

"It's Captain Renge, ma'am," he said, shuffling his feet in a little uncomfortable dance that reminded Robin strongly of a child in need of the water closet. His eyes cut to the side, and Robin followed his dark gaze.

The Benne pilot who had given her a hard time yesterday was leaning against the mantlepiece, smirking. The tarnished honey pot was upended over the mantle, a golden stream of honey oozing slowly off the edge and down the elaborate stone scroll-work, where it bubbled and pooled at the very edge of the fire in the hearth, mixing with the cinders.

"What a clumsy thing that tick-boy is," Captain Renge said, her face carefully blank and her tone light. Her hair was pulled back into an impeccable braid, and Robin jammed her hands into her trouser pockets in an effort to dispel the urge to viciously yank the tempting tail.

"I weren't neither," Seti whispered, his voice strained. "But she says, 'Sealies do as they're told,' ma'am. I thought, you being a Sealie and all, you'd want the honey, and that means I don't have to listen, 'cause you a pilot, too, but Captain Renge, she says . . ." He trailed off and looked down at his boots, brown cheeks flushing crimson in shame.

Robin resisted the urge to cross the room and pummel Captain Renge. There was already one in this room who'd behaved in a manner unfit for her station. There didn't need to be two. She wasn't going to give the Benne woman any more ammunition than her religion already afforded. Instead, she crouched and put her hand under the boy's chin, lifting his gaze to meet hers.

"What did she say, Mr. Seti?"

"That you didn't count. That you weren't a real pilot. That you were just a leech, like me." Seti winced. "She said they promoted you because you and Captain Perwink was . . . that you . . ."

"Thank you. That's good enough. I think I understand," Robin said, teeth clenched. "Back to the kitchen with you, Mr. Seti, and bring back another pot of honey."

He looked up at her, eyes round. "But she'll just make me . . . an' it'll be a *waste*. The bees will be so cross—"

"I know," Robin said. "And I'm sorry for it. But I need to make a point. I'll just have to hope they'll forgive me for it."

Seti looked unhappy, but went. Robin straightened, and every pair of eyes followed her as she strode across the room. She stopped just out of swinging distance and looked Captain Renge up and down. "Hmm," she said thoughtfully, loud enough for her words to carry into the lounge's corners. "You don't look like an idiot."

Renge's carefully blank face tightened, but otherwise, she made no indication that the insult had hit home.

"And you don't look like a Benne," she said. She had the gall to reach out and tug Robin's sparrow-brown braid. Insulting. Robin didn't move, didn't wince or pull away like Renge had clearly expected of her.

"Wow. Hair pulling," Robin said once Renge had let go. "That's mature. I could have sworn we were all grownups, here. And officers."

"Some of us are officers," Renge said through clenched teeth.

"And those of you who aren't?"

Renge grinned, toothy and wolfish, clearly missing the intended insult. Instead, she offered one of her own, lifting both scarred hands and waggling her thumbs meaningfully under Robin's nose.

"I see," Robin said. She held her arms to the side, spreading the edges of her capelet and making her medal of valor clink. "So, the rest of us are what, then?"

"Not welcome here," Renge hissed.

Robin dropped her hands to her sides and made a show of thinking that over. "Well, that's funny, " Robin said. "Because I could swear I was welcome. I mean, I have commissioning papers and everything, and I distinctly recall getting . . ." She looked down and started in mock surprise when she caught sight of her rank pins. "Why yes, there they are." She pointed a finger at her own throat.

Renge took a step forward, getting right in Robin's face. Robin craned her head back, as if the extra height Renge brought to bear offered her no more concern than finding a housefly on a bread loaf. She smiled placidly. She'd faced down far more frightening foes than Captain Renge, and that was just within the slums of Pyria. What she faced in the skies above greatly outweighed Renge and her petty insults.

"We don't want you here," Renge snarled.

Several pilots crowed their agreement, fists pumping in the air. A few others disagreed, and suddenly, there was a shouting match. Clipped, posh Benne accents hurtled abuse after abuse at Robin and each other, tossing about the words, "dirty tick," and "scrubbed-up snob."

Renge grinned. "Look what you've done," she said. "You've turned us against one another."

Robin shrugged. "You did that yourself."

"We don't need you!"

"Then why am I standing here in a pilot's uniform?" Robin snarled, loud enough to drown out the rest of the arguments.

Silence filled the room. Voices cut off mid-shout. Renge's face screwed up, as if she'd just swallowed something sour.

"You'll never be one of us," Renge hissed. *"Parasite."*

"And I thank the gods every day for that," Robin said, raising her palms showily, as if in prayer.

"We have worked hard to be here. All of us!" Renge snarled, throwing her own hands wide to indicate the other officers. "What have you done to deserve what you have? How have you suffered?"

"Suffering!" Robin scoffed. "You call being a pilot in the Air Patrol suffering? Your wage is twice what my father makes in a year! You get a hot breakfast every day! You never have to steal to make sure you can do your job! You have everything, and we have to scrounge. You sit here and play your silly war games, and it is the Sealies who have to pay for it, the Sealies who suffer for it, the Sealies on whose back you ride!"

Renge swung a fist at Robin's face, her lightning-quick pilot's reflexes too fast for Robin. Unlike the brat from the canteen, the notion that Renge would try to punch her *was* so absurd that Robin hadn't even expected Renge to contemplate a physical attack. Renge caught her square in the jaw, though, and Robin reeled backward, fetching up hard against one of the tall breakfast tables. Two other pilots jumped forward to put themselves between Renge and Robin. They didn't restrain Renge, or try to drag her off, but they made sure to block her way.

Robin put out a hand to steady herself. Nobody stepped forward to help. With her other hand, Robin touched the bandages on the back of her hand to the side of her lip. It felt swollen and hot, but they came away clean.

"You're a child," Robin said quietly, straightening. "You can't stand to have me in your sandbox. Well, guess what? I have every right to be here. More than a right, I think. Unlike the rest of your colleagues, I didn't get my ass shot up by the Coyote. And doesn't that just twist you up inside? First pilot to survive a dance with the Coyote, and it's a dirty little Sealie."

"It should have been you!" Renge screamed, fists balled at her sides in impotent rage. "It should have been you instead of Wade! He was a good pilot!"

"That he was," Robin spat, and even in her own ears, her voice sounded low and dangerous. "At least one of us is honoring what he's sacrificed." She took a deliberate step past the pilots who blocked her way. Neither man moved to stop her. Robin walked to the hearth and righted the overturned honey pot.

"I hope that, in the future, you'll be a bit more conscientious, Captain Renge," she stage-whispered. "In case you haven't noticed, there's a war on. It's a shame to waste anything so callously."

"It's only honey," Renge said. "Nobody but a Sealie would care."

A small cough interrupted the furious silence, and Robin looked up to see the same lieutenant colonel from yesterday standing in the threshold, face as furious as a thunderclap and moustache quivering.

Robin's insides quivered, as well, and she bit at the insides of her cheeks to keep her expression steady. Oh gods, this was it. They were going to reprimand her for behavior unbecoming of an officer. They were going to demote her. They were going to ask for the bonus pay packet back.

The lieutenant colonel crooked a finger.

Renge's face glowed with triumph.

"Captain Renge?" the lieutenant colonel said in a deceptively singsong voice. "My office. Now."

Robin bit harder on the inside of her cheek to keep from grinning smugly.

Renge shuffled around her supporters and, eyes downcast, followed the lieutenant colonel out of the lounge, docile as the cow she resembled. Her milky fair complexion burned, and the glare she threw back over her shoulder promised many more confrontations in the mornings to come, but Robin didn't care.

Let the scrubbed-up cow work herself into a lather. The only enemy Robin wanted to give her attention to were the Klonn. Robin glared around the room, daring anyone else to challenge her right to be there. The rest of the pilots took the hint and went back to their breakfasts.

A small tug on her capelet brought her attention down to the returned Bill Seti, an unopened pot of honey clutched in his hands and a look of adoration painted on his face. Robin crouched down and met his wide-eyed gaze.

"Ma'am?" he whispered. "That was rudding fantastic! I've never seen a Sealie stand up to a Benne like that before."

Robin reached out and ruffled his black hair. "Who taught you that word?"

"I hear it in the canteen all the time," Seti said, childishly defensive. "If the mid-flights can use it, why can't I?"

Robin smiled. "Fair enough. Just don't let your mother hear

you say it." Seti's face fell. She understood in an instant. "I'm sorry."

"It's okay," Seti lied. "It was years an' years ago."

"I'm still sorry."

Seti looked away, tiny jaw clenched. "It's not fair, but it's the fate the gods chose for her. She's been reborn, I bet. She's prob'ly got a big house, and a nice family, and lotsa money."

"It's still not fair, though." Robin sighed and scrubbed at the spot between her eyes, where a headache had begun to gather. "It's the poor who pay when the nobility play at war."

"What's that mean?" Seti asked, blinking swiftly. Robin ignored the way his lashes clumped together with moisture.

"If I have any say in the matter, nothing you'll have to worry about when you grow up," Robin said, and ruffled his hair again.

He held out the honey pot, and she took it, placing it deliberately on the table beside the sugar bowl. Then she went about assembling a breakfast filled with delicious things she could smuggle out for Al. Little Bill Seti scampered to his side of the table and beamed at her when she dolloped a spoonful of honey into each of the prim little teapots.

Was it petty? Sure. Did it make her feel better? Oh, hells yes.

❁

Robin was formally given Wade's glider—the sweet, crotchety old thing; Robin was glad she got to keep flying in it—and asked to pick her mid-flight three days later. She had passed the flight training with little concern and, her instructor said, about a week faster than most newly commissioned pilots. Robin claimed it was because she had already spent so much time in the air as a mid-flight herself, but she knew that command still suspected Wade had been actively teaching her. *Well, let them think that*, she decided. *Maybe they'll get it into their heads to train up and promote more of us.* She threw herself into her lessons as she threw her body weight to the side to help the glider bank more steeply—completely and with as much force as she could muster.

Mama was right. Clearly, the gods knew what they were doing.

Sweaty and grimy from her morning exertions, Robin scanned the canteen for the particular forge-drone she'd had her eye on, scouting through the crowd of mid-flights and apprentices hurrying in from their forges and repair hangars and gliders. They were flushed with the thrill of camaraderie and honest work, painted in grease and oil and happiness.

Catching sight of her target, Robin clutched the orders she'd been asked to deliver and strode across the room to where Al was seated with Fron. This time, when she sat, the snotty blond kid didn't get up and leave. Instead, he stared into her face, blushing, and obvious.

He could stare openly now, now that she was more than just a lowly Sealie. Prig. Though it was the papers in her hands that had caught his hungry gaze this time, and not her previously admired rear end.

Robin wasn't in the mood to make ridiculous small talk. She had no patience for the people who had, in the past week, suddenly stopped ignoring her and tried to cozy up.

Most of the other captains were doing it because she was proving to be some kind of wonder-kid, and base myth-making already had her chasing the Coyote across all points of the compass, instead of just over a forest. Some stories had even claimed she'd shot him down, though those ones had been disproved when the Coyote had appeared above the forest outside of Lylon yesterday morning, circling intently over the place where Robin had kicked his aeroship. It felt strangely like he was calling her out, daring her to come kick it again, and she didn't like the shiver it sent zipping up her spine.

Only Al, Officer Vender, and the generals who'd read her report knew what they thought was the truth, and Robin hadn't told them everything. So what if the rumor mill was pumping out wildly outrageous claims about her abilities, and disgustingly intimate lies about how, exactly, she had earned her commission? She knew as well as any other captain that your reputation on the ground often found its way to the enemy's ears, and that such reputations only served to help dishearten them in the sky. So the whole world wanted to think that Robin Arianhod had single-handedly taken on the Coyote and sent him back to Klonn with his tail between his legs. Fantastic. It would only make other Klonn pilots reluctant to engage her.

Fron cleared his throat, and Robin forestalled him by slapping her envelope onto the table. The outside had the seal of the king emblazoned in one corner, and the words, "Letter of Promotion —Sergeant—Mid-Flight," clearly inked out in the other.

Fron set aside his lunch and stared hard at the envelope. So did Al. The color drained from Al's face, and his eyes sparked with jealousy. Before he could say anything, Robin flipped the envelope over, and into Al's lap.

It took Fron a second to register what had happened, and then he was gone, shoving away from the table and stomping out of the room.

Scrubbed-up prig, Robin thought. *As if I was going to hand it to him without him ever earning it.*

"Robin?" Al asked, voice wavering, dark eyes wide and brick-wall face slack with shock.

"I know you want to be a mid-flight," Robin said. The tables around them had sunk into complete silence, every nearby ear straining to hear what she said. Robin ignored them. "I know you want to get away from the forges and into the air, and I know none of the pilots would pick you because you're too much weight."

"Hey," Al protested, weakly, but he was still staring at the envelope sitting face down on his lap, dark eyes wide and lips trembling. His fingers twitched, but his hands remained steadfastly in the air, away from the envelope, as if he was scared it would burn him.

"I'm small," Robin said. "I need counterbalance. I need someone who can put their shoulders into the turns; I need someone to move the glider like I can't. But most of all, Al," she said, reaching out to take one blackened hand in her blood-spotted one, "I need someone at my back I can trust."

She looked pointedly at the gossips around her. Al met her eyes and smiled, turning his hand over to twine his thick fingers with hers. Then he grabbed the commission packet and stuffed it into his pocket, jamming it carelessly into a ball.

"Okay," Al agreed. "If this is the only way you'll let me . . ." He trailed off, the tips of his ears going pinkish.

"Let you what?" Robin asked. "Work with me?"

"Yeah. Sure. Work with you." He patted his pocket. "Just . . . I have one condition."

"What?" Robin asked.

"I want to paint a robin on the nose of the glider."

"What?" Robin asked again, though this time, the tone clearly implied that Al had sweated away most of his brain at the forge.

"Everyone runs from the Coyote when they spot him, yeah?" he asked, excitement firing in his eyes. "Well, we're gonna make those Klonn bastards start running from *us*."

CHAPTER SEVEN

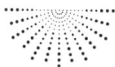

AND RUN THEY DID. AFTER A MONTH OF TRAINING SESSIONS TO find their rhythm, Robin and Al engaged with the enemy above no-man's-land for the first time. They came away with three bullet holes torn into the wing of the glider and three corresponding aeroships smoking in the dirt below.

Robin refused to experience that sort of death—the nameless bitter defeat, body turned into raw meat amid the stench of burning canvas and the whine of sputtering Klonn engines. She had no desire to be down there, mired in the winding trenches and the endless mud, in the disease and despair of the front. So she fought harder, trained longer, took more missions, and slept less than her fellow pilots. She worked *harder* and *longer*. She took more risks. She flew out of the sun and into the crosshairs of the enemy. She attacked aggressively, decisively, and left the fancy flying and noble rules for the air shows. Her gun sang. The aeroships took their turns waltzing with her glider, but in the end, it was always Robin and Al who returned home. Only Robin and Al. It was exhilarating.

Soon enough, Robin had to damn near chase the Klonn across the sky to get her shots in. As Al had predicted, the Klonn fled because they knew it was going to be them or her, and by the gods, Robin Arianhod would make damn well certain it sure as hells wasn't her. The minute the aeroships were close enough to make out the crude but glowering bird Al had painted on her glider's nose, they banked and fled in the other direction. Nobody was willing to dance with her. As Robin's down-count rose, so did her reputation.

And as her reputation rose, there was less muttering to be heard in the officers' mess. There were more slaps on the back when she walked through the slums to trade chocolate for charms. The Sealie children gave her wildflowers, the Benne pilots gave her grudging respect, and the officers gave her medals. Robin clinked as she walked, and soon had to trade the medals in for rows of ribbon-covered buttons that now stood in place for the honors on her capelet.

Robin was quickly becoming the worst kept secret in the war. Not that she had ever really been a secret to begin with.

Desperate to ensure that this fame was earned, Robin worked daily at her craft, spent hours practicing targets in the gunnery range, and hand-to-elbow with Al in the guts of her own glider.

Nobody knew that glider better than she did, and nobody could make it soar like she could. The misty banks of the clouds called to her, and, as the Wise Woman once predicted, Robin was helpless to ignore them.

Flying was her greatest happiness. Even amid the shells and shrapnel.

And then, the Coyote came.

It didn't matter what time of day or night Robin was deployed, what hour she was shot from the zeppelin that carried the gliders high into the sky. It didn't matter whether she was alone on a strafing run, taking down the Klonn-manned anti-glider cannons that speckled the front line, or if she was in formation; it didn't matter if she was twirling her way through a dance with another 'ship. Wherever she was, whenever she was, she would turn her head to the side, and the Coyote would be there.

Regular as rudding clockwork.

At first, he shot at her. Robin shot back. Neither scored a more tangible hit than a bullet hole through a wing. Then, the Coyote simply began to shadow her, bobbing behind her tail like she had to him the first time they'd danced. Teasing.

He would appear like a hobgob out of the aether. Jolting panic would make her fingers clench on the control stick, her breath come too fast, her focus shattered. She would turn to face him, and he would turn away. Eventually, the blinding panic and itch to fight subsided when she'd spot him. It evolved instead into frustration.

He wouldn't fight her, no matter what she tried. Day in, and day out, the Coyote's aeroship would block the light as he flew directly above her, taunting, or his cabin would practically brush her glider's belly if he came up from below. Out of the clouds and out of the sun, no matter where Robin was, as long as she had passed the lines of the front, the Coyote would just *be there*.

She screamed at him. She made rude gestures through the windscreen. But he still would not fight. He would play tag until she was exhausted and could no longer keep the glider in the air, until she clenched her teeth and her arms trembled, until Al had to pat her on the shoulder and tell her she'd been up too long. And still, he wouldn't fire on her.

It didn't escape her notice that he'd somehow improved his fuel reserves, as well, the rudding annoying ass. He was a calculating bastard, that much was clear, and more and more, Robin had to remind herself that there was no such thing as hobgobs, not really. They were just stories for children. The Coyote was no boogie man, no reanimated corpse brought back from death by gears and copper wire and a soul stolen with perverted magic. Those were just Air Patrol base stories. He was a man, a soldier, and a damn good pilot.

And all of those things could be killed.

Eventually, it became clear that the moment the Coyote arrived, there was nothing she could do but turn back. She couldn't maneuver enough to fight with him so godsdamned close, and she could finish no missions with him clinging to her wake. If she shot at him, he would simply depart, leaving the foul breath of his tailpipes in her throat. When the Coyote arrived, all Robin could do was give up. She'd even tried doubling back once, hoping she could fool him into thinking she had given up, but the infuriating coal-bag had been waiting for her when she'd come back out of the cloud bank.

She hated every second of it. Renge and her horrible posse were delighted. There was fresh torment waiting for her every time she walked into the officers' mess lounge for breakfast. She could have just skipped it and gone straight to the hangar, but Robin was trying to prove a point. She belonged where she was, and running away to the canteen would not help her.

Every morning, there was a wasteful display of Renge's contempt, a pointed and clear display of the relative economic stability of her own people. A shrine to the All-Mother was erected right on top of the mantel, followed by various attempts to leverage Robin's ignorance of Benne custom into humiliation by singing religious songs over breakfast, to which Robin clearly did not know the words.

As news about the Coyote spread, the rumors that Robin was cursed also began. Then there were rumors that she was blessed, rumors that she was a demon-spawn, rumors that she was a hobgob herself, and then, most absurdly of all, that she was somehow in league with the Coyote. Distrust ran rampant, and some of the officers even left the room when she walked in.

A small beribboned box of chocolates and an extravagant bouquet of hothouse flowers were left on Robin's regular table one day. The note proclaimed them to be from the Coyote. As

Robin knew that the Coyote would never sign his notes with that name, it was obvious they were just more needling.

Renge had made a joke out of the most horrific enemy they had. It was disrespectful to the dead he had claimed. It was disgusting. And when Robin confronted her—publicly—nearly everyone, Benne and Sealie alike, had agreed on that point, at least. Even as Renge denied that they had come from her.

And because Robin couldn't catch the meddling, scrubbed-up cow at her shenanigans, there was no way to bring it to her superiors. For as much as they supported Robin as a pilot, they treated her differently, as well. They couched their orders as demands instead of requests, the way they did with the Benne officers, and more than once, Robin was subjected to the "Sealies live to do as they're told" lecture. She'd nodded along, mouth clamped shut, and said, "yes, sir," and, "thank you, sir," when the silence prompted it. As degrading, humiliating, and incensing as this treatment was, it was worth it just to be able to fly.

It was after yet another of these instances, on a horrible, sunny afternoon when the Coyote had chased her out of the sky yet again,that Robin decided to console herself with tea at a table in the lonely back corner of the common mess. Al, sitting opposite to her, poured sweet honey liqueur from his battered flask and into her cup when Robin wasn't looking. She gave him the stink eye over the rim when she tasted it, realizing what he'd done, but didn't stop drinking. They sat together in deep, frustrated silence, and Robin had to consciously relax her jaw. It was clenched so tight it had started to make her neck ache.

She was, to put it mildly, furious. It wafted off of her like a dark cloud, and the rest of the Sealies were giving her a very wide berth. The audacity of the Coyote's open taunt and the arrogant, smug smirks on what little of his face she could see when she caught him looking through his own windscreen at her had her seething.

"I hate him!" she barked. "He's doing this on purpose!"

"Robin," Al admonished.

"Next time, I'll shoot him down. I really will!" She brushed her shoulder with crossed fingers to ensure she wasn't fouling up her chances by saying so.

Al put his flask back in his pocket. "Robin—he's doing it to annoy you, and he's succeeding. You know that."

"He's an obsessive prig, is what he is!"

"He's trying to get you upset enough you'll make a mistake, and he's winning at that, yeah? So calm down."

Then, around them, the hangar went suddenly silent. Robin looked up. A general stood in the doorway, hesitating on the threshold as though uncertain whether or not stepping into the common canteen would ruin his shoes. The man himself was olive-complected, resplendent in his moss green uniform, crisp and clean, with sideburns that seemed to be trying to stage an invasion of his chin.

Robin snapped to attention, standing along with the other soldiers in the room. The general scanned the faces of the gathered ranks until, as she feared they would, his eyes zeroed in on her. He beckoned with a jerk of his chin. Grimacing, Robin made her way through the blatantly staring crowd. Al followed in her wake, stubbornly proclaiming his allegiance. The general frowned at Al as they both stopped before him and snapped off smart salutes.

"Captain Arianhod," he said by way of greeting, pointedly ignoring her sergeant.

"Sir," she replied with a deferential nod, keeping her face carefully blank.

"The Coyote troubles you still, I hear."

Robin flushed, her fury doubling.

How dare you reprimand me like this in front of all these people! she thought. *In front of my people! Especially after ignoring Al!* Robin felt her cheeks get hot, and she was shamed by the reaction.

She cleared her throat and, in a forcefully calm voice, said, "Next time, sir. I swear."

He was looking at her too intently to allow her to brush away the bad luck, but she resolved to do it the moment he was gone. Al reached up and made the gesture on her behalf.

"Next time might come sooner than you think, Captain." He raised his hand, and Robin's gaze dropped to the thick, snowy white envelope in his grip. "You have a love letter."

The people around them let out a collective gasp.

Robin felt the blood drain from her face, and, for a very brief moment, she thought she might actually swoon. One of Al's square, strong hands pressed against the small of her back, ready to catch her if he had to, but she swallowed hard, blinked the black sparks away from her eyes, and took a deep breath.

Surely her reputation hadn't become that well-known among the Klonn. Surely the Coyote couldn't know where she was *stationed*. Except, there the letter was. She stepped forward and plucked the envelope from the general's pinched fingers. With trembling hands, Robin split the royal blue seal open.

The only sounds in the room were the hollow shuffle of feet, the deafening thud of her heart in her own ears, and the heavy silence of anticipation. The paper was thick, bright white, and clearly expensive. The ink was dark and fat, almost raised off the paper, and the script was in an elegant, well-trained hand.

It said:

To The Robin:

I tire of our slow courtship. Let us dance.
Let it be tomorrow, at noon, and let it be in
the place we first met.
Yes — your wings have changed. But I
know who you are.
And I remember what you did.

The Wolf

A stylized paw print graced a second dollop of blue wax in the bottom corner, and Robin felt for a moment as though she might be sick. On the small of her back, Al's hand curled into a fist.

"When?" the general asked. His voice held no surprise. The seal had made it clear who it was from, and what its purpose would be.

Robin swallowed hard and forced her own voice not to tremble. "Tomorrow, noon. The place where I marked the map with blood."

There was a long silence as the general screwed his eyes shut for a moment. The lines around his eyes and under his chin suddenly seemed deeper, and the obvious show of weakness scared Robin more than the contents of the letter had. "Sir?"

The general took a deep breath. "We can ill afford to lose you, Captain Arianhod. But the risk is far outweighed by the chance to be rid of the Coyote once and for all." He nodded once, more to himself than to Robin, and then met her eyes squarely. "Very well. You may answer the Coyote's challenge with your guns, Captain. Take him down."

Around her, the mess erupted into wild, enthusiastic cheers. Al's hand slid up her spine to her shoulder and patted her once.

"Yes, sir," Robin said.

The general nodded again, once, firmly. "May the All-Mother protect you tomorrow."

"Thank you, sir," she said, accepting the spirit of the blessing for what it was, if not the actual blessing itself. Besides, the Benne's All-Mother was a goddess, wasn't she? Robin could let herself believe in the All-Mother along with all the rest of them.

"And, Captain," the general said before he turned and walked away, "make sure you make the bastard pay."

Robin's rage toward the Coyote shifted in that moment. It became something bigger—no longer small and dark, fisted behind her heart. It blossomed, pushing up against the underside of her skin, became something warm and triumphant. Robin felt the feral, predatory grin slide across her face. She welcomed it.

"Yes, sir," she said. Fear tried to swell in her breast—fear of death, fear of losing—but it was drowned immediately by the desire for *revenge*.

Tomorrow, she would take back the sky she so loved. Tomorrow, it would be her or the Coyote. And it had never before been her.

✸

Robin was afraid that she wouldn't be able to sleep that night, but somehow, she managed to close her eyes at sunset and wake a few hours after sunrise, feeling rested. If she'd had any dreams, she didn't remember them. A quiet sense of calm had settled over her, like a downy blanket, and it seemed to extend to the entire house. She dressed quietly, and was about to head out when the gentle tick of a pebble hitting the plyboard over her window caught her attention.

Al.

She crept out of her room before her parents awoke, pausing briefly to look in on them. Papa was curled around Mama, his bushy moustache pressed against her forehead like an affectionate kitten. Robin raised her palms and prayed silently that their sleep would stay peaceful. Then she swung her capelet around her shoulder, the love letter tucked into the inner pocket, donned her pilot's goggles, and let herself out.

Al was waiting for her on the step, hands jammed into his pockets and shoulders hunched to ward off the early morning chill. They nodded to one another before moving on in silence. The walk to the base was cold—she wished she'd thought to grab a scarf. Winter was now well on its way. Frost clung to the stones in the shadows and iced the ragged teeth of shattered windows. It had rained in the night, transforming the soot and smoke that usually hung in the air into a greasy black mess on the uneven paving stones; she had to tread carefully to avoid the places where the slicks had frozen into dark ice. The buckle on the strap of her goggles was cold against her scalp, and Robin felt more animate because of it. Every pore tingled with expectancy. Every hair was on end. Every scent and sound seemed sharper this morning. Her sight seemed clearer. Her whole body was alive with anticipation.

When they arrived on base, they went straight to their glider. Desperate for some kind of action, for some way to be proactive, for something to do with her hands and her unspent energy, Robin stripped off her capelet, draped it haphazardly from the glider's wing, and then rolled up her sleeves. Al peeled back the canvas on the front, careful not to crack the painted robin. He handed her a spanner without comment, and shoulder-to-shoulder, practically cheek-to-cheek, they tuned the glider's heart.

"Robin, can you move your arm to—yes, that. Give me the— huh, yeah," Al said when she tossed the hammer to him. He pounded for a moment on a bent gear tooth, then dropped the hammer back into the toolbox with a clatter loud enough to make Robin wince.

"What am I doing?" Robin asked, standing back from the nose and wiping at the grease she'd smeared on her forehead.

Al blinked at her, and then smiled. "Tuning the system alongside your mid-flight, Captain. Hasn't the general already scolded you about doing work below your rank?"

Robin sighed and dropped down onto the dew-wet grass beside the gravel runway. She stretched out her cramped legs and rotated her stiff shoulders, and sighed again. "I mean, why am I letting this jerk get to me?"

Al came around to sit beside her on the ground, wiping the grease off his hands with a rag. He leaned into Robin, shoulders touching and knees bumping, eyes on the sparse, thready clouds that drifted above them and the place where the sky was seeping into a rich, robust red. "He's obsessed, like you said. You've outmaneuvered him. You can stay ahead of his guns. No one else has done that."

"Yeah, but he's not shooting at me! And now that godsdamned love letter."

Al just grunted. Robin shifted so she could face him and tried to ignore the meaty hand that Al let drift to the inside of her closest knee. She wasn't in the mood for roughhousing, but she appreciated the friendliness of the gesture, all the same. "It's more like he's trying to learn how I fly. Do you think that's it? Is he shadowing me to learn how I fly? So he can eventually shoot me down?"

Al frowned. "I don't know. He could have shot us down yesterday, and he didn't."

"He *what?*" Robin asked, aghast. "Al, why didn't you say something? How close was he?"

"Real close," Al said, picking morosely at a blade of grass.

"And you didn't warn me?"

"I thought we were dead!" Al snapped suddenly, ripping at the blades. "He was already beside us before I saw him, and I thought we were *dead*, and . . . and I was scared. I was a coward! I didn't say a thing! I couldn't."

"Oh, Al," Robin said softly. She laid one of her scarred palms on his knee, comforting. "It's fine—"

"It's not, though!" Al snapped. "I'm supposed to have your back, and I didn't. I failed you!"

"If he was that close, it's only because he's been sneaky. I think someone's done something to his rudding aeroship, you know? It runs too quiet. I've been thinking about it since that first time Wade and I faced him. Someone's been tinkering with his engine."

"Robin," Al interrupted. He cupped his hand over hers on his knee. "He saw you. I mean, he *really saw you*. I looked up, and he was beside us, practically right under our wing, and he was *looking* right at you. I could see his mask and eyes and everything. He was studying you."

Robin shuddered, her skin tightening in fear. "That's . . . horrible."

Al licked his lips and leaned closer, comforting her back. "I wouldn't let him get you, not if I could help it."

"Yeah, but what if you *can't* help it?" Robin asked. And then she shivered all over and squeezed her eyes shut. She dug her free hand in behind her knee, fingers curled into her trousers, and tugged hard, using the pain to ground her. The pain was real; it was an honest feeling, gave immediacy to the vague panic and fear that hung over her like a thunderhead.

She was being hunted. She felt as though, if she were to look up at the sky right now, she would see the man who seemed so determined to steal it from her bearing down on them from behind a cloud. She could almost feel the Coyote's eyes on the back of her neck, and all the hair under her braid stood up, as if anticipating the first stutter of gunfire that was about to rip through her flesh.

Something warm and damp puffed against her face, and it took her a second to realize that it was someone's breath. Robin jerked backward, eyes flung open in panic. Someone was looming over her, blotting out the sunrise. Robin shoved hard at the shadow, panic twisting tight behind her ribs. It was the *Coyote*. He was here, and—

Al sprawled back against the gravel of the runway, skidding and throwing up dust, hands out to catch himself.

"What in all the hells was that for?" he snarled from his sprawl. He sat up, staring at his palms, at the places where the gravel had bit into his skin. There was no blood, thank the gods.

"By the omens, Al! Why were you *sneaking up* on me?" Robin snarled back, jerking to her feet.

"Sneaking up . . . Robin!" Al huffed. "You were just sitting there, waiting to be kissed. I don't—"

"Waiting to be *kissed*," Robin repeated, aghast. "What makes you think that—?"

Al scrambled to his feet, gesturing sharply. "You touched my leg, and you leaned in, and you turned your face up—"

"I was trying to comfort you! And I . . . I was thinking! I wanted the sun on my face!"

"Omens, Robin, you must know how I—"

"Gods, don't *say* it!" Robin shrilled, taking a scrambling step back even as he stepped forward, arms up, presumably, to embrace her. She brushed her shoulders with crossed fingers.

Al froze, gawping at her hands. "Did you just . . . as if I'm an ill omen?"

Robin realized what she'd done, how she'd done it without thinking, and jammed her hands behind her back. "No!"

"You did! I just saw you. *Robin!* Look at me," he said, grabbing her shoulder as she tried to turn away, tried to get away from the mortification, to *run*. "I didn't mean to scare you. I'm sorry."

"You didn't," Robin lied, and pushed herself back again.

"You pushed me," Al accused, stepping forward to follow her.

"I was thinking of something else," Robin said. She went to the glider to fetch her capelet, suddenly feeling cold.

"Clearly," Al sneered. He made a frustrated sound right behind her shoulder. "Robin, will you look at me? Please?"

"No," she said, focused on doing up her buttons without getting streaks of grease on the capelet's cream trim.

"Robin!" Al said, and from the corner of her eyes, Robin saw him throw up his hands in frustration. "I can't honestly be that bad a choice! You have to marry someone, and there's no one else who'll have you!"

Robin's blood froze.

"Excuse me?" she snarled, turning to meet his gaze, jaw hard with indignation, chin out. *There's no way I just heard that*, she thought. *There's no way Al would say something like that, not to me.*

"Or is there?" Al asked, voice soft, and slightly wounded. He crowded her close to the body of the glider, intent on her answer. "The Sealies think you're getting jumped-up. The Benne think you're out of place. It's just me who knows you, Robin. And you know me, too. We could—"

"No!" Robin gasped. "No."

"What's so wrong with me that—?"

"It's not about *you!*" Robin ducked under his arm and whirled around, braid flying, to face him again. "None of any of this is about you!"

"I just want to keep you safe!" Al roared. "I don't want you to go dance with that maniac!"

"And I don't want to give up the sky!" Robin roared back.

"Don't think I didn't hear you say you were only trying to kiss me because no one else would want me, Alistair Brigid! I am not a romantic charity case!"

"Of course not! It's not that! It's . . . please, Robin," Al begged. "You've noticed, right? Tell me you've noticed everything I've done for you. How I've readied the forges and hauled coals, how I've walked you home—hells, how I painted the damn robin on our glider? Tell me you've noticed."

"Al, I . . ." she said, then hesitated. What could she say? That she hadn't? That she had and had honestly hoped that she was just misinterpreting the signals? That she wanted his comfort and his companionship, but was too scared that if it didn't work out, she'd have messed up the only friendship worth anything to her? "I can't think about this right now," she said instead, chickening out.

Al's face darkened, hurt flooding his eyes. "Don't run away from me, Robin."

"I'm not running! When have you ever known me to run away?"

"Right now!" Al said. "You're being a coward."

"About what?" Robin snapped, stubbornly refusing to admit how she felt because if she did, if she had to say it out loud, then Al would hate her. And she couldn't stand to have Al hate her.

"I wanna kiss you!"

"I noticed. I'm not stupid."

"So, then, kiss me back."

"Al, stop it," Robin huffed. She pushed him away so hard that he stumbled and had to grab the wing of the glider to stay upright. A wounded expression flashed across his face, twisting his blocky features into a grimace. "I can't do this right now," she said again. "I have to think about the Coyote. I have to avenge Wade. Please understand."

Al's eyes narrowed. "What does that mean?"

"Exactly what it sounds like."

"Do you *know* what that sounds like?"

"Don't be thick, Al!" Robin snarled. "You know that Wade and I never . . . gods! Are you jealous?"

Al crossed his arms, his lower lip sticking out in an obstinate pout. "No. Maybe."

"You can't be jealous of something that never happened."

"Then what did?" Al said, studying her face. "Because something's changed, Robin. You're different. More focused. Angry."

"I am not!"

"What aren't you telling me?" he pushed. "What happened up there with Wade that was so bad you won't even tell me?"

"Nothing!" Robin screamed, throwing up her hands.

"You're lying!"

Tears of frustration burned at the back of Robin's eyes, and she swiped at them with the back of her hand, not wanting to be caught bloody well crying in front of her own glider. "He . . . saw me, okay! The Coyote saw me that day, too. He looked right at me, and he *smiled*. And I can't shake the feeling that . . . that he chose not to kill me, and I don't know *why!*"

Al reached out to embrace her, but Robin wasn't going to let him get close enough to try to kiss her a second time. "Don't," she said, and he stopped short, his face shutting down, becoming unreadable. Robin took a few deep breaths, and then forced herself to turn and meet his dark eyes. "The love letter. I have to . . . to go brief," was all she said.

For a tense second, it seemed as though Al would not move out of her way, that she would have to shove him aside to get past. His eyes dropped to her mouth again, and Robin bit her lips, afraid that he was going to try to kiss her a second time. Then the moment passed, and Al took a step to the side, turning his shoulders so Robin could go by untouched.

Robin's eyes burned with unshed tears, but she was just angry enough at herself for even wanting to cry that she managed to keep them in check. She forced herself to walk away from slowly, calmly, back stiff and eyes forward, hiding the fact that she was doing exactly what he'd accused her of—she was running away.

When she was halfway back to the base offices, far enough that Al wouldn't be able to see any small gestures she made, she touched the tips of her fingers to her lips.

Rudding hells, she thought bitterly. *That wasn't at all how I hoped my first kiss would go.*

CHAPTER EIGHT

FOR THE FIRST TIME SINCE HER COMMISSIONING, ROBIN ESCHEWED the officers' mess for breakfast and made her way straight to the common canteen. She didn't want to ruin her morning with another match with Renge and her cronies, especially since she was trying so hard to regain the calm confidence she'd had before Al had gone and ruined it all. The mess hall was just stirring, the staff wheeling out jangling carts of plates, cups, tarnished knives and forks, filling the air with the jingle of metallic music. Robin filled her plate as the cooks put out the first of the giant, dented serving tureens. Then she poured herself some tea, added a daub of honey, and went to their favorite table. A few minutes later, Al came in, fetched his own breakfast, and sat beside her.

But he didn't say anything.

What was there to say? Nothing that would improve either of their moods, that was sure. Nothing that couldn't wait until . . . after.

Robin ate, but tasted nothing. The food was fuel to keep her going in the air, or else she wouldn't have bothered. She wasn't hungry.

They remained locked in tense silence as they broke their fasts, and slowly, the hall around them filled. Robin half-anticipated being disturbed by people asking to see the love letter. She was dreading it. They didn't need the distraction of hundreds of people wishing them luck when they needed to focus. Luckily, the base seemed sluggish and reluctant to start cranking this morning. Even with the sun up, it was cold, and they were more concerned with shuffling in from the winter-breathed air outside, heading straight for the warm porridge, than they were with hounding the captain in their midst.

"I'm not sorry for trying to kiss you," Al said, as soon as the noise had risen to its familiar pitch, and was loud enough to drown out intimate conversation. He looked ahead, not meeting her eyes. "I might try again after this all of this is over, if that's all right with you. With a warning this time, of course."

"Al," Robin began, loud enough so only he could hear. She stopped there, however. She didn't know what she could add that didn't sound like an apology, or an excuse, or pity.

"No, it's okay," Al said. He stood and gathered up their collective dishes. "I get it. I'm good enough to be your mid-flight, and nothing else."

"That's not fair," Robin whispered.

"No, it's not," he agreed. "But they're your rules, not mine."

"Al."

"I'm going to drop these off," he said, nodding at the dishes, "and then you and I are going to go finish what we started with the navigation systems, yeah? And we won't talk about this again until after."

"Fine," Robin said, nodding.

She felt awful. She knew that she was taking advantage of the friendship between them by not setting Al straight immediately. But she also knew she couldn't afford to compromise their ability to focus as a team any further than it had already been strained.

Not now. Not today. Especially today. Guilt and worry churned in her guts as she watched Al make his way over to the bussing station and leave their dishes in the giant washbasin. Before he had turned around to come back, Robin had schooled her nerves and her expression. When they returned from this ridiculous dance, when this was all over and the Coyote was defeated, Robin would have a talk with Al. She would figure out how she felt, and what she wanted to do about it. Until then, there was only one man she could think about.

✺

When they got back outside, Robin sat on the ground as Al began the pre-flight check, handing him the tools he needed before he asked for them.

"Humph," he said, as she passed over the key used to tighten the winch system. "Guess that's the good thing about having a pilot who was once a mid-flight. Care to pass me the grease pat, too, Captain Arianhod?"

"Har, har," Robin said, but did as he had asked, pinching the edge of the paper packet carefully to keep her leather gloves clean. She supposed she could have done it bare-handed, but her fingers were cold, and she would have to strip off her gloves to fly soon enough.

When Al was satisfied that the steering system was in order and that all the flaps were moving smoothly, they pushed the glider into the queue for loading on the aircraft carrier zeppelin. Al glanced at his pocket watch. "Nine twenty," he said. "Just enough time for a visit to the water closet."

"I'm good," Robin said, eyes on the sky. She studied the clouds, trying to gauge how fast the wind was up there, and how clear it might be above them. She wondered whether it would be smarter to stay in the cloud bank and drop down on the Coyote from above, or whether she should try to sneak up underneath the cover, if she thought he was going to try for the same.

Al grunted, and suddenly, there were warm hands reaching down Robin's shirt.

"What? Hey!" she said, and slapped his wrists.

Al laughed and yanked his hands back, one of them clutching the love letter. "I haven't actually read it yet, you know."

"You could have asked!" Robin said.

"Ah, yeah," he said, taking a step back as Robin reached out to snatch the letter back. She lunged again, and he held it above his head, dancing out of the way and laughing as she leapt for it. "But then I wouldn't have been able to cop a more glorious feel than any woodland god before me."

Robin laughed, too. This felt right; this was what she and Al were to each other. This was what it was supposed to be. This was good. "You're a dirty, rudding—"

"Uncouth," another voice cut in, and Robin stopped dead, spinning on her heel to glare at the interlopers. Captain Renge and a handful of other pilots were making their way past the queue of gliders, headed toward them. "And to think, I was the one reprimanded for behavior unfitting for an officer."

"Omens," Al grunted and dropped his hands to his sides, swiftly hiding the love letter in his coverall pocket.

Renge stopped a good few feet away from Robin, probably to make sure she stayed out of range, and grinned. Robin felt the confident calm she had been cultivating all morning start to blister.

"Captain," Robin said, nodding stiffly. "To what do I owe the displeasure?"

Renge jerked her chin at a tall man standing just off to the side. Wade. He was leaning on a pretty nurse, his blond hair unbrushed, weary circles under his eyes, but his smile bright. His armless shoulder was bound tightly, and without the bulky protective padding, Robin could see that the medics had removed his limb as close to his torso as possible.

"Wade!" Robin said and happily shook the hand he shakily offered. "They're letting you up and around?"

"Captain Arianhod," he said. "Never thought I'd live to see the day a Sealie wore the wings." He tapped one of the rank pins at her collar. His voice was careful, neutral, but the smile that sparkled in his eyes was genuine. It was a relief to hear.

"You look good," Robin said, and then realized that it might have been insulting to say that. "I mean, despite the—no, not despite. I mean—I'm so sorry, Wade. I should have done better. I should have come back faster. I shouldn't have—"

Wade sent her a soft, slightly miserable grin. "You saved my life. You brought me home. You have nothing to apologize for."

Robin reached out, and when he didn't flinch away, she laid a gentle hand on his bandages. "Maybe a little?"

"Nothing," he insisted. It looked like he was planning to say more, but was interrupted when Renge called out:

"Oh dear, Wade, what have they done to your glider?"

"Hey, get away from there!" Al snarled, stalking over to shoo Renge and one of her cronies back. They had lifted the nose flap and were poking at the painted robin.

"Hardly a terrifying specter," Renge sneered.

Robin bristled. "Makes the enemy turn tail fast enough. Or maybe it's the fact that I'm good at flying and, you know, tend to shoot them down a lot."

"You arrogant, smug, dirty little tick," Renge started, stalking around the glider to stand toe-to-toe with Robin. "I'm going to—"

"Going to what, Captain Renge?" Wade asked, shuffling over to stand behind Robin's shoulder. He placed his hand on her arm meaningfully.

Renge's mouth puckered. She swallowed hard, and then said,

"—wish you good luck, Captain Arianhod. May the All-Mother protect you against the Coyote."

"Thank you," Robin said graciously. "Her among the many."

Renge turned on her heel and stalked off across the runway, heading back toward the officers' quarters. Two others followed close in her wake. The remaining pilots each took a turn shaking her hand, and wished her the protection of the All-Mother before they left. Al made faces at their backs.

Wade, the last of them, pulled her into a gentle, one-armed hug and whispered into her hair, "Give that coal-bag payback for my arm. May the gods of luck be sitting on your shoulder."

Robin smiled up at him as he pulled away. "And may the All-Mother grant you a speedy recovery, Captain Perwink."

"Send him to hell, Captain Arianhod." He snapped off a wrong-handed salute, and then, leaning on the nurse, he tottered back toward the infirmary.

"Send him to hell, Captain Arianhod," Al echoed in a high, mocking, pinched Benne accent as soon as Wade was out of earshot. Robin swatted his stomach. He gave her a grimace and continued in his regular voice. "What was that supposed to be? Your scrubbed-up Benne pilot, come to wish you luck? Humph. Where was he when Renge was torturing you, huh?"

Robin narrowed her eyes at Al. "In the hospital, recovering from a terrible loss of actual limb that he suffered while saving my life. You're out of line, Sergeant Brigid."

"Excuse me? Since when did we resort to line-of-command crap, Robin?"

"As soon as we needed to."

"You mean, as soon as you became a scrubbed-up snob like them."

Robin rocked back on her heels. "I am not!"

Al turned red and looked away. His ears flushed, and he bit his lower lip.

"Oh, gods, you really are jealous!" Robin spluttered. "There's nothing to be jealous of! I already told you that."

"And I didn't believe the rumors. I didn't!" Al muttered. "But then, the way he just hugged you . . ."

"Oh, for gods' sake," Robin said, throwing up her hands. "There can't be a bond between a mid-flight and her captain after they've survived so many battles? He's not allowed to be my friend, just because he's Benne?"

"He's not your friend," Al snapped, turning back to face her. His expression was hard, angrier than Robin had ever seen it before. His sudden rage caught her flat-footed. "He's a pilot, and the minute he leaves this base, you know that he'll forget you ever existed. He'll marry that rudding nurse, and it won't matter one bit that he's got no arm, 'cause he has *money*. You ain't nothing and no one to him."

It felt like a slap in the face, but Robin wasn't going to show it. Instead, she crossed her arms and scowled. "So now I'm nothing to Wade? A second ago, gossip said that I was his lover."

"It can be both, Robin," Al said. "Sealies are nothing to them. You can be faceless and still be just an obedient little girl who lays back and—"

Robin lashed out, but he caught her wrist before the back of her hand could connect.

She could, however, scream at him. "Stop it, Al! Just shut up!" she shouted, yanking her wrist free and turning her back to him.

"Robin!"

"Don't talk about him, about *me*, that way!"

"'Sealies live to do as they're told,'" Al recited grimly. "You wouldn't be the first."

Robin scrubbed her eyes with the heels of her hands. She took a few deep breaths, struggling to regain the detached calm she had enjoyed in the early morning stillness of her parents' home. "Go secure the glider's nose flap, Sergeant Brigid," she ground out, turning to face him with her head held high.

Al stared at her with stunned surprise, mouth working like a landed fish.

"That's an order, Sergeant," Robin snapped. "The Coyote's waiting."

"Aye, ma'am," Al spat back, bitterness in every syllable. He offered a mocking salute, and then firmly turned his back to her, marching off to see to the glider.

Robin walked over to the zeppelin gangway and slumped against the railing, weary and cold. "I hate this godsforsaken war."

✺

The gliders were loaded and lined up in order of release—Robin's glider was the first on, as it would be last off. She'd requested that the zeppelin take her to a higher release altitude than the others. As the ground crew began the slow process of spooling the zeppelin out, Robin climbed into her cockpit and settled herself behind the dash. Al hopped in and helped the carrier's crew secure the buckles on the glider's entry flaps. He was frustratingly mute, seething quietly, making it quite clear that he would punish Robin for pulling rank on him for as long as it took her to break down and apologize.

That, Robin decided, *is never going to happen. I'm not going to be the one to say sorry first.*

The zeppelin rose on its tether. The grinding whine of the mechanical winch on the far side of the carrier bay jammed at Robin's ears, high-pitched and as reassuringly familiar as the scent of honeyed tea in the canteen. The bottom of Robin's stomach dropped out as they ascended, and she closed her eyes, reveling in the momentary feeling of weightlessness.

Al threw himself down into his own seat, back-to-back with Robin. If he'd ever felt the same sense of wonder at the sensation of floating up into the air, he'd never said. As soon as they had stopped at the first altitude mark and the carrier crew hitched the first glider's front wheel to the slingshot track, Al leaned over the backs of the seats to speak directly in her ear.

"You never told me that he *already* knows who you are," Al accused.

It wasn't an apology, so Robin didn't mind answering. "I didn't know. Not for sure."

"Didn't know, or just decided that it wasn't any of my business?"

Robin craned around in her seat. "Don't be an ass."

"I'm not being an ass!"

"You're being a complete ass!"

Al scowled, dark eyebrows pulled down over black eyes. "Fine, I'm being an ass. I am the king of the asses. I'm sorry."

Robin sighed. "Then I'm sorry, too," she admitted. "I don't want to fight with you, especially not right now." The angle hurt her neck, so she turned back around and strapped herself in. Ahead of them, the launch door opened and the first of the gliders shot out into the air.

"Why do you think he sent the letter to you, Robin? Why hasn't he shot us down yet, if he remembers you?"

A chill crept up her spine as she remembered the way his gaze had seemed to call to her. She stripped off her gloves and jammed them into her belt, then rubbed her arms to try to stave off the goosebumps. "No idea. It creeps me out, though."

The last glider before Robin's was loaded onto the slingshot, and the launch doors closed up after it disappeared into the clouds. Al dropped back down into his seat, and Robin heard him clipping himself into his harness. The zeppelin crew's flagman flashed the "prepare" signal, and she returned it with a thumbs-up.

The ground crew pulled her glider into position, and the winch squealed as they ascended to the altitude Robin had requested. A few minutes later, and with another signal from the flagman, the glider's front wheel was hitched to the slingshot track.

"Ready, Mid-Flight?" Robin asked.

"Ready, Captain," Al confirmed. "Let's go."

The launch doors opened up again. Robin pushed her goggles down over her eyes, and the world turned amber. She flashed a double thumbs-up. The flagman snapped his hand downward, and with no more warning than that, the glider shot forward and soared out into the sky. Robin whooped in glee, every nerve in her face and fingers tingling.

"Gods, I love that part!" she crowed.

"Ugh, I don't," Al groaned. "I think I left my breakkie back there."

Robin circled the glider around, doing a mandatory sweep for any aeroships that might try to attack the carrier, and saw none. The zeppelin was already descending, the steel cables and winches pulling it back groundward as it bobbed in the swift currents of the wind.

Robin turned the nose of her glider south.

She let out a deep breath and closed her eyes for a second, centering herself with reassuring thoughts. She wasn't scared. She wasn't worried. She was a great pilot. She'd made every other aeroship she'd faced turn tail or turn into wreckage. The Coyote was just one man, and she could beat him.

Robin wasn't stupid enough to fly directly to the meeting location, so she circled the front for a bit, avoiding other altercations and ensuring that nobody was trying to sneak up on her. After an hour, they crossed into enemy territory.

"Twelve minutes," she informed Al, remembering the sound of Wade's voice as he'd announced the same thing to her, all those months ago.

Just as they were approaching the bloody fingerprint on the map, a soft metallic snick caught her ears and she opened her eyes. A faint ticking followed, and then another snick.

"Noon," Al said, putting away his pocket watch.

They traveled on in silence. Robin counted backward from one hundred, eyes scanning the cloud bank below for any telltale shadows. The glider gave a weird little shiver, and Robin pushed gently at the yoke, gaining a bit more altitude to avoid whatever turbulence had caused it. Robin thought she might have heard a splintering sound, but couldn't be sure; it was drowned out by the metallic *click* of Al removing his safety harness.

"No, you know what? I'm not through," Al said, as if picking up a conversation that had dropped. A second later, he was hovering over her shoulder, one square hand a warm, tingling presence at the back of her neck. "There's one more thing I want to say before he shows up."

"What?" Robin asked, staring up at him in confused shock. "What are you even talking about?"

"Kissing you."

"No, you idiot. Shut up and let me fly, Al."

He heaved a theatrical sigh. "Robiiiiiiiiiiiiin . . ."

"Aaaaaaaaal. The Coyote is looking for us. For me."

"Can't we just talk about this seriously for half a moment?"

"What's there to talk about?"

"Oh, so it was nothing?"

"Al, I'm trying to focus right now."

"But I just—"

"Fine! Fine, okay? We'll talk about it when we get back on the ground, but not right now. I need to stay—" Before Robin could finish her thought, the crackle of splintering wood sounded again, and this time, she was sure it was real. "Did you hear that?"

"Omens, I actually did," Al said grimly. "I'm gonna get my toolbox. Hold on." He moved out of her line of vision. Robin heard the hatch in the floor clunk open, and the cabin was suddenly filled with the loud white noise of wind.

"Put your safety harness on first, you idiot!" Robin called.

"What?"

"Listen, I think we should turn around! If something's wrong . . ."

"Nothing's wrong. We just checked it together! Just keep your eyes out for . . ."

"Al?"

"Holy rudding omens . . . Robin! Look up! He's here! Dive! Dive!"

Robin shoved the yoke forward and Al tumbled past her, slamming against the dash. "Get your safety harness back on, you rudding ass!" she snarled, and twisted the glider to the left, banking steeply and sweeping against the upper canopy of the forest. Al scrambled toward his seat, hauling himself hand over hand by the rungs welded to the floor.

Behind her, the buzzing rumble of an aeroship grew louder. The Coyote's aeroship was still quieter than it should have been, but Robin was getting good at picking out the fainter hum of her nemesis. He was hot on their tail. Robin twisted around in her seat to try to sight him through the side windscreens, but he was too close to see.

The sharp cough of a gun rang through the cabin, and the glider shivered.

"Al?"

"Left wing!" he snarled.

"Forget the repairs. Get on the gun!" Robin called. She jerked hard to the right, hoping the damage to the wing's canvas wasn't so severe that it would impede the maneuver, but the glider didn't respond. She tried to bank again, yanking hard enough that the handles cut into her palms, slicing through her calluses. The yoke trembled, and the glider made an embarrassing attempt to turn, sliding sideways with no real control. "What the hells is wrong with this thing?" Robin snarled.

"Robin, he's under us!" Al shouted from the rear of the glider. Their own gun answered the Coyote's, and Robin yanked to the left again. The glider responded this time, turning sharply and dancing higher on the updraft, allowing Robin the advantage of getting behind the Coyote.

The painted wolf snarled at her from around the exhaust pipes, and Al swung the gun hanging beneath the glider around, aiming for the beast's yellow eyes. A few bullets pinged off the metallic exterior of the aeroship, and the Coyote veered away.

"Follow him!" Al snarled.

Robin shoved at the yoke. Nothing responded. "I can't!" Robin cried. "There's something wrong with the steering!"

"No, I checked it myself!" Al shouted, his voice getting closer as he hauled himself up the cabin and came around beside her, jamming his bulky frame under the dash so he could get a look at the steering column. "I know it was fine when we queued up. No one else was near the . . . oh, hells!"

"Did Renge? You didn't check?"

"I checked, I checked! I swear I did!" Al yelled over the roar of the Coyote's aeroship coming back around.

Robin felt her stomach drop away again, but this time, it wasn't because of an altitude change.

"What has that crazy cow done?" Robin snarled. She hauled hard on the yoke, and the glider pulled up just enough that they buzzed over the head of the Coyote. His guns flared again, and the sound of ripping canvas echoed through the cockpit. The glider tipped to the left, dropping horribly. A glance to the side told Robin why—half the wing had come clean off. It was enough to get them to the ground with, but nothing she could use to maneuver. "Renge is gonna get us killed!"

"I think that's the point!" Al said, hauling himself upright. Then he pointed over her shoulder at the windscreen. "He's coming back around! He's going to drive us too low to catch an updraft."

"Not if I can help it!" Robin snarled, and yanked back hard on the yoke.

The glider wobbled in midair. Robin yanked harder, and with

an inglorious *crack*, the whole thing fell apart in her hands. The handles came off, and she looked down—blue sky peered back at her through a hole in the floor as the steering column fell to the earth in pieces. Trees shivered where they landed.

"Oh, rudding hells," Robin breathed. The glider sank, its weight pulling them toward the tree line in a grotesque parody of elegance.

CHAPTER NINE

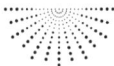

ROBIN SURPRISED HERSELF BY OPENING HER EYES.

Red and orange blurred above her head, and for a brief, terror-inducing second, she thought it was flames. The memory of heat, the crunch of impact, the scent of burning canvas assaulted her mind. She remembered the feel of the yoke crumbling in her hands, and the horrible, consuming rage.

She wondered if Renge would ever be disciplined for sabotaging her glider, or if they would just put it down to mechanical failure. The next time she saw the backstabbing, scrubbed-up cow, Robin was going to bash her stupid, smug face in with a gearbox.

The flames above her swayed and through the gaps, she saw bright, unashamed blue.

The sky.

Home, said something deep inside of her, something underneath the pain that was making itself known to her, buried so deep inside her heart that she wondered if this yearning to fly had once sprung from an egg. *Oh, to be up there, away from the misery and desperation of the ground.* The sky slid and slipped around inside her field of vision, the trees spinning and whirling against her eyes. She blinked a few times to make it still. Through the tapestry of autumn-rusted leaves, she saw a speck of brown.

What a funny little bird, Robin thought, watching it swoop so far up in the air that it became barely more than a brownish mote against the high ceiling of the sky. Yet, she could still hear its song: clear, trilling, and cyclical. Then the bird swooped down, surprising another flying lower in the sky, and they turned in circles together, their songs sharp and joyful as they mated between the clouds.

I just did that, too. Sort of, she thought. *Swoosh! Right on top of the enemy. Just like that. Oh, I think I've hurt my head.*

But seeing the two birds together tugged at something else in Robin, something half-buried behind the pain, and the anger, and wonder. It was ... *it was* ...

"Al," Robin gasped. Had Al managed to reattach his harness? She couldn't remember. She couldn't turn her head, couldn't feel her arms, couldn't see him. He wasn't *here* ...

Where's Al?

The cyclical birdsong came again, joined now by the bird's mate. Her attention stuck to it, and the other things—the pain, the panic, the fear and exhaustion—slipped away as her thoughts grew muzzy again. It was difficult to keep more than one thought in her head at a time. *That's a skylark, isn't it? Or a meadowlark? Doesn't matter, I guess. It's a pretty pleasant sound to die to*, Robin thought before the blackness crashed over her. She wondered briefly, in that last second, if it would be her last thought.

She was strangely content with it if it was.

❂

Robin woke a second time, pulled back to the world by the sound of a pair of very tall, very shiny, black boots cutting through the deadfall on the forest floor. She knew the sound belonged to tall shiny boots because, when she opened her eyes, they were the first things she saw. Winter hadn't quite crept its white fingers of frost this far south—not yet, anyway—so the leaf mould was wet and slightly warm where she lay. It made a sort of muddy squishing sound, overlaid by the dry rustle of the leaves that hadn't yet succumbed to the dampness at the bottom of the forest.

She blinked at the boots, willing her mind to return to sharpness. She tried to force it, but that just made a tender spot at the back of her skull ache fiercely. The only sensible thoughts she could produce were *where's Al?* and *those are big boots*. Robin's sense of proportion was all out of whack from hitting what felt like just about everything she'd passed on the way to the ground.

The breeze shifted, and she smelled sweaty men, dank forest, burning canvas, spilt oil, and blood. The concoction balled up in her throat, making it hard to swallow.

"Are you awake?" hissed a deep voice from the air somewhere above the big black boots, heavily accented. It was said in Saskwyan, so she assumed it was meant to be a question for her.

Robin already knew she was awake, so she didn't bother to reply. It seemed an absurd thing to ask. And besides, she wasn't certain her tongue would even work. It was dry and plastered to the roof of her mouth.

Robin let her eyes fall upward, following the boots to a pair of completely impractical ice-blue trousers. Black stripes ran the length of the outer seam. She swallowed so hard her dry throat clicked. She knew that uniform. Everyone knew that uniform. The wide black belt was studded with silver, and both a fierce-looking pistol and an archaic, white-hilted sword hung from holsters over his hips. She followed the stripes to the low hem of the ice-blue jacket, up the double row of flashing silver buttons, past the black scarf to the tight, choking collar and, above that, the leering silver countenance of a wolf.

Fear seized her body, and Robin went perfectly still. Her tongue seemed to get heavier, and the pain in her head blossomed into a whole-body ache as she tensed, caught between the urge to fling herself at her enemy and pummel him, and the desire to throw herself to her feet and flee. The urgent throbbing in the back of her head, echoed now in other parts of her body—ribs, left ankle, palms—wouldn't let her do either, however.

All she could do was lay there like some stupid, docile farm animal, just waiting to be clubbed, or shot, or gods knew what else these people did to prisoners of war.

"Ah, it *is* you," the Coyote said behind the mask, voice muffled by the lupine nose, consonants sharp. The voice was younger than she expected it to be, not as robust as a full grown man's. When she looked again, she realized that the body filling out the ice-blue uniform was more lithe than she had assumed. "I am glad you survived, though I must say, I am quite cross at you for missing our date."

Robin turned her head, trying to glimpse beneath the mask, blinking against the way the sunlight cut through the canopy and stabbed into her vision. Her head felt too small for her brain, pushing behind her eyes and across her skull in a way that wasn't letting up.

Another soldier stepped into her field of vision, silhouetted against the red leaves. Fear zinged down Robin's spine. The colors still reminded her of fire. Fire, and the glider, and . . .

"Al!" She tried to sit up, but one of the Coyote's black boots came down on her ribs. He didn't press hard, but the sudden rocket burst of agony that flared through her torso was enough to make her writhe back in pain. She'd probably cracked a rib or two when her safety harness had broken away.

"Stay put," the Coyote hissed. "Do not let them see you move."

"Get off!" Suddenly, the fearful reverence, the respect of the Coyote as a concept, as an other, as a demon, evaporated. He was just a man. She could see him. He was touching her. He was *real*. Which meant that Robin could fight him. "Al!"

A sharp scream echoed hers, and Robin craned her head,

struggling to see past the Coyote's leg, down her own battered body and torn uniform, through the glare of the setting sun and the sharp, dark shadows of the forest, searching for the source of it. There was a mound of shadows several meters away—tall figures that resolved themselves into three more Klonn soldiers in impeccable navy-blue uniforms, crouched around a supine body.

Five on two. Not good odds, she thought. *And me injured, besides.*

Air base scuttlebutt and urban legends about the Coyote jammed up in her imagination, shoved at her, tried to make her panic: tales of cannibalism and secret laboratories where the Coyote reassembled Saskwyans into mechanical monstrosities bound to obey his sadistic king. Robin swallowed heavily and counted backward until her mind stilled.

The Coyote is human. Just human, she reminded herself. *And humans can be hurt.*

Once she was sure she could speak again without her voice shaking, she said softly, "Let me up."

"Your mid-flight," the Coyote replied in near-perfect Saskwyan. It wasn't a question. His voice was low still. Soft. Almost as if he wished to comfort her, which was ridiculous. She must have hit her head harder than she thought. "You do not want to see him."

"The hells I don't!" Robin snarled and got her hands around the Coyote's foot. She twisted, trying to wrench his ankle and lever him to the ground. But he just shifted forward, putting more pressure on her ribs. Robin spasmed and let go, the agony making stars pop behind her eyes and her fingers twitch.

Oh yes, humans can be hurt, all right. And boy did she hurt.

"Trust me, you do *not*," the Coyote insisted. "It is not what I would want to keep as the final memory of a trusted colleague."

Another gasping, panicked gurgling scream echoed through the forest. The Coyote's silver helmet turned toward it, betraying the direction Al was in.

"What have you done to him?" Robin hissed. She didn't want to obey his orders, but there was something in the way he'd warned her to not let the other soldiers see her move, hear her speak, something in the way the Coyote was talking through tight lips, as if he didn't want to be caught either, that worried her.

"I did nothing."

"You shoot down gliders—you steal the bodies."

There was a sound that might have been laughter if it hadn't been distorted by the helmet. "Theft! No, my dear Miss Pilot. Prisoners. Those who live, anyway."

Prisoners, Robin repeated to herself. She couldn't hold back the shudder at the thoughts that phrase produced. Every hair on Robin's body leapt up as a chill settled over her flesh.

Fear curdled in her stomach. "What do you intend to do to me?"

"Do *to* you?" the Coyote said, and a smile lit what little was visible of his face. "My dear, what do *you* fear I will do?"

She wasn't going to fall for that. If she told him what she feared, he might make it come true. "If you take them prisoner, why don't we know? You haven't ransomed anyone back," she said instead, wishing desperately for water and forcing herself to speak through the cracking, anyway.

"I have no desire to give them up," the Coyote replied. "I keep them."

"For how long?" Robin asked, unable to raise her voice louder than a fearful whisper.

"For as long as I am allowed," he said, and there was a sad gravity to the pronouncement that was confusing. "Just as I will keep you."

Fear spiked again in Robin's chest, throbbing along in time with her ribs. "You'll never be able to keep me."

The helmet angled down, and through the visor slits, Robin saw a pair of light gray eyes narrow. The Coyote huffed an annoyed snort. "Persistent *and* mouthy. Be advised that it is only because you were once a mid-flight that your life has been spared this day. Otherwise, you would be dead as any other Saskwyan pilot I run to ground. It is not their kind that I seek to hold."

He leaned back slightly, turning his attention to the soldier on the other side of her, and snapped out something in guttural Klonnish. The other man nodded sharply and moved closer to Robin, one hand going to the pistol sheathed on his thigh holster.

The Coyote removed his foot, and Robin took that as permission to be *seen* to be alive. She sat up so slowly, being as gentle as possible with her ribs, breathing shallowly. When she tucked her knees up, her ankle screamed in protest and she had to clamp her lips around a grunt.

Broken? she thought. *No. But sprained, at least. And badly. Rudding hells.*

Neither the Coyote nor the guard moved against her as she tried to stand, and so, Robin pushed herself to her feet, taking a moment to close her eyes and swallow against the pain. She wasn't going to show them any weakness.

She lifted her head to squint through the shadows at the others in the distance. "I want to go to him," she said. "He's alive."

The Coyote cocked his head to one side, eyes narrowing. "How compassionate you are. No worry for yourself? You are, after all, surrounded by the enemy."

She rubbed the place where his heel had dug into her flesh, trying to work some feeling back into the already forming bruises. Carefully, she put weight on her ankle. Knives shot up her calf, but her ankle didn't buckle beneath her. She forced herself to ignore the pain and rose onto the balls of her feet, preparing to run if need be.

"I'm not scared of you," she said, puffing up her chest and trying to feel half as calm and assured as she sounded.

"Yet you turned tail before the battle was properly joined and fled."

Robin grimaced, and decided there was no point in lying to him. After all, she didn't want him to think her downfall was in any way his doing. She did have *some* pride. "My steering column was sabotaged. Garrote wire, is my guess."

The Coyote sighed, like an overindulgent instructor. "I would call it a shame that the Saskwyans are so fond of building their aircraft of canvas and wood, if it did not provide me with such an advantage."

"What advantage?" Robin sneered. "You pick off the crippled ships. You would never have downed me otherwise. And my flying style has your men baffled. You get outclassed by a healthy glider every time."

"Not for much longer," the Coyote said lightly. He turned his helmet up to the sky, as if he too yearned for it the way Robin did.

Robin waited for him to explain what he meant by that, but he seemed reluctant to furnish his gloat with any sort of details. When the silence drew ominous, she discreetly brushed her shoulders with crossed fingers, just to be sure. But the Coyote caught the movement from the side of his vision and turned back to her. He reached out with one black-gloved hand, slowly enough that it was clear he didn't mean to strike her. Robin cringed, but stayed still. All he did was brush the side of one thumb along her cheek and up her temple.

"This has healed nicely," the Coyote said softly, almost to himself. Ever so slowly, he reached out and grasped her wrist firmly. His fingers were wiry and strong, and Robin would have had to allow him to break her wrist to keep him from turning it palm up. He stripped off his glove with his teeth, and then, black leather dangling from his mouth, brushed his fingers gently across the telltale circular markings that stood out against her palm. They were red and swollen from her fight to control the glider's doomed nosedive, overlapping the other, deeper cuts and puffy white ridges of scars. "And these, as well. What an interesting new development. Since when are Sealies the pilots of Benne gliders?"

"I'm not a pilot," Robin said, the lie flowing out immediately, reflexively. That was something else her instructors had drilled into her head—never appear to be as valuable to the enemy as you are. Her capelet was nowhere in sight, and she had a vague recollection of it being ripped from around her throat by the crackling branches she had fallen through.

"I have watched you, my dear. I know your face, and I know your flying style. Your warding against ill-luck betrays you," he said, in a softly mocking tone that she would have called flirting if it didn't sound so wrong coming from him, here and now. His fingers continued to stroke her palm. "You are certainly a Sealie. So, I reiterate—since when do Sealies pilot Benne gliders?"

"But I'm not!" Robin protested. She'd heard the stories of what happened to glider pilots captured by the enemy. If losing a thumb to a Pyrian guard was horrific, the thought of having both her hands cut off by a crazed Klonn general made her woozy. She yanked her arm back, hard, but the Coyote didn't let go.

"Please, do not lie to me, my dear," the Coyote said, gently chiding. "I will not allow you to begin this on a lie. You kicked my 'ship. I know your face, even without the goggles."

Robin's heart seemed about ready to stop. She bit her tongue and refused him the pleasure of an answer. She could be a stubborn bastard, too.

"You are an engineering sergeant, or you were, before they promoted you. Do not bother denying it. You have all the skills of a mid-flight." It wasn't a question, but this time, his steely gaze compelled Robin to answer.

"I was. I do."

"Good," the Coyote said. "Then you shall be spared."

"What? Why?" Robin blurted, and then immediately wished the words back.

"Would you prefer that we did not?"

"No!"

He leaned in close, hauling her body nearly flush against his own, and bent down to her ear. The cold nose of his mask brushed against the fine hair at the nape of her neck, and she shivered. His breath smelled like apples, and made goosebumps pop up all along her skin. His voice, when he spoke, was low and husky with gravel. "Then kindly be silent while I attempt to save your life."

Without another word, and without waiting for Robin to reply, he straightened to his full height—at least another head and a half taller than her—and brusquely released her. Robin stumbled backward, wincing as she put weight on her sprained ankle. The Coyote swiftly made his way across the forest floor to join the other soldiers.

Robin cut a glance at the guard, and he met her eyes with an impenetrably blank look, the expression of a career soldier determined to follow orders, no matter how inane. She took an experimental, limping step forward. The man's hand tightened on the butt of his pistol. Robin sighed and held her hands out to her sides, indicating that she had no intention of challenging him, and he relaxed again. Then she turned her attention to the shadows in the distance.

Al, her heart screamed, silent and burning in her chest. She balled her hands up and pressed them against her thighs, shaking with the desire to punch, to scream, to fight, to flail, to do *something*, anything except stand there and be . . . impotent.

The wind carried the sound of muted conversation back to her, too jumbled by the air spirits to make out.Even if she could have heard what they were saying, she didn't speak the language. A real Benne pilot might have had lessons in Klonnish, but nobody had bothered to educate the Sealie sergeants. No one ever expected *them* to have to negotiate for their freedom in a prison camp.

One of the shadows threw up his hands and shouted, *"Nema!"*

From the hollow ring of his voice, Robin recognized it as the Coyote.

She knew that Klonnish word, at least—but what was he saying "no" to? A horrible premonition seized her around the throat. She took another limping step, but this time, to the side. When the guard didn't immediately lunge for her, she broke into a flat-out run, dashing toward the most dense copse of bracken she could spot. It hurt like rudding hells, but she gritted her teeth and ploughed forward. A protesting ankle and stabbing pain in her ribs were nothing compared to what a bullet between her eyes could do.

A shout and the pop of gunfire rang out between the trees, but Robin kept her head down and crashed through the briars. Thorns and prickling leaves scratched at her arms, stung her skin, tugged at her vest and shirt and bootlaces, but she didn't dare slow down. She feigned to the left, cutting a false path through the brush, and then swerved forward again, trying to dodge into the little spaces that she hoped the tall Klonn soldiers might not be able to manage.

Robin burst through the brush into a blasted clearing. Wreckage still smoldered at the edge of a shallow crater, dirt and blackened leaves thrown up in piles around its oblong rim. She skidded to a halt, horrified by the devastation around her. She realized, after a few seconds of staring, that this had all been wrought by her crash.

What little remained of her glider smoked under its blanket of deadfall. Ammunition shells and missile shrapnel was lodged in the tree trunks all around them. Her powder box had likely exploded on impact. Some of the brush was still on fire, licking along the damp ground, searching for tinder dry enough to feed it. Robin took only a moment to wonder that she had survived the crash at all. She must have been thrown clear, she decided. Or Al had pushed her.

Gods, no, Al, she thought, mind a frantic blur of half-formed strategies and discarded plans. *This is the dumbest idea you've ever thought up, Captain Arianhod. What will you do now?*

Robin dithered at the edge of the clearing for only a few seconds as she made up her mind whether to keep running, or double back and find a way to save Al. But a few seconds was all the Coyote needed to catch up. A crash echoed out of the undergrowth, and then, before she could throw herself out of the way, a pair of strong, leather-clad fingers were digging into her throat. Robin felt her feet leave the earth and flailed. Her struggles only made him tighten his grip.

"Little idiot!" the Coyote snarled, glaring up into her face. "Such a headstrong, foolish Sealie. The Benne, at least, have the good grace to know when they are captured." He shook her once, roughly, and Robin kicked out, slamming the toes of her boots against his knees, his shins. His hand tightened again, and Robin gasped. She went still, trying to dig her nails into the leather covering his long fingers in a desperate bid to free herself.

Her lungs burned, begging for air. Her heart fluttered frantically against the hollow of her throat. Darkness crept into the sides of vision, heat pressing against the back of her eyes. Then, just as suddenly as he'd had her up in the air, Robin was back on the ground, coughing messily into the leaves and inhaling lungful after precious lungful of vegetation and rot.

The Coyote grabbed her by the braid, yanking painfully on her hair until she managed to pull herself upright, arms wrapped around her abused torso, and then back up onto her screaming legs. He used his grip to pull her back toward that first clearing, where she could hear Al screaming again, loud and agonizing. She clutched at the Coyote's arm in an effort to lever him off, but he just dug his fingers into the fine hairs at her nape and dragged her along like a reticent dog. Robin had no choice but to stagger and stumble in his wake, unable to see where she was going, fighting to keep pace with her throbbing ankle.

"There!" the Coyote barked. He shoved her down, forcing her

to kneel, and released her. Robin raised her eyes, half-turning to lunge at him, and then froze.

"Are you pleased?" the Coyote sneered. "This is what you wanted, was it not? To see your mid-flight? Then look!"

Robin couldn't have defied him if she wanted to.

If it wasn't for Al's voice, she wasn't sure she would have recognized the mass of burnt flesh, blackened exposed bone and rolling, terrified brown eyes as her best friend. The scent of loosened bowels, charred meat, and utter fear assaulted her nose, and she choked back a cough. His face, in some horrific turn of fate, or the sick whim of some petty god, was still mostly intact—red with pain and twisted into a grimace so fierce Robin thought she could hear his teeth cracking as he clenched his jaw. His eyes were screwed shut now, bushy eyebrows all but singed away.

"Do something," she hissed, voice squeezing out of her in a thin, reedy plea. She couldn't look away, though she desperately wanted to. She would not disrespect Al like that. "For the sake of the gods, please, help him. He's drowning in his own blood! *Do something!*"

"Do what?" the Coyote whispered back, his baritone voice cutting through the pained whines and blowing breaths that made something in Al's ruined chest bubble and pop. "Do you think our Arts of Healing so advanced, little Miss Pilot? Even the Klonn cannot stop death."

"Gods, no!" Robin moaned, and something inside of her, twisting and sharp inside her ribcage, cracked open. "Al!" she cried, giving voice to the anguish in her chest that had nothing to do with her broken ribs. Just as surely as she couldn't look away, she couldn't help but touch him. Grabbing the only part of him that looked like it wouldn't cause him even more agony, she arched forward and cupped his cheeks in her hands. Something clear and wet dropped onto his forehead, and it took Robin a second to recognize it as her own tears.

"Al!" she sobbed. "Alistair Brigid, you open your eyes right now! That's an order, Sergeant!"

Something in her tone must have penetrated the pain, because he obeyed, lids snapping wide and black doe eyes rolling down to meet hers. "Rrrrrrrnnn," he whined, and Robin stroked his high cheekbones with her thumbs.

"I'm here, Al. Oh, gods, hold on, okay? I'll get you help. Just don't go, okay? Don't go!"

Something had once been a hand wrapped around Robin's wrist, and she fought back another gag. It was hot, burning against her own skin, and slick with blood and pus and something else that Robin didn't want to think too hard about, something that reminded her of the juices that sweated out of a roast when her mother cooked.

"Rrrrnn," he moaned, and it took her a second to realize it was supposed to be her name. "Rrrrn. Swrrr. Wnt go."

"Swear I won't go?" Robin parsed. She swallowed and tasted death in the air, blood and hatred and humiliation. "Yes, Al. Dammit, hells yes. I won't go, I promise. I won't go."

"I," Al corrected. Somehow, he found the power to shake his head, just once, back and forth.

More sobs pressed against the back of Robin's larynx, and she had no choice but to let them out. "Okay, okay," she whispered. "You won't go. You promise. You swear. You won't go."

"Nnnt wthout Rrrn." His jaw strained, forcing more air into the ruin of his lungs, and Robin could do nothing to make it easier, to take away the pain, or, gods help her, to make it end sooner. To just . . . get it all over with. The gods must have heard her, though, and she regretted the wish instantly, because, between one heart beat and the next, Al went still.

Silence jammed into her ears, and she strained for just one more breath, one more heartbeat, one more painful whine. None came. She wanted to scream. But she would not. She refused to ruin the dignity of his death in that way.

"Gods guide you safely to your next life," Robin strained to say. She hated herself for crying in front of the enemy like this, hated that they got to see her in this weakness when she had worked so hard to be strong before the other pilots, before her parents.

She leaned down and gently, carefully, pressed her lips against Al's.

This was not the kiss he deserved.

Robin wasn't even sure she had wanted to kiss Al, wasn't sure she had wanted to encourage him to try to cultivate honey in a place where no flowers may ever grow. But now, the choice was taken from them. Gone. It was unfair! To have it whisked away so horribly, so finally, before Robin could even make up her mind!

Al's lips were still warm, still soft, and it broke her heart a little bit more. She reached up and stripped Al's goggles off his head. She slipped them over her own, pushing them down to lay against her collarbones like a gruesome necklace. And then a voice shattered the quiet.

"How could you?" It was so filled with pain, so graveled with tears, so full to the brim with a terrible, desperate loathing that it took her saying it a second time to even recognize it as her own. "How *could* you?"

The Coyote bent down and wrapped his hand around her throat again. Robin pressed against it, trying to throw him off balance, wanting to jump up with fists flailing.

"I wanted to help him. I did," he insisted under his breath, words just for her, even as Robin's face twisted into a scoff of disbelief. "However, I could not. Not without . . ." He turned and glanced out of the corner of his eyes at a man standing off to the side, a look of aloof disinterest in his pale eyes, the silver leaves of a general growing on his shoulders. "You must trust me, or I will not be able to help you, either."

"Velph," the general said, followed by a string of words that Robin didn't understand.

The Coyote straightened and shook his head curtly.

"Velph," the general growled, and the Coyote cut a calculating glance at Robin.

"Get up," he hissed. "Stand, now."

"Bug off, you rudding coal-bag," she hissed back.

"Get up, or I will drag you up again, and trust me when I say, my dear, that it will be a humiliation in which neither of us will take any joy."

Robin scowled. Then slowly, carefully, she uncurled Al's fingers from around her wrist and laid his arm across the ruin of his chest. The Coyote extended a hand, and Robin batted it aside, choosing to struggle to her feet without his gentlemanly garbage.

The Coyote drew his sword.

Fear bubbled back up through her guts. "What are you doing?"

"For his sake, I am making sure."

"Making sure of what? Hey!" Two of the other soldiers had grabbed her arms—one hand each jammed up under her armpits, the other ones locked around her wrists—and dragged her away. "Let me go! Stop! Making sure of what?"

"Do not watch," the Coyote said, gripping the hilt in both fists and raising the sword like a cudgel.

"No!" Robin screamed, even as the soldiers yanked her off her feet, pulling her further and further away. "No, you can't! Wait. Stop! You can't just leave him alone out here like that! What about the rites? Hey, stop!"

But all her mid-flight muscle was useless against the height the two Klonn soldiers leveraged against her. Her feet came off the ground, and she twisted in the air, kicking but only hitting their steel shin guards. Her left ankle shrieked.

The Coyote, silver mask glinting in the sparse sunlight, looked over at his commander.

The general nodded once.

"No!" Robin screeched.

And then the Coyote drove his sword into Al's heart.

CHAPTER TEN

ROBIN WAS ALREADY TRUSSED AND BLINDFOLDED, WRISTS BOUND tight behind her back, metal cuffs threaded through a metal loop bolted to the bench, when the Coyote climbed into the transport wagon. She knew it was him because the soldiers squeezed in shoulder-to-shoulder on either side of her made her lean back so whoever it was could pass, which only meant that he had to be someone important. The person rapped on the dividing wall between the back filled with benches and the driver with what sounded like the butt of his sword, and said what Robin assumed was the Klonnish word for "drive" or "go" in the Coyote's voice.

"Did you just . . . leave him out there?" Robin asked, throat dry, voice tight with fury. Around her, the transport wagon shivered to life as someone started to crank the engine.

"Silence," another soldier snarled from right beside Robin, and she curled her shoulders inward and absolutely did not cringe. She was surrounded on every side by Klonn, literally packed in, and it would be very easy for one of them to decide to use their pistol for more than empty threats.

"And what else would you have had us do, my dear?" the Coyote asked, settling in directly opposite to her.

"The rites, the funeral—"

"The remains of your glider are giving off quite a lot of smoke. Your people will find your mid-flight, if they follow it."

"But the Coyote *never* leaves bodies—"

One of the other soldiers said something in Klonnish, gesturing at Robin as if she had a point. The Coyote gave an inelegant snort and replied waspishly in the same language. Then he turned to look straight at Robin and added, so she could understand: "For this one, we make the exception."

"Why?" Robin choked.

"Because you asked it of me."

The transport's engine revved up, and the whole thing lurched. Robin had a stern stomach—you had to, to spend as much time in a glider as she did—but being unable to see the landscape moving around her as the transport chugged away made her head swim sickeningly.

Or maybe that's the crash, she chided herself. *Lots of trees to hit your head on on the way down. That's the only way to explain why he's being so ... so ...*

But she didn't have a word for what the Coyote was being. It wasn't "kind." It wasn't "thoughtful."

After all, she was a prisoner of war. But it also wasn't what she'd expected.

Anticipation kept her skin pimpled, her hair standing upright, her teeth bared. And yet, what was there to anticipate? She didn't actually know. No one had hit her yet. No one had roughed her up. No one had even really pointed a weapon at her. The only person to have laid his hands on her was the Coyote, and even then, it wasn't to harm so much as to hold her in place.

The transport wasn't a large vehicle, and it reeked of the gasoline that ran it. The Coyote's knees bumped Robin's, and she drew back her legs. It jolted her ankle, and she hissed and winced as the shock of the unexpected touch startled her.

"You have made it worse," the Coyote tutted. A hand touched

her left knee, and then, without warning, her calf was yanked upward so that her boot landed on his thigh. "Why did you try to run on it?" Fingers plucked at her bootlaces.

"Let me go!" Robin shrieked, wriggling against his hold. She careened into the soldiers on either side of her, trying to wrench her leg back. Fingers dug into the joint of her shoulder, the back of her knee, the insides of her elbows. "Get off!"

"Be still, fool," the Coyote snapped. One long-fingered hand curled around her heel, fingertips pressing in just enough to make Robin whimper and go still, just enough to imply the promise of more pain if she didn't cooperate. "Or they shall make you stay still."

As the Coyote resumed undoing her laces, one of the soldiers said, in very halting Saskwyan: "Should you really . . . ? A medic can—"

"Enough," the Coyote snapped.

The soldier fell silent after a quick, "*Ai, deh.*"

Robin, equally cowed, stayed as frozen in place as the sway of the transport allowed. He peeled her boot and sock away in one swift motion. Strangely, the first thing Robin worried about was how rank her feet might be after so many hours jammed inside her footwear. Of course, she was ridiculous for being worried about that in a transport crammed with sweating people in what felt like wool uniforms that reeked of black smoke and blood.

The Coyote's touch was light on her swollen ankle, warm in a way she didn't expect, even through the leather of his gloves. Robin was glad for the blindfold suddenly, for the way it covered pretty much everything from the tip of her nose to her hairline. There was something so deliberately reverent about the Coyote's touch in the dark closeless of the transport that it was very nearly *intimate*.

"Why are you being kind to me?" Robin whispered.

"Would you rather that I was not, my dear?" the Coyote replied, voice equally low and soft.

Beside her, the soldier who had spoken in Saskwyan, who clearly understood what she was saying, sniggered. Robin remembered where they were, then, and yanked her foot back. The Coyote sighed as if she was being a particularly obstinate child, but said nothing else. The rest of the journey was as silent as it could be in a rumbling, juttering transport stuffed with the enemy. Robin tried to memorize the turns, the directions she was being taken, but the truth was that she'd had no idea where they'd even started from and had no way to tell where they were headed.

Klonn, obviously, she reprimanded herself. *But which part? Were we south enough to be within easy distance of Lylon?*

The humid closeness of the truck combined with the darkness of her blindfold and the last of the adrenaline that was finally wearing off, and Robin felt herself start to nod. She scrunched her eyes, took deep breaths, everything to try to stay awake, but eventually, someone shook her leg softly and said: "Wake. We do not have much time."

Robin jolted back to consciousness, hips and ribs and ankle burning in pain. She kicked out with her booted foot, and it connected hard with the Coyote's shin. He grunted and shifted away.

"Stop it now!" he hissed. "Listen to me!"

"Why should I?"

"Because I left your Al to be found when my general would have much rathered I did not. I have done him the favor of a Sealie burial, and so, I ask a favor of you in return."

Robin wasn't chastened, wasn't convinced, not really. But she was willing to listen. She shut her mouth and thrust out her chin, waiting.

"You must trust me. Please," the Coyote said, voice barely audible. It was only then, listening to the way it echoed off the metal walls of the covered transport, that she realized they were alone. Utterly alone.

With the enemy.

"Let me out," Robin hissed back. "Just let me go."

"I cannot."

"Then get away from me!"

"I cannot. Please. *You must trust me.*" There was an earnestness in his plea that Robin hadn't expected, and it threw off her panic just enough for her to think rationally about this. Was this a real, honest request? Or was this the start of some strange sort of mind game? Some psychological torture?

The Coyote said he took the mid-flights. That he *kept* them. Was this how it began?

"I have no reason to trust you," Robin snarled back.

"I am well aware, my dear," the Coyote said ruefully. "And yet I ask it of you, all the same."

"Give me one good reason. Ah-ah!" Robin said when he tried to interrupt her, her voice a dry scrape, frustration and fear balling up on the back of her parched tongue. "One that doesn't use my best friend's murder as a bargaining chip."

The Coyote said nothing. He went so quiet, so still, that for a moment, Robin feared he'd simply left the transport, disgusted by her demand. Tired of the game. Perhaps he even had his pistol drawn and aimed at her head *right now*, and she'd *never know*—

"Because," the Coyote said eventually, and Robin was so caught up in the hive of her imagination that she actually jumped at the sound of his reply. "I need you to."

"That's not . . ." Robin coughed once, and swallowed, trying to work some saliva into her mouth.

"Here," the Coyote murmured, and there was the welcome metallic snick and scrape of a canteen being opened. He tucked his fingers under her chin lightly, urging her to tilt her head back. Robin allowed herself to think about poison for only a second. Then the cool, clean water splashed against her lips and Robin was so *thirsty*, and it was *so good*, that she gulped down as much as she could. Trickles of water escaped the corner of her mouth, and when the canteen was empty, the Coyote dabbed at her wet face and neck with what felt like an actual godsdamned *silk hanky*.

Robin bit back a hysterical chuckle at the thought of the fierce Coyote, in his lupine helmet, dabbing fussily at her mouth with a lace-fringed hanky like an old grandmother.

"Better?"

"Yes. But it's also not an answer. 'I need you to' isn't good enough."

The Coyote put away his flask, and then gently maneuvered Robin's foot back inside her sock. The boot, he left off.

"Because," he said again, drawing out the word. "Because, Miss Pilot, you are not the only prisoner here."

❁

In Saskwya, thievery was punished with the forceful, bloody removal of a thumb. This was usually done on the spot by the soldier who caught the perpetrator, and with whatever sharp implement they happened to have at hand, clean or not. Robin still had both of her thumbs, despite the number of factories and burned-out homes she'd burgled, and she offered a prayer to the gods, much as she did every time she defied her parents, scavenging for glider parts and things of value in the debris, that tonight would not been the night she was caught. She flipped her house key between her fingers, tugging at it where it was attached to her undervest button with string, tapping it restlessly with her thumbnail.

She was standing on the street, a few blocks from her parent's house. Al's house, yes, that's where she was. She was standing outside the Brigid family home, crammed with little children and cousins whose parents had been killed in the raids, three people to a bed. But no—

No. There was no house there. It was gone.

In its place was a smoking hole, a spray of brick and bone and blood, and Robin took a step back, horrified, her boots ringing out on the heaving stones of the street. She clung to a wall as the streetlamps swayed back and forth, and thought, *Omens, an earthquake! We're not supposed to get earthquakes this far inland!*

The rolicking stopped, and Robin swung her arms around one of the iron poles, as if holding it down with her body would keep the streets still. A heavy haze had settled with the dusk. The perpetual clouds of soot that blew in off the factory fields had mingled with the evening's heavy fog, obstructing her view. Red brick dust choked her lungs, and Robin coughed, hard and long.

A white blur of movement caught her eye, and her heart shot up into the back of her mouth, fear crystallizing on her tongue. A cat sat primly cleaning a paw on a nearby wall, looking for all the gods as if the world hadn't just rattled around its ears. A fellow nightpad, and harmless. She began picking her way carefully among the rubble, keeping to a slow and careful pace that wouldn't attract the unwanted attention of the curfew constabulary. She heard the dogs in the distance, but they never got closer. With a start, she realized that nothing seemed to be any closer than it had a moment ago. Where was she going?

Home.

Home?

The haze shifted, and Robin caught sight of her bedroom window, a block away. The ragged ends of the rags stuffed into the gaps in the board fluttered in the chill autumn breeze; they looked like ghost hands, beckoning her on. Her stomach unwound slightly at the familiar sight. Relief flooded her veins, and she sighed. The cat made a noise that sounded strangely like an echo.

A soft *swooshing* noise plucked at her ears. Robin froze.

"Omens," she cursed quietly. She stepped back quickly, out of the dim orange spotlight of the streetlamp, and put her back against a half-crumbled wall. She lowered her head so the darkness of her dirty cap hid the shine of her dusky cheeks from the sweep of the searchlight that crawled along the ground.

The urge to run was strong, but she defied it, keeping still. The light swept across the heaved flags of the shattered sidewalk, climbed over a downed garden wall, over the ruined remains of someone's private beehive, and then dropped away into darkness. Robin counted to ten to give the glider ample time to pass, tracking its tail across the sky.

The cat yowled and leapt away, at least as reluctant to be caught out as Robin was. Each noise made Robin more impatient, more desperate to get out of the open, more sure that this time would be the time the soldiers caught her. When she felt it was safe to move, she slipped forward again.

And then, somehow, Robin was already inside the house. She stood in the hallway, Mama's loom hanging off her arm, a gearbox glowing orange from the forge in her hand, but not burning her skin. Not hot, not at all.

Robin hefted her burdens and crept toward the parlor. Yes. This is where these went. She set the gearbox down on the sofa so she could place the loom on Mama's small table. The heated metal made a hard cracking sound, followed by the horrific *fah-woosh* of a fireball catching air. The thick, coating, acrid smell of smoke plowed across her tongue.

"Robin!" someone called from the other side of the flames that leapt to consume the sofa. They surrounded Robin, faster than a blink.

"Papa!" Robin called back. "Mama?"

"Robin!" A silhouette appeared on the other side of the flames, dark and dancing as the sinister light shifted. Hands reached out to the fire.

"Don't touch it!" Robin warned. The figure didn't stop, and the flames parted at their touch.

"Papa? Mama!" Robin howled. "Help me!"

But it wasn't Papa. It wasn't Mama. It was Renge.

Her mouth was pulled back in a tight, painful rictus of smugness, her teeth somehow too long, too sharp. There was a bloody knife in her hand, a thumb in her other, and it was . . . oh gods, it was *Robin's* thumb. Her teeth were growing as she advanced. They just kept *growing*. Her nose elongated, turned black, jaws slavering, lupine—

Robin screamed, loud enough to wake herself up.

Robin jerked awake and sat up, eyes wide to drink in what little light was available. Something white flashed in the corner of her eyes—*the cat!*—but no, no, there was no cat. The instant she was upright, Robin moaned and curled around her midsection, one arm cupping her battered ribs. Her left ankle throbbed in time, tight and hot.

Every part of her protested so strongly that Robin let herself flop back down. The nightmare faded, got fuzzy. Darkness danced at the edges of her vision, making it hard to concentrate.

Her favorite scent in all the world was that of freshly cleaned cotton. She turned her head as far as she could without moving, stuffing her nose against the pillowcase, and inhaled deeply. Mama had just washed the sheets. There was fresh-baked bread and honey for breakfast. And there was no war.

Safe, she thought for a moment. And then, *No, wait, no, not safe!*

She made herself sit up again, biting back groans all the way. *Never mind the pain*, she scolded herself. *Where are you? And how do you get out?*

The room was slowly coming into focus as her eyes adjusted. A slim bar of light ran along the bottom of one wall, the golden quality betraying it to be a gas lamp. *Light under a door, then. Bright hallway. Not good for escaping unseen.* She turned her head to the other wall, and was rewarded with the milky glow of the moon and stars through high, thick glass windows. *Better, but a wide-open field won't be much better, and I don't see enough shadows from trees.*

Robin licked her lips thoughtfully, and then gagged. They were sour, sort of dusty, powdered with a chemical aftertaste. *Stupid,* she berated herself. *You should have known better than to accept a drink of water from the flask of an enemy soldier.*

She felt clear-headed now, though, without the overwhelming urge to sleep pressing under her skin. Whatever drug had been in her system, it must have passed. *I'm lucky to be alive,* she thought. *The Coyote kept his word there, at least, but why?*

"You are not the only prisoner here," he'd said. Did he mean Res and Woden? Were they still alive? Were their pilots? Would the Coyote try to use her fellow Sealies as leverage against her to get her to—to do what, exactly? She still had no rudding idea why she wasn't dead.

Thinking about it wasn't going to make the answers any clearer—she was no Wise Woman, to read and interpret dreams —so she decided to turn her attention to her predicament, instead. Robin wiggled her toes and fingers, just to prove that she could, and then moved on slowly to every other joint, working her way inward through her wrists and ankles, elbows and knees, finally her neck and shoulders, and her spine. Everything seemed attached and mobile, though her left shoulder screamed when she forced it into motion, and her left ankle proved to be heavily bound in something very constricting. Her feet were bare.

The most painful part of her proved to be her hips, where her safety harness had dug hard when she'd been thrown against it, and her bottom ribs. She straightened slowly, biting her lips to keep the little mewls of pain suppressed and to avoid any further jolting of her abused midsection.

Where's Al? Is he in here? She strained her ears, but the only sounds echoing in the darkness were her own. And then she remembered.

Heat pushed behind her larynx—a scream, a sob, hysterical laughter, Robin didn't know. She only knew that if she made the sound, someone would know that she was awake. She clamped her hand over her mouth to keep in whatever it was that was trying to escape. Her hand was shaking so badly she feared bruising her own nose, so she bit down gently on a knuckle and waited for the shivering to pass, eyes squeezed shut. Gasping filled her ears, and she realized she was the one making the small, pathetic sound, suffocating in her pain and panic. She forced herself to breathe at a normal pace, forcing her chest to unclench, and touched the back of her hand to her lips, deliberately conjuring up the memory of Al's rubbish attempt at a kiss.

Robin wished she'd taken the time to say something to him that morning. Instead of letting what had happened the night before get in between them. Instead of the tense silence, the arrogance of assuming they'd get out of this alive. She wished futilely that there'd be time to . . . to . . . Robin didn't even know what. Time to explain why not? Time to say yes? Time to at least give it a try?

Now, there was time for nothing.

Robin clapped her palms over her eyes, determined not to sob like a child. She didn't have time for *this*. She needed to get out, get away, get safe. That's what Al would have wanted.

Is that how I'm going to hold him in my heart now? Convince myself to do things because it's what Al would have wanted? Force him to become my god of morals and ethics? I'd rather have him here with me, alive, and making bad choices and . . . and—gods, just shut up, Robin. Shut up and focus.

She forced herself to suck back the grief. She mopped her face with the back of her hands, and resumed casing the room. It was not, as she'd expected, a prison cell. It was a *bedchamber*. And a fancy one, at that. Too fancy. Revoltingly fancy, really. *Wastefully* fancy.

Now that her eyes had become accustomed to the dark, Robin

saw that there were sconces ringing the room, too. They were shuttered so low that they hadn't seemed to be lit at all. It gave the place an eerie, orange glow that made it hard to determine how big the room was, hiding the corners in a sort of false twilight. Robin forced her mind away from tales of spirits and malevolent gods that roamed the border between day and night. She was a soldier. If she could handle dances with Klonn aeroships and being shot at, she could sure as hells handle a strange, poorly lit room.

She was sitting on a large and very ornate bed in what had to be a private bedchamber. There were an inordinate number of pillows, and the coverlet was made of something soft and comfortable, which immediately ruled out a hospital or field-medic's tent. She tried very hard to not think about why someone would install an injured enemy soldier in a very luxurious bedchamber and not within the presence of a medic. She didn't like the answers her slightly hysterical mind had to offer, so she forced herself to scout her surroundings instead.

She swung her feet to the edge, and dropped quietly onto carpeting so rich and lush that it hardly even whispered as she stood. The pain from her ankle radiated up her leg and she grimaced, shifting her balance over to the other foot. *Hells*, she thought. *No way I can run on this. But I could sneak, if I have to.*

Her boots were lined up neatly beside the bed, and she slipped them on. The flat knife she kept hidden in the tongue of her right boot was miraculously still inside its camouflaged leather pocket, but her more obvious boot knife, the one whose hilt stuck up out of the top of her left boot, was gone.

One blade is better than none, Robin thought.

Her empty belly growled its unhappiness, and her head throbbed. Her ribs ached less, so she downgraded her earlier assessment from "broken" to just "bruised."

All the same, she knew she was in no shape to fight her way out.

Hobbling, she went to the door. It was locked, so she made a circuit of the room, counting out how many paces long each wall was, noting where there was a washstand, a vanity whose mirror was draped in black lace, a wardrobe, and windows. She threw back the curtains and stared at a dimming sunset. She'd slept through the afternoon. Maybe she'd been asleep for days.

The world outside the window was nothing but a wide, rolling lawn bordered by the brilliant tapestry of autumn forest. There was no road, no creek, no landmarks to indicate location, nothing for her to recognize and match against the aerial map of Klonn's forests in her mind. She had no clue how close or how far away she might be from the bloody fingerprint.

Robin pressed her cheek against the chilly glass of the window and gazed up at the sky. Sharp, hard longing welled up, and she fisted her hands in the drapery. The seam of the valance started to rip, and she forced herself to let go. The windows were heavily mullioned and crisscrossed with metal bars cemented into the casement. The cement, when Robin bent to peer at it through the thick glass, looked pale and new.

Where in the hells was she, that someone had installed bars outside of what was clearly the window of a very fine house? And why here? Why *not* one of the horrific prison camps? Why *not* a field hospital? Had they anticipated capturing her alive? More than once, the Coyote had chased her quite close to the ground during a dance. Maybe that's what he did—literally ran the gliders to ground. Maybe that was the plan all along.

Maybe he had *always* wanted to keep her.

But what if I hadn't survived? she thought. *Al didn't.*

The renewed thought of Al brought a sob from between her lips before she could fully clamp down on the sound. Robin jammed her fist against her mouth and waited, but there was no indication out in the hallway that she had been heard. Hobbling back to the bed, she sat in the center of it. She used one of the ridiculously luxuriant pillows to cradle her ankle, and lifted her palms upward. Warmth and wetness pricked her eyes, built a hot lump in her throat, and she swallowed hastily, blinking rapidly, and then gave in. She wept.

Her heart ached so fiercely she feared a god had its hand wrapped around it and was squeezing her to death. Her back burned with long, shuddering sobs, and her nose and eyes stung. When she felt she couldn't possibly cry any more, that she had used up her lifetime's allotment of tears, she raised her palms and began the prayers that would, she hoped, help guide Al's wandering spirit back to Saskwya, where it could be reborn again as a Sealie, innocent and safe. She knew the Klonn hadn't buried him with the proper rites, and she was damned if she was going to let Al wander the woods of Klonn for the rest of time, alone and unloved, if their own people didn't find his body.

Finally, she forced herself to stop. She would not cry any longer. Not until she knew where she was, and if it was safe enough to show that kind of weakness. She had grieved Alistair Brigid, and would indulge in her sadness only when she was once again safe in the comfort and quiet of her own home. Now, she had to focus.

Now, she had to escape.

She raised her hands and began the prayers to the gods of luck, the gods of young men, and the gods of travel—anyone she thought might help. Her lips tingled with the sting of her misery, and she did her very best to forget what it had felt like to almost kiss a kind friend she would never see again.

CHAPTER ELEVEN

SOMETIME LATER, A MAN WEARING THE BLACK UNIFORM OF A seneschal swung open the door and stepped into the room. Like all Air Patrol apprentices, Robin had studied the different iterations of Klonn military garb. She never thought she'd see one of these close up. Only diplomats and high-ranking officers had the honor of a personal secretary and valet. Whoever was holding Robin and occupied this house, he or she was important.

The seneschal hadn't knocked, and he said nothing when he came in. He didn't even meet her eyes. He carried a large porcelain ewer that steamed gently and filled the air with the scent of lilacs, which he carried over to the washbasin and set down in a matching bowl. Then he went to each of the gas lamps that ringed the room and, with a key he pulled from his pocket, turned the darkness into blazing warm light. His expression remained as blank and unreadable as the soldiers in the forest, just this side of disdainful.

Robin stayed on the bed, sitting perfectly still, and watched every deliberate motion he made with care, as if such mundane tasks would provide the secret to her escape. She wondered how he felt about imprisoning a fellow human like this. If, indeed, he even saw Sealies as human. From the talk she'd sometimes heard in the pilots' lounge, she wondered if all soldiers, no matter what side of the war they were on, thought of their enemies as inhuman, soulless monsters.

The seneschal returned to the hall, and before Robin could stand and barge out the open door, he brought in a long, flat box bound with a flouncy blue ribbon, and offered it to her. When Robin refused to take it, he placed it on the foot of the bed, within her reach. Then, still without saying a word, he folded his hands behind his back and glanced meaningfully at the bow.

"You can't be serious," Robin said with a snort. Wonder turned to mulishness, and she stuck out her chin in defiance. "What if I don't want to open it?"

He may not have understood her words—she had no idea if he spoke Saskwyan or not—but her tone made her opinion quite clear.

"Then my heart will be broken," said the Coyote from the hallway. The seneschal stepped back just enough to let him enter. He was still wearing the helmet, and a lazy, smug smile to boot. His clothing was less formal, though—crisp black trousers, sharp dress shoes, and an almost painfully white blouse under an ice-blue waistcoat embroidered with silver wolves. Of course. "Come, come. Open it," he urged.

"I don't want a gift. I want to know where I am," Robin countered.

The Coyote waved the question away and stepped meaningfully to the side of the bed, waiting expectantly with his hands folded behind his back, just like the seneschal. Robin crossed her arms across her chest, just for variety. The seneschal's fingers settled around the hilt of the knife sheathed on his hip.

Robin gave into the urge to roll her eyes and picked up the box. It was light, and didn't rattle. It didn't smell like petrol or cordite, and there were no ticking sounds, no whirring gears. She pulled at the ribbon.

She almost would have preferred a bomb—inside the box was a dress. An insult of a dress in royal blue silk trimmed with bleached white lace. Lace. *Ugh!* There were hair ribbons of a matching blue, and a tiny satchel of cosmetics pots. Petticoats, bloomers, *bustles*. Horrible. There was even a second smaller box, containing sparkling drop earrings and an absurdly ornate necklace that resembled nothing so much as a dog's collar made of diamonds, hung with a cascade of sapphires.

Klonnish soldiers—and, in mimicking them, the nobility—wore blue. Saskwyan palettes tended toward the mundane, the camouflaged, the easily cared for: the olive drab of Ground Patrol uniforms and the fawn of the Air Patrol, the shades of flame amid the Benne nobility that deliberately set them apart from their enemy. The insult in this "gift" was obvious and pointed.

Robin spread it all out on the bed and raised an eyebrow at the Coyote. "This is a joke, right?"

"Of course not," the Coyote said. "I assumed . . . well, a good wash and a nice new dress always seem to do wonders for the moods of fine ladies, and my guests are always welcome to—"

"First," Robin interrupted, standing on her good foot and jamming a pointed finger at the helmet's lupine nose plate, "I'm not your guest. Second, I'm no fine lady. And third, I'm not your dolly."

The sound of the seneschal's dagger being drawn was a sharp, clear hiss in the jammed, startled silence of the room. Robin couldn't be sure, but she thought she saw, just for a second, sheer vulnerable *panic* in the Coyote's eyes. He didn't do anything so obvious as lick his lips or swallow hard, but his pale eyes flicked to the doorway just once before the smug sneer was back.

"There is no need for that," he said in Saskwyan, then added something in rapid Klonnish that Robin couldn't possibly hope to catch. He waved dismissively at the seneschal, and the man resheathed his dagger, turned sharply on his heel, exited, and yanked the door shut behind him.

Again, the Coyote didn't do something quite so obvious as sag on the spot, but the lines of tension around his eyes immediately eased, and his shoulders went loose. Relief screamed out of his posture like a signal flare, for all that he had barely moved.

"Do not do that again," the Coyote said, his voice weary. Robin wished she could see more of his face, read his expression, understand what was happening. But every part of his face, except his mouth and chin, and the sliver of his eyes, was hidden.

"Do what?" Robin asked, taking an experimental step toward the door, seeing how close he'd let her get. She was barefoot, and hobbled; she wouldn't get far. But it was better than staying here, docile. Alone in a room with the man who had stalked her across the sky.

"Defy me so openly. Especially in front of him." He made a disgusted sound in his throat and, in a flash, had her wrist gripped hard in his hand. "And stop testing boundaries, as well. There is nowhere for you to run to in this place that they would not find you in a trice. You waste your time and energy dwelling on that which will not be."

"What game do you think we're playing here?" Robin challenged, flicking a gesture between them. "This little back and forth of yours, the dress, calling me 'my dear'—which is rudding condescending, by the way. What is all this?"

The Coyote rocked back on his heels, a grin spreading on his face. "You do not fear me."

"Of course I don't fear you!" Robin snarled. "I told you that. Not anymore. And especially not when you're acting like some Benne prig with a stupid crush."

"But you used to?" the Coyote asked. He reached out and brushed his leather-clad thumb over her cheek again. This time, Robin had the freedom of movement to duck away from the motion. "Back when this was bruised? Did you fear me then? Tell me, my dear, who struck you that day?"

"A scrubbed-up little calf who thought his father's position meant he could tell me what to do," she shot back with a meaningful glower.

The Coyote surprised her by throwing back his head and offering up a full-bellied laugh. "Oh, this is going to be difficult."

"*What* is?" Robin snarled, hands balling into fists as she fought down the urge to slug another self-important prig who was asking for it.

Instead of answering, the Coyote had the gall to turn his back on her and smooth the dress down over the coverlet. "Do you not like it? I will admit, women's fashion is not entirely my forte. But I have never had a lady decline so luxurious a gown before."

Robin stood very still and tried very hard not to make it look like she was thinking of reaching for the knife in the tongue of her boot. She waited until she was absolutely certain that he couldn't see her before she dipped down to retrieve it.

"Give dresses to women a lot, do you?" Robin sneered.

The question did exactly what she wanted. It made him straighten, affronted by the insult inherent in the barb. This put him in the exact right position to stab up under his ribs and into his kidney. She lunged forward, blade flashing in the light of the gas lamps. Robin's reflexes were quick.

The Coyote's were quicker.

He whirled on his heel, snatched her hand out of the air, braced his palm against her bicep, and heaved Robin up over his shoulder to slam against the mattress on her back. The air wuffed out of her as her bruised ribs were jolted, and she groaned, curling in on herself, all the fight knocked out of her, along with her breath.

"This is exactly what I mean," the Coyote said, staring down at her, his hand still wrapped around her wrist. He squeezed hard, grinding her bones together, and Robin held on to the little knife for as long as she could. When the pain became too much, she whined and let go. The knife dropped into the Coyote's waiting hand. She figured she'd never see it again, had played her one ace too soon.

And then, inexplicably, and within full view of her, he tucked it back into the tongue of her boot. Right into the pouch she thought he didn't know about.

He must have been the one to take my boot off when he brought me in here, she realized. *That's when he found it. Why didn't he say anything then? Why didn't he . . . ?* "Wh . . . why?" Robin asked when he let go of her, cradling her bruised wrist against her belly.

He leaned over her slightly, looking nearly comical from upside down and tilted to the side. "Because, my dear, we are going to be partners. And I want you to trust me."

Robin snorted. "Fat chance."

"Your only chance," the Coyote corrected, and he tapped his index finger deliberately in the middle of her forehead. "Use more of that wily brain I saw when we danced, my dear. And less of that Sealie brawn." Then he paused and lifted the fringe of her hair between his fingers, rolling it as if considering the texture. "Fascinating. It is spreading."

Robin batted him away. "Go jump in a frozen river, you rudding coal-bag."

"Such strong language from a Sealie," the Coyote chuckled again. Then he stepped back. Robin scrambled as much as her injuries allowed and swung around to face him, kneeling on the mattress, flicking her braid back over her shoulder. Something white flickered in the side of her vision, but she kept her eyes on her enemy.

"Leave me alone."

"Very well," the Coyote said, taking a dramatic step backward and spreading his arms to the side like a showman. "Get yourself dressed. Dinner is in one hour."

"*Dinner*," Robin echoed, aghast.

"Yes. I would have you dine with me," the Coyote said, as if asking your arch nemesis to a meal like a besotted beau was a normal occurrence. "I will relish sharing the right way to do it with you."

"You mean the *Klonn* way."

"Is that not what I said?" the Coyote asked with an impish head tilt. And Robin had to remind herself that this was a tactic, a ploy, some sort of strange torture. Because the Coyote, the scourge of the Saskwyan Air Patrol, absolutely *was not* flirting with her. "Clean yourself up. You reek of blood and smoke. And put on the dress. You will like it once you see how well it looks on you."

"Not rudding likely," Robin shot back.

"Then you will look *proper*, at least." He chuckled again, and then backed the rest of the way to the door. A light rap on the frame in a complicated pattern, done behind his back, had the door opened from the outside. He had slipped through it, and it was closed again behind him, before Robin even managed to get her feet on the floor.

Omens. She hobbled to the door and yanked on the knob, but it was firmly locked, just as she'd expected. *Now what?*

Robin turned back to the bed and regarded the dress with contempt. She was half tempted to strike the glass from the gas lamps and hold the fabric in the flame, but that would probably set the room on fire and trap her with no way to escape. She filed that thought away for later—maybe she could set fire to the curtains when her ankle was healed enough to allow her to run.

Then she thought of the wealth of jewels she might escape with, if she only managed to do so while wearing them, and what they might mean not only for her family, but for the Air Patrol. The necklace alone could probably fund the construction of at least three new gliders.

Wash, the bastard had said. And now that the idea was in her head, she couldn't ignore the realization that she . . . well, she *smelled*. Dried blood and dirt scratched at her skin, crusted around her cuffs and collar, and Robin had to admit that the thought of a wash and fresh clothing was rather appealing. The sleeves of her shirt were in tatters, and her leather pants had suffered the brunt of her unsuccessful flight through the forest. Neither covered much of her limbs anymore, and the buttons had popped off her undervest in her struggles against the soldiers, leaving it to gape obscenely. Much as she hated to admit it, the dress would be better protection against the elements than what she currently wore.

Grudgingly, she gathered up the cosmetics pots and dumped them on the vanity. Al's goggles were hanging from the post that held up the mirror, and she snatched them up, cradling them close to her heart. *Oh, gods! I still have them! I didn't even check . . .*

She set the goggles aside with the solemn reverence the last relic of a loved one deserved and, with a grimace, turned her attention back to the cosmetics. She had no idea what half the creams and powders were for, but the hair pomade and lip rouge were familiar from Mama's collection. There was something whitish and creamy that came away on her fingers thickly. If this was supposed to be some sort of blemish-covering cream, it certainly wasn't made for the Sealie complexion.

She wiped it off on the swath of black lace that covered the mirror and closed the jar. There was a small bottle of what Robin assumed was perfume, as it smelled pungently of rotting lilacs, and was overwhelming when added to the scent of the water in the washstand. She hid that bottle behind the wardrobe.

There were also fresh bandages and an unguent that smelled strongly of mint. It reminded her of the molasses-like cream Renge had given her for her palms, and she could well guess what it was for.

Struggling around her hurts, Robin managed to get herself out of what was left of her tattered uniform. She frowned to see that her unwanted host had also provided the necessary undergarments for the dress, along with the silken chemise and bloomers, and the heavily starched, multi-layered petticoat. She left the underbust corset in the box, firstly because she hadn't the faintest idea how to lace herself into such a thing alone, and secondly because her damaged ribs wouldn't thank her if she tried. Also, for all that Al had admired them, her breasts were not so big as to need that kind of support.

Washing quickly, lest the seneschal walk in on her while she was unclothed, Robin donned the undergarments, smeared the unguent on her hands—still powerfully blistered from her attempt to land the glider—and bound them with the bandages. She sat at the vanity to attempt to wrestle her hair into some semblance of order. It felt tangled and greasy, her scalp aching from where the Coyote had wrapped his hands in the tight braid. She found a brush in the vanity drawer, but no comb, no hair-pins, no ornate decorations, nothing that could be used to stab someone's eyes with. Omens. Her host was proving to be annoy-ingly clever.

Sighing, she pulled the swath of lace off the glass—and screamed.

"Oh, oh, gods!" she gasped and jumped up from the chair, nearly toppling when she forgot about her ankle and put her weight on it.

In the mirror, the horrifying white thing backed away, large and puffed and angry. Robin's eyesight blurred in fear, and though her pilot-stern stomach held fast, she felt like every other bit of her insides had crumpled into a ball of terror. She whipped around, head craning, ankle screaming, trying to spot the thing that was casting the reflection.

Nothing. No one. She was alone, completely alone in the room. A whimper leaked from between Robin's teeth, and she clapped a hand over her mouth, forcing herself to breathe shal-lowly, to listen.

No other sounds save the crackle of the wick and her own breaths filled the shadows. Still, she was breathing so hard . . . what if there was something there? Something in the corner that

. . . Robin turned back to the mirror. The white was still there. But there was nothing behind her. Robin held perfectly still, and the thing in the mirror did the same. Robin blinked until her vision was clear, and then, suddenly, realization slammed into her like summer lightning.

In the mirror, her face had turned yellow-green in shock, her fingers spasmed into horrified claws. She saw it happening, but she couldn't feel it. Her hands were numb with confusion and terror. Her feet were moving, she was backing up . . . and then the end of the bed smacked against her thighs and she sat, eyes wide, mouth open, staring.

"Omens," she breathed. She reached up and yanked at a lock of hair that had fallen over her forehead, pulling it around so she could stare at it with her own eyes. Her braid, when she pulled it over her shoulder and into view, was streaked through with white.

In a panic, she turned and looked at the bed—the pillow was littered with long brown hair. With trembling fingers, she pulled at the tie and detangled her braid. Clumps of dirty, sparrow-colored hair came away in her hands, spreading across the carpet like deadfall. Only the white hair remained.

"What could do this?" she wailed. Nobody answered. "What could make hair turn white?"

Shaking, she forced herself back to the vanity, to meet her own honey-brown eyes in the reflection. They were wide and scared-looking. Carefully, she picked up the brush and, starting from the bottom, worked her way through her braid. She had to stop frequently to pull off all the dead hair and dried foliage from the bristles. The white didn't brush out. It didn't go away.

"I'm a ghost," she said. "A nowhere person. Oh, gods. Am I not a Sealie anymore?"

She had heard of the ghosts, of course, but she'd never met them. The babies born blessed by the gods, with colorless skin and white hair and rabbit eyes, the people who could pass anywhere because they had no hair color to delineate their heritage. They were the lucky ones, that's what people said. They could be at home everywhere.

Robin didn't feel lucky. She felt punished.

What had she done, what had been so horrible that the gods felt she deserved to lose her heritage, her culture, everything that she had fought so hard for, had given up her hands and her best friend for? Why had they stolen everything that made Robin a Sealie? Was it because she had stolen first, and frequently, to get her glider in the air? Was it because she had failed to down the Coyote?

"I'm sorry," she said, raising her palms to the ceiling, eyes squeezed shut. "I don't know what I've done. I'm sorry. Just please, please . . . give it back!"

She opened her eyes and looked in the mirror, but her hair remained white.

"Okay, okay," she whispered to herself. "Calmly, calmly. There must be a reason. I just don't know it yet. I need to stay calm. I need to escape. Stop being vain, Captain, and start being smart. Use that brain of yours." She tapped her index finger against her forehead, in the same spot the Coyote had.

She took a few minutes to breathe deep and slow, the way they taught pilots who flew too high and banked too fast. Even though it was a simple exercise, it made Robin feel more in control. Her hands stopped shaking, and she used the leftover wash water to rinse her substantially thinned hair clean. With the blue ribbons, Robin managed to bind it into a single braid, and coiled it up at her nape to cover the bald spots, and to keep it out of yanking range of the Coyote.

She smoothed her eerie fringe with the pomade, and rifled through the little pots until she found a moisturizing cream—that went under her eyes and on her nose, where the crying had left the skin raw and dry. She put on a little of the lip and cheek rouge. She had no idea if Klonn women lined their eyes with charcoal the way Sealie women did. As she found no smudging stick and no matches, she guessed not.

She disdained the flimsy blue slippers in the box and put her sturdy boots back on instead. Her wrapped foot was tight, but the lacing supported her weak ankle enough that she thought she may be able to walk on it for a short distance. Then she stepped into the dress and managed to wriggle around enough to fasten up the ridiculously small buttons that climbed up the center of her stomach. The dress was dismayingly low against her chest, but at least her musculature kept it from gapping too much at the front. Her shoulders were far too broad for a Klonn noble-woman's fashion. The collar was square cut, and made her look mannish. The skirts billowed behind her, dragging on the carpet. Robin felt muffled by the sheer volume of the shimmering fabric.

When she was finished, Robin stared at the door expectantly, wondering if she was supposed to knock to let them know she was done. Then she decided that if the Coyote had deemed she should play dress up, then he could damn well wait. She crawled back up onto the bed, spread out her skirts, closed her eyes, and counted backward from one hundred. It helped keep her mind from wandering to places that she frankly didn't want it to go.

CHAPTER TWELVE

ABOUT AN HOUR AFTER SUNSET, JUDGING BY THE QUALITY OF THE light outside, the door opened again. The seneschal was back, and this time, he waited on the threshold expectantly. Robin stood and limped to the door. If he saw her brown boots under the tangling swish of her skirts, he didn't mention them.

The seneschal offered his arm, and though she had absolutely no desire to take it, to play out this farce of civility, she needed the support to walk. They traveled in silence, and Robin kept her eyes open and her mind sharp. She catalogued each arrogant-looking Klonn in their ice-blue uniforms as they filled out the frame of each portrait hung along the wall. She studied each ridiculously fussy vase on a pedestal. She counted each doorway and hall, each overwhelming spray of flowers in the corners, trying to find a way to remember. She even counted the stuffed dogs. They were enshrined under glass bells with plaques declaring them the loyal companion of this dead duke or another. Even in death, they had not escaped the eyes of their masters. Robin felt sympathy for them—watched and prized and never able to get away.

Would she, too, be one day stuffed and mounted behind glass?

Would her plaque read: "Robin Arianhod, War Prize of the Klonn. She was docile and obedient. Eventually."

The seneschal picked one of the many heavy, dark wooden doors that dappled the corridor, and opened it with a key that looked exactly like all the rest on the ring that hung from his belt. Robin couldn't decipher anything unique about this key or this door that would help her ensure she stole the right one later. She'd just have to take the entire ring.

The room they entered was huge, easily the size of the officers' mess back on base. Every lamp was turned all the way up, and a great, glittering gas chandelier sparkled from the vaulted ceiling. The warmth of the flames behind their glass made the room cozy, even for all its great size, and Robin shuddered at the way her perceptions had been so twisted without her permission. The Klonn were not supposed to be anything but terrible and sterile. *Cozy* was not supposed to be within their parameters.

The walls were adorned with a thick blue paper covered in elaborate geometric designs and spackled by portraits of important-looking men and women, the latter painted with elaborate hairstyles and dresses that pushed their breasts up obscenely. They were all draped in a revolting amount of jewelry and medals, no matter their age or gender, and it made Robin sick to think of how much she could fetch for just one of the rings that dappled those painted fingers, how much good that money would have made back home. She wished that the portraits contained the real thing, so she could snatch the knickknacks and stuff her pockets with their wealth.

Two place settings had been made up at the far end of a massive, ornately carved table. They were shrouded behind a large potted plant, sat right in the middle of the table like an overgrown centerpiece, which gave the two chairs an illusion of intimacy.

Robin swallowed hard and detached herself from the seneschal. She lifted her chin and limped proudly to the seat to the left of the large carved chair placed at the head of the table. Lupine motifs loped across the arms and around the back; it was clear whom that one was meant for. A sharp panic welled in the hollow of her throat, and she reminded herself that her fear of the man was all superstitious drivel. He was a not a hobgob or a specter, and she could damn well sit beside him and eat. She'd already traded barbs with him—she could do this.

The Coyote wasn't there yet, and she decided not to wait for him. She certainly didn't owe him the honor. Instead, she plopped into the chair the seneschal pulled out for her with as much deliberate, sullen resentment as she could summon.

There was bread in a basket, and a butter dish within reach, and water trembled in a finely cut glass that perspired gently in the heat of the room. A massive hearth, set into the wall behind her and old enough to make her guess that wherever she was, it was *old*, crackled with fire. Robin had to pretend that she didn't hear its sound, pretend that it didn't remind her of the orange light that had filled the cabin of glider as she and Al had plummeted toward the forest floor. Her shoulders still curled up around her ears, all the same.

Under the silver dome covering her plate, Robin found a gently steaming, artfully arranged display of vegetables, rice, and meat cut so finely and cooked so little that it shook like a leaf in her hand when she lifted her fork to inspect it. It was practically still bloody. Gross.

She had heard that the Klonn sometimes ate their meat practically raw, but she had dismissed it as the folly of the Saskwyan people trying to demonize their enemy. To see the truth of those rumors before her disturbed Robin more than she cared to admit. If this rumor had proven to be true, then what others might be as well? The stories told in the pilots' lounge crowded against her imagination with more insistence, and she shoved them back with a vicious refusal to linger.

She hesitated with a gob of rice on her fork, and then decided it was all or nothing. Either they would poison her, or they wouldn't. Either way, she wouldn't be at her best if she starved herself. If she was going to heal enough, if she was going to be granted the food and drink she would need to regain her strength, then she would consume it. Though she may have to playact complacency in order to continue to get it. It was a revolting thought, but there was no other option for now, not that she could see.

Trust me, the Coyote had begged, and for a second, fear had flashed through his eyes. But fear for which of them, exactly? Or fear of whom?

Robin shoved that thought aside and tucked in. She didn't bother to look up when she heard the door to the room open and close, and the booted footsteps approach. A bottle of wine was set down on the table between the two place settings, and the Coyote dropped into his chair. Robin looked up, and then froze, startled.

He wasn't wearing his mask.

Her first thought was, *Gods, he's young.*

Up close, face bare, he was sort of handsome (though Robin despised having to admit that to herself). Not traditionally, not the way that Wade was devastatingly good-looking or her father was solid and objectively handsome. The Coyote's nose was just a hair too narrow, his eyes too washed out to properly be called gray, and his complexion was pale and sickly to the point of being practically blue. He would have looked ephemeral, like a charcoal sketch that had been rubbed too often and was fading to nothingness, if it wasn't for the black anchor of his hair. A scruffy, half-arsed goatee obscured his chin. Younger than Wade, then, but certainly older than Al. *No more than twenty, at the most,* Robin thought.

Her second thought was, *Gods, he looks weary.*

A surge of guilt and loathing flooded her thoughts, and she stopped her perusal. It was an insult to Al's memory to even study the face of the man who had killed him so openly. The food sank like a cold stone in Robin's gut, and she set down her fork and pushed her plate away, no longer hungry.

"I see that you were too famished to wait," the Coyote said conversationally in Benne-perfect Saskwyan, unaware of the irony of his proclamation. He propped his chin on a hand and watched her with slitted eyes. He was wearing another of those fancy Klonn jackets, all shining black fabric and that tall, wide band of a collar the Klonn always seemed to prefer, with embroidered edgings.

"You look like a proper lady," he said, reaching out and brushing one bare knuckle across the side of her neck. He hesitated for just a moment when Robin recoiled, then settled his bare palm on her bare forearm instead, a parody of comfort. Robin's skin pricked with the realization that, outside of his clinical inspection of her palms, this was the first time they'd touched flesh-to-flesh. "We will have to find a better cut of dress for you, though—such arms. And the noble palette does not suit your skin tone, which is inconvenient," he said with a sniff. Then he reached out and pinched a lock of hair that had escaped its ribbon, rolling it between his thumb and middle finger.

"Don't," Robin said, and jerked back. He let the hair fall, rather than tugging at it.

"How remarkable," the Coyote said. "I have read of such instances, of hair suddenly losing all color after a trauma. It *was* quite a colorful crash—and you have been asleep for over a day. I suppose a transformation such as this would take time. Your hair was still brown in the forest."

Robin looked down, shamed. His keen, assessing gaze, so frank, so intent, made her uncomfortable.

"It is . . . fitting, I think," the Coyote whispered. "Yes. Your people call albinos the 'nowhere folk,' if I am not mistaken. How poetical. And in this case, apt."

Robin stared hard at her lap and concentrated on saying

nothing. Each word was like a slap to the face, and she refused to let him see her flinch. A task made worse by the fact that he seemed not to understand just how insulting it all was. A Sealie could never be a *nowhere* person, unless they were utterly without a hive of bees to direct them home. Nowhere people belonged to a world without boundaries—the ghost-haired were not from *no*where. They were from *every*where.

Robin was far from her mother's hives now, and it was possible that she would now never have any of her own, either, but she was not without a home to return to. All she need given was an opportunity to do so.

Through with his inspection of her—for the time being, at least—the Coyote removed the dome from his own plate and began to eat. The wobbly, undercooked meat slipped around his mouth, and Robin swallowed against the sour urge to be ill. She raised her hands to thank the gods for what little of the meal she had eaten. They still deserved their due, whether she had enjoyed the meal or not, and she still believed in them, even if they had abandoned her to the nowhere folk, either for plot or for purpose. She *needed* to believe in them, needed the anchor, the familiarity, the comfort of the ritual.

But before she could close her eyes, the Coyote grabbed hold of her closest wrist, tugging her hand back down to the tabletop. The quick flash of fear was back in his eyes. They flicked to the door, once, subtly, and Robin's heart stuttered to realize that the seneschal was still there, glowering at her through the fronds of the plant.

"None of that, now," he admonished, voice pitched low and soft. "You are in Klonn now, my dear, and you will comport yourself accordingly. Do not give our hosts any more reason to despise you. Please?"

Robin met his gaze, held it for a moment, trying to decide if the cold civility she saw reflected in the gray of his eyes was anything other than what it seemed. Finally, she nodded once, and the Coyote released her wrist, pointedly returning to his dinner. Dismissed out of hand. Insulting.

Robin swallowed hard, and lowered her hands to her lap. She kept them palm up, though, and finished her prayers in her head, daring the Coyote to read her mind and stop her.

Instead, the Coyote reached forward to pour them each a glass of wine. He set hers down in front of her, and then reached for his own. As he picked it up off the table, his eyes flickered toward the door, narrowing for a fraction of a heartbeat on the place where the seneschal still stood, perched like a gargoyle, overseeing their meal. Then he turned to her and offered her a smile that was tight around the edges.

"To the Seven Arts," the Coyote said in salute, and when Robin didn't raise her glass to the toast, he huffed and tapped the edge of his wine glass against hers, where it stood still on the table. Robin tilted her head, eyeing him shrewdly. What was wrong with him? What manner of torture would require him to behave as though he were afraid? When she still didn't move to pick up her glass, he nodded toward it, eyebrows lifted. Robin waited for him to sip his first, just to be sure, before she finally grabbed her glass and took a mouthful of her own.

It was laced with honey. The unexpected familiarity, the taste of home, made tears spring into her eyes. She blinked them back furiously, determined not to show even the smallest speck of emotion in front of him. It was a losing battle. She set down her glass and covered her face with her hands so the Coyote wouldn't see, but it was too late.

"Oh! Oh no, please, do not cry," the Coyote said, seeming to be genuinely distressed. One of his spidery hands landed on her shoulder, a mimicry of a concerned lover's caress. "I thought it would be a nice gift for you. You must not cry. "

Robin pulled her hands down to glare at the Coyote with raw eyes. "I'm not crying."

He sent another furtive gaze darting at the seneschal again, and Robin was beginning to see why he kept his helmet on so much—much as he tried to hide it behind his officious pronouncements and grand gestures,he actually seemed worried about her. There was a kernel, hidden deep under his performance, of true concern, true fear. Of genuine *truth* that the helmet would have hidden. But why?

I keep them, he'd said about the other mid-flights. But there was no indication that they were still here. That they, too, were being insulted by ridiculous, overbearing clothing, or what was probably supposed to be a fancy meal. They weren't here, being offered honeyed wine and touches that were probably meant to be comforting, but that just made her more and more uncomfortable.

"That is another habit we must break you of," the Coyote whispered, hiding his mouth behind his wine glass, as though he feared someone might be reading his lips. It didn't make sense. He was the *Coyote*, the scourge of the skies. He was ruthless, dishonorable, brutal—not fearful, kind, and concerned. Something wasn't adding up.

"What habit?" she asked.

"Contractions. No one in Klonn is low-bred enough to utilize contractions. You must say, *I am*."

"I won't," Robin hissed back, defiant and just about sick to the teeth with being told what she could and couldn't do.

The Coyote slammed his knife point down in the table, and when he let go, it remained there, embedded, the handle shivering.

"*Will not*," he corrected, evenly. But there was something in the action, something in the horrible, sudden, tight blankness in his eyes that—

He's playacting, she realized. *He's pretending to be overbearing and cruel. Why? Why this show? Why any of it?* The puzzle itched at her brain in places she couldn't reach, teasing and just beyond her grasp.

Instead, Robin stared at the wine and bit her lip hard enough to keep all the horrible cusses she wanted to spit at him contained. It would do absolutely no good to get him angry. She had to hold on to her rage—keep it close, keep it secret within her, let it keep her powerful.

The Coyote removed the knife. She remained quiet as he finished eating, and then he haughtily rang a little bell that had been sitting, unseen by Robin, beside his chair. The seneschal came and cleared their dishes. Robin wondered if there were any other servants in the building. It would make her escape all the easier if there was only one.

On the other hand, there could be hundreds, and perhaps Robin was only seeing him. She gritted her teeth against the frustration. She hated not knowing where her horizons lay.

The seneschal returned with two small dishes of a rich, moist cake made of chocolate, and Robin's defiant willpower crumbled enough that she ate alongside the Coyote in small, hesitant bites. It wasn't healthy, but it was fuel, and that was all that mattered just now. And, yes, okay—it was godsdamned delicious.

When both their plates were empty, the Coyote sat back, running his finger around the rim of his wine glass, making it hum a clear, perfect note. Robin raised her eyes at the sound and saw, for the first time, that there was a dark black bruise on the side of the Coyote's face—the one that was furthest from her, the one he had hidden with his hands whenever he turned to her, making it look like boredom or exhaustion. She studied his posture and realized that he was slumped, shoulders curled inward around some sort of hurt she couldn't see.

Surprised at the surge of pity that filled her, she asked: "What happened to you?"

His finger paused on the rim of the glass and he huffed, as if answering was beneath him. Then he answered, all the same. "I was punished. For leaving behind your mid-flight."

Robin's heart quavered. He described his punishment so

matter-of-factly, she had to wonder how often it had happened before.

"Why would your general beat his best pilot? That doesn't make any sense." Then, suddenly, it dawned on Robin.

Everything the Coyote had said in the forest, every whisper in her ear, even the way he spoke made it screamingly obvious, and Robin wondered how she had ever missed the clues.

Robin ducked as far behind the plant as she was able, and raised her own wine glass to hide her mouth, the same way he had. "*You're* the other prisoner," she whispered.

The Coyote grinned, his smile filled with self-loathing and defeat.

"There now. How very clever you are," he said and leaned out to chime the bowl of his wine glass against hers in a bitter salute. "I knew you would come to the truth, eventually."

CHAPTER THIRTEEN

THEY WERE SILENT UNTIL THEIR GLASSES WERE EMPTY. The Coyote, it seemed, in quiet shame. Robin, in furious, chugging thought, so lost in the gears and cogs of her mind that she jumped when the Coyote stood and put his hands on the back of her chair. It seemed to be a clear signal that whatever sort of charade this dinner was meant to be, it was over, because the door opened and half a dozen navy-blue-uniformed soldiers descended on the room, clearing their dessert plates, collecting glasses, and standing at attention at various spots around the room.

Robin jumped up, too. She couldn't bear the thought of him hovering over her exposed neck—he'd already shown a penchant for putting his hands around it, after all. The Coyote reached out, and without so much as a "please," took her hand and placed it in the crook of his arm with a pointed look. Officious, high-handed ass. Robin forced her fingers into a flex, countering the desire to pinch down hard and maybe try to rip at the sensitive bundle of tendons under his skin.

Perhaps he *was* a prisoner. But there was also the possibility that he was lying to her. All she knew for sure was that he had shot down dozens of her colleagues, and she wasn't going to trust him, not as easily as all that. Not because he'd simply asked her to and spun her a fancy tale. Not until she knew for sure what it was that was actually happening inside these walls.

The Coyote escorted her back into the same long hallway the seneschal had brought her down; though, with her limp, it became more of a slow shuffle than the graceful promenade of nobility. The Coyote's gait was stiff with performance and his own unseen bruises, and Robin wondered how much of the show was for her benefit, made for the sole purpose of garnering her favor, and how much of it was for their captors—whoever they might be. Assuming he was to be believed, of course, and was not, himself, her true captor. She was starting to cultivate a headache trying to unravel this knot.

He led her along the hall and selected, seemingly on a whim, another door identical to the one that had opened to the dining room. This time, they entered a small salon, the sort where a family might spend their evenings in a rousing game of cards, or playing with their children, or reading to one another.

The Coyote released Robin's arm as soon as they stepped inside, and turned immediately to the door to begin a conversation in low, rapid Klonnish with the seneschal, who had followed them with fresh glasses, the wine bottle, and a thick folio. Robin took several deliberate steps away from them, just to see if he would let her. She'd test boundaries all she rudding well wanted, and to hells with what he commanded. Neither man paid her any mind. They seemed to have decided that, in this particular cage, it was safe to let her off her leash, so she turned to take in the room. It was decorated in the colors of Klonn, all icy blues and pale greens, and so artificial. The furniture was stiff and ornately carved. Robin ached for the warm earth tones preferred by her own people, or even the rich reds and oranges and yellows that made the Benne nobility look like autumn leaves caught in a whirlwind when they walked down the streets. She missed overstuffed sofas and plain chairs with deep seats, and the flickering flash of sparkling thread embroidered into everything.

Above the massive fireplace on the far wall was a large painting. A family—the man looked remarkably like the Coyote, though his eyes were a deeper, richer blue, his face narrower, his cheeks more gaunt, his facial hair far fussier. There was a little boy who stood beside him, while a woman she presumed to be their mother sat in the front, holding a chubby toddler with an affable expression. The eldest boy had silvery eyes and held himself stiff, his lip curled with familiar disdain. Robin had doubted that someone like the Coyote could ever have been a child, but here was the proof. The woman was beautiful, with a sort of beatific radiance that shone out of the canvas. Robin saw the same peace and joy in the younger boy, a cloud of black curls ringing his head, a slightly mischievous curl to the side of his pillowy baby lips.

The gears in her mind whirred and whirled, and a foggy understanding began to take shape.

Robin peered over at the Coyote again; he stood in the doorway still, signing a small stack of papers that were balanced on the seneschal's leather folder.

"*Deh*," the seneschal was saying. "You may have this. It is acceptable." His words were heavily accented, but undoubtedly *Saskwyan*. Which meant, he'd *wanted* her to hear him, to understand him. Which also meant that he'd understood everything they'd said over dinner. There was more in Klonnish, and Robin wished again that she'd been afforded the training the other officers had been offered in regards to communication with the enemy. Perhaps, if she'd been given more time, if their need to get her into the sky as soon as possible hadn't been so urgent, she would have been.

Anxiety over what their hosts might have planned next warred with the need to keep pretending to be . . . whatever it was the Coyote wanted of her. Docile? Vapid? She still wasn't sure what her role in all of this was supposed to be.

Robin hobbled toward a table set against the window, where a board of alternating white and black squares was laid with little carvings of courtiers and kings and knights. She pretended to study them as she cased the latch on the windowpane, eyes drawn to the bars and fresh cement that held them to the outside wall.

Frozen turds, she thought. *This window, too. They've got this all figured out, haven't they?*

"Do you know this game, my dear?" the Coyote asked over her shoulder, and Robin startled. She winced and sucked in a deep breath as both her ribs and her ankle protested. The thick carpeting had prevented her from hearing his approach. He was just a few steps away, the bottle and glasses in his hands. The seneschal had left the room, the door firmly closed once more.

There was a loud, obvious click as it was locked from the outside. Hells.

Alone at last. Or are we? Robin wondered.

She resisted the urge to upend the table and scream. "No, I don't know the game," she said instead, grating the words out between clenched teeth.

The Coyote waved her into the seat opposite him with a magnanimity that bordered on the hostile. For all the farce of being treated like a guest, she was still being given orders to obey. She sat. He handed her a wine glass.

"It is a war game," the Coyote explained.

Now that she could see him head-on, she could catalogue his bruise in full—it spread from his hairline to his jaw, and was getting darker every moment, the flesh around it raw and red with tiny scraped pricks. *Someone kicked him*, Robin realized. *Kicked him right in the face. Good gods. Probably knocked him down and booted him a few times, too, the way he's holding his side.*

"It is called chess," he went on when Robin didn't say

anything, too horrified by her revelation to reply. "It is a game of strategy and patience. I am very good at both."

He looked up at Robin over the board, eyes glittering, and Robin understood that he wasn't talking about just the game. He was patient, that much was clear. He had been playing this game, this give and take with their captors, for a long time.

Hells, this probably is his house, Robin thought, glancing again at the painting over the mantle. *Have they taken it over? Or is all of this a ruse? Is he victim, as he pretends to be, or master, as the painting implies?* The headache got a bit tighter, perching right between her eyes.

"I like strategy, as well," he said. "Take, for instance, Pyria." He studied her face for her reaction, so she bit the insides of her cheeks and gave him none. Did he know that's where she'd grown up? Was this some kind of bait? "It is the closest city to the southern border. At the advent of the war, it became an industrial town." He spread his spider fingers and smiled. "And then we bombed it. With no factories, there are no jobs, and with no jobs, people start to become frugal and desperate. Your home nation is eating itself alive, my dear."

Robin thought of Mama, without her loom, and of her own scavenging expeditions. She thought of the neighbors who had lost their thumbs and hated, *hated* the man who sat smiling before her, so smugly pleased with his own cleverness.

"People are suffering in Pyria," she snapped.

He frowned, looking at her with a shrewd, calculating gaze. "Indeed. Our strategy held true."

He was still for a long moment, assessing her. And then, as if he had come to the conclusion that her righteous anger was entirely dismissible, he looked back to the board and explained how each of the pieces could be maneuvered. Robin wanted to fight with him, against him and his flippant affirmation, against his *pride* in the atrocities he'd orchestrated, but the ease with which he'd maneuvered past the opportunity for her to do so quashed her ability to respond as she'd like. The topic was closed, and his posture, his intent attention on the game pieces, said that it would not reopen anytime soon.

The rules of the war game seemed ridiculously complicated, but Robin paid attention because it was better than letting her mind roam over her inability to pin this slippery bastard down. Every time she thought she was confident she despised him, he'd go and say something else that ruined it. And every time she resolved to pity him, he'd do the same.

"Shall we begin, then?" he asked.

Robin blinked at him. "What, you mean actually play?"

"Of course!" he chuckled, and it held only the faintest thread of strain. "I was not lying when I said I quite enjoy chess."

Robin swallowed hard, eyes bouncing around the board. "I . . . I don't think I . . ."

"If it will make it easier for you to understand, I shall play first." Robin nodded, mouth dry with worry that this was some sort of test she was about to fail. She took a gulp of her wine to wet her throat. The honey sat heavy on her tongue, and she wouldn't cry—she *wouldn't*.

The Coyote tapped the base of his wine glass thoughtfully on the tabletop, and then moved one of his pieces. Robin had no idea to what advantage the move was, but she was sure there had to be one. She leaned in, pretending to study the board. She raised her hand to her chin to make herself look thoughtful, blocking the view of her mouth from the room. She had no idea if anyone was peeking at them through the wall panels or from behind the curtains, but paranoia had begun to infect her.

"Who did they take from you? Who are they threatening?" She reached down with her free hand and played the first piece she touched.

The Coyote stretched his mouth at her, reviving that uncomfortable smile, but didn't answer. He played a second piece.

"It's someone, though," Robin pressed, playing her second

piece, copying what he did because she had no space in her head to keep the rules straight just now. "Or you wouldn't be cooperating. So, who?"

The Coyote played his third, then raised his glass to hide his lips. "Did I not call you clever, my dear?" He paused, a small bit of anguish flickering across his face before he steeled it. "I have a brother. A boastful man who praised the flying ability of his sibling far too often to far too many of the wrong people. And that is all I will say."

Robin's eyes cut to the portrait. The younger boy stared back at her, helpless and vulnerable-looking. Robin played her next piece and hissed, "But you could just fly away. I don't understand. You have an aeroship."

"And where would I go?" the Coyote asked. "The Benne will not take me. Frankin is aggressively neutral and will harbor neither fugitives nor deserters. No aeroship could fly as far as Telniem, and pirates litter the skies above the deserts. I am just a man, and my king has ordered my cooperation. Or else."

"If this is all true, then I feel sorry for you," Robin ground out. "But I still won't help you do . . . whatever it is you need mid-flights for."

The Coyote shook his head—he wasn't going to discuss it here. "My dear—" he began instead.

"Stop calling me that," Robin snapped. "I'm not *your* anything."

The Coyote folded his hands in his lap and regarded her thoughtfully. "You gave me no name to call you by. Shall I call you simply the Pilot with the Robin-Nosed Glider?"

The thought that he might use that to guess her true name filled Robin with dread. She wished, suddenly, that Al had chosen any other bird to decorate their aircraft with. Now that she had a better idea of who her enemy was, it made her extremely uneasy to think that her captors knew even that small a truth about her.

Any other bird, she thought, dithering, mind racing. The memory of the two brown birds in the sky above the crash, crying out their fierce joy, bubbled into her mind. "If you have to call me something, then call me Skylark."

The Coyote's mouth twisted. "The Skylark and the Coyote. It sounds like a child's tale." Robin shot him a surprised glance. "Yes, I know what your people call me. I find I prefer it over the moniker the king has chosen. Wolves hunt. Coyotes scavenge."

Robin took several deep breaths, flicking her eyes around the room and reaching out to push one of the foot soldiers on her side of the board forward a space. "And that's what our hosts do? Scavenge?"

The Coyote met her steady gaze and winked.

"Tech?"

He tapped his glass again. Robin thought for a moment, recalled the questions he had asked her in the forest, and wasn't sure she liked where the memory was leading her.

"Mid-flights?" she whispered, trying not to move her mouth at all.

He winked again.

"Why?"

He tapped his glass.

"Where are they?"

He tapped.

Robin flopped back in the chair, hollow and gutted. Adam and John, all the mid-flights she had known who'd been shot down, gone. Hauled away, probably screaming as they watched the Coyote stab their pilots through the heart, like Robin had watched him desecrate Al. Robin wondered where those mid-flights were now.

Don't be stupid, Robin scolded herself. *It's obvious. They're dead, or he wouldn't have needed you.* She looked up and found that he was watching her, waiting, it seemed, as she put the pieces of the puzzle into a coherent pattern. She grimaced.

He smiled again, and the light, confident tone crept back into his voice, making it richer, more enticing. "Ah, there it is. I will never forget the first time I saw that charming scowl under your goggles. Although, if I may, it looks even more charming with your hair as it is now. The juxtaposition with your skin tone is striking. It suits you." Performing again. Was the flirtation performance as well, or did he really think that he could charm her?

Robin rolled her eyes and forced herself not to snap at him. She was not some stupid girl, to have her head turned with silver-tongued compliments. Especially when they came from the lips of the enemy. And he *was* still her enemy, no matter the protestations of his own captivity, no matter the shared meals, and the wine, and his apparent protectiveness.

"So, was it me you were after, then?"

"And your mid-flight, as well. Two at the cost of one. Quite a bargain for my efforts."

Robin gawped at him, horrified. "Don't trivialize it."

"We are at war, Skylark," he replied sadly. "You must forgive a soldier his gallows humor."

"I don't have to forgive you for anything," Robin snapped.

The Coyote set his wine glass down with enough force that the game pieces rattled.

"You could thank me, then, at least," he snarled, frustration bubbling up in him. The congenial facade cracked, and for the first time, Robin caught a glimpse of the raging firestorm that surged below it. She saw the danger in him across the table that she had always known was there when they faced off in the sky. "Believe me, the courtesies extended to you tonight were not solely the result of your sex. No other we have held has had the pleasure of bathing, or a fine meal!"

Robin puffed out a laugh. "I'm sorry, but you want me to thank you? Ha!"

He looked wounded for a moment, like he really had expected her to be grateful. "Mind yourself," he warned, but he was projecting again, raising his voice for their unseen audience, as if there were more than just the seneschal watching. "The cold pantry is uncomfortable at night."

Robin scoffed. "Isn't that a bit barbaric, threatening to lock a prisoner in a food cupboard?"

"Come now, enough of this. Be reasonable and we can—*nema*!"

That last order was directed toward someone standing behind her. Robin leapt up and turned. The seneschal stood there—damn those thick carpets; she hadn't even heard him enter the room—and before Robin could properly duck, he laid the back of his hand across her face. The inside of her cheek bashed against the edge of her teeth, and Robin tasted blood. The slap was meant to insult more than hurt, and her cheeks burned with the humiliation of it.

Blood dribbled from the corner of her lips. Robin, never one to walk away from a fistfight, hauled back and let her fist fly. The Coyote intercepted, catching her wrist easily.

"Let go!" she snapped.

"No," he said, gaze darting between Robin and the seneschal. "I did warn you, my dear Skylark. Now, you have left me no choice."

"Go ahead, then," Robin snarled, defiant, glaring up at him. "Kill me, lock me in an ice box, I don't care. Whatever it is you're collecting us up for, I won't do it. I won't agree to anything, or tell you anything, or do anything. So you might as well just get it over with!"

The Coyote yanked on her wrist, pulling her back around the game table and back against his chest, mouth directly on her ear as he hissed: "I convinced them to treat you like a lady. I told them you were a Benne noblewoman, and it is for that reason alone that they have not taken any further liberties. If they do not kill you outright, they will send you to a prison camp, and you must know as well as I the fate of a Sealie woman within those walls."

Panic seized her, and Robin froze in dread, breath whooshing out in horror. All thoughts of a quiet escape with scores of intelligence fled. All she knew was that she could not let the Coyote ensnare her. Not with his pretty words, or his charms, or his calculating kindness, or even his false, cold cruelty. She could not let him trick her into compliance, but more than that, she could not let him send her to the camps. She had to get away.

Trust me, he had asked of her, and for what? *To trick me? To use me? What is his game?*

Groping out with one hand, her fingers seized on his wine glass. She shoved it into the seneschal's face, splashing the wine into his eyes to blind him, cracking the crystal against his temple. He jerked back, roaring, and she wriggled free of the Coyote, grip loosened just enough in his shock.

As quick as she was able, she ran to the door, ignoring the throb of her abused ankle. She threw herself bodily at the wood, wrenching on the knob.

Locked! Clever bastard. They are too thorough by half!

Robin slammed against the door, putting all of her considerable mid-flight muscle into the effort. The hinges groaned, but didn't give. Had she enough time, she thought she might have been able to loosen them enough to get the door open, but the seneschal was already coming at her, his face a mask of rage.

Robin ducked to the side and dashed to the fireplace, searching for a weapon—there was no poker, no grate broom. She grabbed the end of a slim, burning log and whirled around to brandish it at the seneschal. He stopped up short, just as aware as she that the wine soaking into his clothes would go up in a brilliant blaze the moment Robin touched him with the flame.

Behind him, the Coyote's face was painted with an irritated snarl.

"Enough," he growled.

"Unlock the door," she demanded. "And release me."

"No," he laughed, and then, before Robin even saw it coming, the Coyote crossed the room, lunged forward, and batted the burning log right out of her hand. It rolled along the carpet, the flames snuffing instead of setting it ablaze. "Cease this."

"Never gonna happen," Robin snarled, sidestepping his snatching hands.

"Going to," the Coyote corrected.

"Stop pretending! Stop acting like you actually care what happens to me!" Robin shouted at him. Ignoring the strain on her ribs, she crouched and scrambled for her boot knife. She came back up brandishing it. "You killed Al!"

The Coyote took a step back, surprise written around his eyes at the sight of the blade, that she had dared to draw it in front of the seneschal to point it at him. "Skylark," he warned, low and dangerous, "listen to me—"

"You wounded Wade, and you've shot down dozens of gliders! You! You—!" Robin sobbed, but there was no curse, no epithet, no word big enough, *black* enough to encompass the totality of the hatred she felt.

"Fifty-three," the Coyote corrected, tone carefully indifferent, cold, clinical. Flippant. The seneschal straightened from his wary crouch and took a small step back, out of range of her blade.

Robin was so aghast at the calculated flatness of the Coyote's tone that she actually had to gasp against the shock. "You . . . you think that's *funny?*"

"No, I do not," the Coyote said, lips twisting with what looked like genuine sorrow. A somber sort of seriousness fell over him, like a too-heavy cloak. "How many of us have you shot down?"

"I don't keep track," she said, defensive. "It's not a scorecard. I've got more respect for lives than that."

"Sixty-one," the Coyote supplied, stepping closer, arms down and to the side. "Sixty-one Klonn soldiers, shot down by the pilot in the robin-nosed glider. And in far fewer skirmishes than it took me to achieve a similar count."

The seneschal shifted forward, assuming she was distracted,

and Robin swung the knife in an arc toward his thigh. But the seneschal was too tall. His reach was greater, and he had hold of her wrist before the blow landed. He squeezed, grinding the bones in her arm together. Robin clamped down on the little pained grunt that wanted to escape and fought to keep her grip on the knife. Her fingers went numb, and the choice was stolen from her.

As soon as her blade thumped to the carpeting, harmless, the seneschal swung her arm back, forcing it down. Robin cried out as the seneschal spun her swiftly to the side and stepped up behind her, his free hand suddenly clutching her throat, fingers pressed with just enough force against her windpipe to let her know he meant business.

The seneschal growled something in guttural Klonnish, and the Coyote's face soured around the edges, resignation flickering in his eyes.

"*Nema*," he said, with a pointed look at Robin. "I will do it."

"*Ai, deh*," the seneschal said, and then stepped aside so the Coyote to take his place.

He pushed her forward, frog-marching her to the door.

Robin considered flinging her head back and trying to bash in his nose with her skull, but she was simply too short—the best she could do was bruise herself on his breastbone. Robin was shoved out the door and dragged down the hall. They turned into what was clearly a servant's passageway, barren and narrow, and marched through an empty kitchen.

"You meant the actual cold panty?" Robin goggled as they stopped before a barred doorway.

Behind her, the Coyote sighed, faint and warm against the back of her neck. "Did you think it a lie? You must learn, my dear, to listen when I warn you. You are making it hard for me to spare you, and I do not relish punishments such as these. Now, please, stay. Do not make this worse."

Slowly, he let go of her throat and arm. When Robin didn't

move, he crossed to the pantry door and unlocked it, opening it wide. He met her gaze then, and for a brief flash of a moment, Robin saw sadness, hurt, and concern flicker behind the resignation and cruel glint. She didn't understand him, didn't understand anything about her situation, but she refused to let him—them—see her cowed.

She was stronger than she looked. She always had been. She could handle whatever they put her through. So long as she could dream of the sky, she could survive. So long as she *lived*, she could still escape.

Head held high, shoulders back, Robin walked inside the little closet of her own accord. She turned and met the Coyote's gaze with a glare, daring him to do it, to close her inside.

The door slammed shut, locking her in with the smell of must and slow rot. There was just enough light under the door to throw wavering shadows up against the bare stone walls. The closet was narrow, and small, hardly big enough for her to stretch out in, lined with empty racks that, judging by the sour smell that permeated the stained wood, had once held rows of wine bottles. A small wooden box in the corner held ice packed in filthy straw, which made it unsafe to drink the ice melt if she got thirsty later. A few greasy, old waxed wrappers littered the floor, reeking of the raw meat they must have once contained.

Robin tore at the buttons on the gown, wanting to get the stink of her captors off of her. Bile rose in her throat, the wine and the chocolate and the rice all mingling into a hard, angry ball in her gut. Her fingers shook, and the fabric refused to rip, and she forced herself to slow down and undo each of the small buttons one at a time, her fingers shaking so hard that, by the end of the row, it took her four tries to undo the last one, throwing her into even more of an impotent rage.

Robin sucked hard on the air, which suddenly felt too thick to make its way past the burning stone that had appeared at the root of her tongue. Anger was threatening to crawl into her limbs, and she shut it away. Having a temper tantrum would do her no good.

I can't panic like that again, she snarled to herself. *He's right. I was outclassed. I can't just swing my fists and expect it to turn out in my favor. I have to use my brain. Godsdamnit!*

She threw the dress against the wall, and it landed with a completely unsatisfactory whisper on the floor. Robin breathed hard, and refused to scream, refused to rail or weep or any of the weak, womanly things the Coyote obviously sought to wring from her.

She probed the cut on the inside of her mouth with her tongue, and yearned for the clear, fresh air of the sky with every miserable part of herself.

CHAPTER FOURTEEN

In what Robin assumed was the morning, the door swung open again, with no warning to precede it. She hadn't slept at all. Partially because she wanted to be awake and aware if someone came back in the night. Partially because she couldn't stomach any more horrible dreams. And partially because the pantry was just so rudding *freezing*.

She'd spent the time despising her enforced passivity. She wanted to run, to fight, to fly. To throw a punch, to kick, to scream. Outside of a glider, though, it was painfully obvious that she was outmatched. The only weapon she had left was her wits, and the quicksilver changes in the Coyote's temperament was making her doubt even those. When the anger at her captors, her situation, herself, was too much for her to sustain, she let down her hair, stared at her strange white locks, and missed Al like a raw wound.

The unexpected stab of daylight as the door swung outward hurt her eyes, and she squinted against it, wishing she had goggles with her. Her teeth were chattering hard, and had been for so long that her jaw ached from having tried to still them.

"I trust the lesson has been absorbed," the seneschal said

softly, his words halting and thick, but clear.

"Bug off, you scrubbed-up ass!" Robin snarled. If they had thought a night locked up in there was enough to tame her, they were dead wrong. It had only made her angrier.

The Coyote was there, too, Robin saw as her eyes stopped watering. He stood just behind the seneschal, back in shirtsleeves and what looked to be his uniform trousers and bracers. His waistcoat this time was the fine blue of a summer morning sky. His expression was careful, rigidly placid, like an iced-over pond. The bruise on his face had deepened to a mottled purple in the center, both lids of his eye green. She wondered how his captors expected him to fly for them like that. When his warden-servant turned aside to let him into the doorway, the haughty expression of disdain she was quickly growing familiar with swam back.

He bared his teeth in an indulgent smile. "Winter comes, Skylark. The nights will only grow colder. Refuse to cooperate, and you will stay here, and freeze, as so many of your very stubborn colleagues have done. Or you can come with me, do what is asked of you, and live."

Robin's flesh crawled. She was sitting where some of the other mid-flights had died? She stood quickly, joints stiff from the cold, her whole body aching from the shivers that wracked her. The dress dropped to the floor. She'd been using it as a blanket, but her pride won out over her desire for warmth and she left it there. She refused to be embarrassed to be seen in her underthings.

But the honest truth was: she wasn't sure if she could survive many more nights in the pantry. And she despised that he had so neatly, so perfectly exposed this weakness. Being both a former mid-flight and a Sealie meant that there wasn't a lot of precious, vital, insulating fat left on her body. She could lie, she could stay silent, she could probably even resist painful torture, but the fear of being left alone to die in the cold and the dark was just too much. The thought of being locked up and *forgotten*, of rotting in the dank and the chill, was the stuff of nightmares. In ways that the threat of physical violence could never be, it was utterly and completely *terrifying*.

The Coyote held out his hand.

"You are an insufferable, assuming bastard," Robin snapped, crossing her arms over her stomach, pressing her chilled fingers into her armpits to resist the urge to take his hand, to leech on his body heat. Yet another expression Robin wasn't sure she could parse crossed his face. It wasn't shame or worry this time. It was . . . pity? Or maybe *self*-pity?

"I will not disagree," he said softly, flexing the fingers of his free hand. "But I am also right. Please, choose to cooperate." His eyes were wide and earnest when she met them, and she couldn't help licking her parched lips, hesitating. Was he being honest? Or was this just more playacting?

She didn't know which version of this man to trust.

"For now," Robin allowed at last. "But just for now."

She took his hand. His fingers closed around hers, his skin so warm it felt like he was branding the back of her hand. It made her shiver harder. He bent down and whispered quickly, in her ear: "If you trust me, Skylark, and I hope you will, then I can win us our freedom."

"I wouldn't trust you as far as I could throw you," she whispered back.

"And yet, who else is there for you to place your trust in?"

Omens, she snarled to herself. *He's right, and he knows it. Gods-dammit.* She nodded, just once, eyes on the seneschal, who seemed to be paying more attention to the guard at the door to the kitchen than to his two charges. Then, after a moment of thought, she added, "I don't suppose you'll give me my knife back."

He leaned back, eyes glittering with real mirth, and laughed. It was light and bubbly, a startled sort of honest laugh, and its sheer authenticity annoyed her.

"Didn't think so," she said grumpily.

Tugging gently, the Coyote pulled her into the kitchen proper. There was a thick blanket hanging on a hook on the wall, and with his free hand, he swept it over her shoulders.

"Thank you," she said grudgingly.

"I have called for a warm bath for you. Come, I will escort you back to your room, you will bathe, and then we will discuss what it is that is required of you."

"I'm not sure I want to know," Robin said warily. "But I don't have much of a choice, do I?"

"No," he agreed. "None whatsoever."

He stepped back and motioned for her to go first. Casting a quick glance at the seneschal and the guard, Robin complied, limping slowly into the hall. The Coyote followed. She paused, waiting to be told which direction to turn, and the Coyote frowned.

"Does it hurt? Your ankle?"

Robin saw no point in lying. "Maybe."

"I shall arrange for you to have enough bandages to bind yourself. In the meantime—" He dipped down and swung her up into his arms like a bride without so much as a "by your leave."

Robin flailed as her feet left the floor, and then went utterly stiff in his grip. "What are you—?"

"Oof," the Coyote said with a cheeky grin. "You are heavier than you look."

"Then put me *down*!"

"Of course, my dear Miss Skylark," he said easily and headed down the hall without actually doing so. The guard at the kitchen door looked vaguely bemused, but when Robin threw her arm across the Coyote's shoulders to keep from getting jostled, she caught a glimpse of the thundercloud fury on the the seneschal's face as he followed along behind them. "As soon as you are back in your rooms."

"I'm not your dear," she reminded him. Something in his eyes shuttered, a warmth that she had only now realized had been there because it was no longer present. Had she hurt his feelings? Impossible. Robin dismissed the thought. Surely it was all just more manipulation.

"You have your pride still, I see," the Coyote said slowly. "I respect that."

"You could respect it better by letting me walk," Robin shot back, thumping his shoulder with her fist.

"And you will heal faster if you stay off your foot," he retaliated, wincing theatrically at the hit. She hadn't put that much force into it. He was playing. It reminded her sharply, painfully of Al, the way his brick-wall face would scrunch up, the smirk curled in the corner of his mouth that she would *never see again* and—

"Why do you care?" Robin challenged, not allowing herself to get distracted when she was literally in the arms of the enemy.

The Coyote bit his bottom lip. He looked over at the rows and rows of portraits frowning down at them both, and didn't answer. Robin decided not to push, turning her attention to their route.

Last night had been a blur of fear, and the twist of being hauled awkwardly down the hall. She'd tried to keep track of where they were going, but hadn't quite been able to—this time, she counted the turns carefully, kept her eyes peeled for useful landmarks, and began to build a map in her mind.

Kitchens were useful places to be able to sneak off to. There was food in kitchens. And usually cloth to secret it away in. And fires for warmth. But most importantly, because kitchens needed to accept deliveries from butchers, and greengrocers, and the milk maid, kitchens also quite often had a door to the outside world.

As the Coyote cradled her close, her shivers slowly subsided. Robin was loath to admit that being in his arms was comfortable, but his body heat was delicious, and the feel of his soft shirtsleeves against her bare arms and the backs of her knees reminded her of being carried by Papa when she was small. Exhaustion pulled at her eyes, had her chin bobbing against his shoulder as she warmed up and her body begged for sleep. When they passed the little stuffed dog, Robin knew she was minutes away from being locked in that revoltingly luxurious bedroom again. A prison cell was still a prison cell, no matter how many nice bedclothes it had, or how expensive the wallpaper was. The surge of fear at being locked up and left to starve, and die, and rot swelled against her sternum again, made her breath hitch and her throat convulse.

"Hush now," the Coyote said quietly. He squeezed her once, gently. "Do not make a fuss."

"Or what?" she asked, just as quietly. "You'll lock me away again?"

"Do not challenge me in front of him," the Coyote replied, with a subtle head tilt in the direction of the seneschal. "He is reluctant enough to allow me this freedom of treating you as a lady as it is. He would much rather we treat you as an enemy soldier."

"I don't know if I should be grateful for that or not," Robin sneered.

"Do not," the Coyote corrected her grammar absently, and then fell silent. They were standing in front of a door that could only be the one to her bedroom. The seneschal stepped around them and selected yet another identical key from the massive ring. He unlocked the door on the first try, no fumbling, and Robin really wished she had the time to investigate the key ring more carefully, see what it was that distinguished them from one another for him.

The Coyote set her down on the mattress, and Robin immediately sprang back up. The seneschal closed the door behind them, locking them in. A copper tub filled with steaming water was already sitting on the floor at the foot of the bed. It was so tempting that Robin could practically feel herself salivate at the thought of sinking into all that hot water and just closing her eyes for an hour.

"I could help you into the tub," the Coyote said, and the mischievous, little-boy grin was back.

"Out of the question," Robin answered.

"Ah, well," he said with a smirk and a shrug, folding his hands behind himself. "You cannot blame a man for trying."

"I absolutely can," Robin said. "Besides, you're kinda my arch nemesis."

"Am I?" the Coyote blurted, looking charmed. "Well, then."

"Yes. And now that we're alone, at last," Robin huffed, leaning back against one of the bedposts and crossing her arms over her chest, trying to look as unapproachable as possible. "You wanna tell me what exactly is going on here now? Or do these walls have ears, as well?"

"Not these walls, no," the Coyote allowed.

"Explain, then." Robin sat on the edge of the bed, expectant.

The Coyote toyed with the cuffs of his shirt, a weird, endearingly nervous gesture that Robin hadn't expected from someone who moved so much like he calculated the exact arc of every motion, and made no gestures that were frivolous. "Your bath will get cold," he hedged.

"Better talk fast, then," Robin said.

The Coyote sighed, ran his hands through his artfully arranged hair, dislodging it and sending it into an awkward, almost charming mess. And then he slumped. It was like watching a zeppelin balloon deflate. The strong shape of him withered, his shoulders curling in, his posture stooping. His face, when he finally looked back up at her, was creased and haggard. There were tight lines around his mouth and eyes. For the first time, he really looked like what he'd called himself—a prisoner.

"You know that I am the best pilot in the Klonn Aeroforce; it is not boastfulness when I say that—"

"I do," Robin interrupted. "We've danced, remember?"

"Yes, right, of course," the Coyote said, clearing his throat and running his hands through his hair again, then down to scratch at his chin-scruff. He offered her a cheeky glance. "My dear Skylark, how could I forget?"

Robin shifted uncomfortably, trying not to squirm at his honesty. "I'm not your dear," she reminded him again.

One corner of the Coyote's mouth pulled upward, wry and thin. "Must you contradict all I say? Must you challenge everything?"

"Yes," Robin said simply.

"Do you wish to hear my tale, or not?"

Robin clutched her own elbows tighter, cutting off her body language, deciding not to address his odd crush, or whatever falsehood he wished to instill her with, just yet. "Talk."

The Coyote leaned back against the rim of the tub, dipping his fingertips absently in the steaming water. The ripple sent the scent of strong floral perfume echoing out into the room, and Robin wrinkled her nose.

"I am possibly the very best pilot in Klonn," he started again, and Robin kept her silence this time and listened. "And I have come to be so because I had the luxury of an upbringing that valued the Arts of War, and left me—ah, how shall I say it?— financially and socially secure enough to pursue flying as much as I liked. But we were both children when King Eloy and King Auden began this bloody war of theirs, were we not? We did not understand when we began to train to participate in it what it really meant to do so."

Robin tried to keep the surprise off her face. *How does he know?* she thought. *Listening to him sounds like listening to my most private thoughts spoken aloud.*

"I thought it was very great fun, you see," the Coyote went on miserably. "Being up in the air, just me and the sky and my aeroship. Until I shot down my first glider. The Benne pilot, she met my eyes as she fell, you see. I had to watch her, watching me, as she was swallowed up by the sky. For those last few moments she was alive. And we both knew, without any doubt, that those same moments were to be her last. She would be dead as soon as she —" He pressed the back of one hand to his mouth, and Robin was surprised to see that it was shaking.

"I tried to leave, then," he said. "Just as you suggested, I flew south. Flew until my aeroship ran out of fuel, and then I put her down in a field just north of the Frankin border. I walked the rest of the way, determined to . . ." He sighed and tilted his head back. The steam curled around him like ill-wishes. "But what can one young nobleman do to stop a war when his king is so determined? I have power, Skylark. But not that much."

"What happened?"

"I made it as far as the court of Queen Diramon on the strength of my name, but she would not listen to me. She would not step into our conflict, not even to help end it. She would not send her people, she said, to die for our foolishness." He scoffed and shot Robin a self-deprecating glance. "And then my brother came and fetched me home."

"When was this?" Robin asked, her own words tremulous.

"Four years ago. After that, I was pressed into service. But I was ashamed. I did not want to kill for a king I no longer respected, so I . . ." He held his spread hands a breath away from his face, covering his features.

"Became the . . . the Wolf," Robin said, hesitating over his title.

"The Coyote," he corrected with a wry smirk. "That is more appropriate. I could not bear to shoot down gliders which might make it back to Saskwya, and fight another day. That might give your side the chance to win. You say I scavenge. I say that if I must shoot down my enemy, then I will choose the ones who are already likely to be dead."

"Do you really hate your own people that much?" Robin asked, in awe. "You really want us to win so bad as all that?"

"I do not want anyone to win, nor lose!" the Coyote said, straightening up again, the haughty disdain reappearing. "I want it to be *ended*."

"Me, too," Robin blurted, and then wondered at what had inspired her sudden truthfulness. The words had felt like they were being torn straight from her guts. "I just want it done. Sometimes . . . sometimes, I almost wish our side would lose. Just so it would be over. One way or another."

"If we won, you would never be allowed to worship your gods again, little Sealie." It wasn't meant as an insult, not when he said it with such sadness. Such . . . affection.

"And we wouldn't," Robin said, sending him a cheeky grin of her own. "Not where a Klonn officer could see us, at least. We've had lots of practice since the Great Sickness."

The Coyote barked out a surprised laugh, and some of the weariness fell off of him. "I see."

Silence descended again, but this time, it felt nearly comfortable. Which made Robin feel even more wary. She had no idea if the story he'd just told was even remotely true.

"That doesn't explain why you need mid-flights," she said. "Why you need to keep . . . them. Us." She swallowed hard. "Me."

"The queen gave me a token when I was fetched home," the Coyote said. "A thing she told me had been thought up a hundred years ago by one of the brightest minds of Frankin. A thing that came to him in a bolt of inspiration, almost as though it were derived from a set of divine blueprints."

"But you're trying to . . ." Robin said, more details of the clockwork puzzle clicking into place in her mind.

"I would like to see it remain workable only on paper," the Coyote admitted. "But my king . . ."

"What is it?" Robin asked, and if she sounded more eager than she liked, well, there was nothing wrong with intense mechanical curiosity, was there? "Is it a weapon?"

"No," the Coyote said. "And . . . perhaps yes."

"What is it?" Robin repeated, sitting forward, intrigued.

The Coyote regarded her intently for a moment, eyes narrowed, lips pursed.

"Bathe first," he said at length. "Dress. Eat. Sleep. Take comfort in those few luxuries our prison offers us. And then, I will show you."

❋

As much as Robin hated to admit it, the bath was glorious. So was the thick robe left thrown over the vanity stool. A rough, simple black dress that most likely belonged to a servant had been draped over the foot of the bed, as well. Robin tried not to be insulted by the thought of wearing a servant's uniform in a place where she was expected to obey the master of the house, and missed her leather trousers intensely. It was still better than another frippery dress with so much lace strangling her that she could sell it and buy preserves enough to get the Brigid family through the winter. She could be, if not grateful, then satisfied with that, at least.

Happily, Al's goggles were right where she had left them, too. Seeing them had eased the anxiety that had been twisting up her guts more than she had thought it would. She was a prisoner, there was no mistaking that, but it seemed that the guest-charade had been extended even so far as to leave the few personal items she possessed unmolested. Whether this could be used as a bargaining chip later or not, she didn't know. She could make herself crazy trying to guess the Coyote's motivations and intents, so instead, she just thanked the gods that the goggles were still there and made a vow to never leave them behind again, if she could help it.

They were all she had left of Al. She wasn't going to abandon them, too.

As soon as the Coyote left her to her toilette, and before she succumbed to the bribe of the bath, Robin had cased the room for any sort of usable weapon. Predictably, she found none, so she'd resigned herself to the indulgence of hot water. A cake of soap had been left on the rim to wash her hair and clean the sticky wine from her skin. The soap smelled of lilacs, and Robin wondered if every bath product in Klonn would reek of these particular dead flowers, or if it was just the Coyote's personal taste.

She dressed and went through the motions of brushing out her horrifying white hair, trying to ignore how her hands trembled as she pulled it back into a serviceable plait. The small bald patches were covered adequately, at least, and her vanity reared up.

It will grow back, she told herself, and tried to ignore the fact that she felt like she was lying. She then put on Al's goggles, and pushed them high on her forehead to keep the wisps of white from getting in her face, keeping them out of the corners of her eyes. She didn't want to have to see her hair. She didn't want to have to think about it.

And then someone knocked on the door. The clink of keys on a hip, echoing through the keyhole, made it obvious who her visitor was even before she saw him. Robin was already standing, wary, ready to bolt or scream or crack him over the head with the vanity stool if need be. Instead, the seneschal just opened the door, and stood there on the threshold, holding it open in an unmistakable order to come with him. This time, Robin obeyed it.

"You will not disappoint him," the seneschal said as she stepped back into the hallway. This, too, was an order.

Whether or not Robin was going to follow it was a completely different story altogether.

CHAPTER FIFTEEN

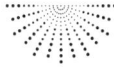

THE SENESCHAL LED HER—SLOWLY, IN DEFERENCE TO HER LIMP; A surprising consideration she had no doubt the Coyote had engineered somehow—up a flight of stairs and down another long hall. Here, too, the doors looked exactly identical to all the others she had seen. Whatever the original purpose of the room he eventually chose—which, Robin guessed by the bookshelves and the many little tables and cabinets, was likely once a study—it was now clearly a workshop. Oil and gas lamps littered every available table and shelf, and the place practically blazed with light. There was a window open at the back, but the air was not fresh. It stank of aeroship fuel and grease, the fumes so thick that all other smells were masked.

Scattered along every horizontal surface were tins of oil and grease, wrenches, gears, some hosing, half-coiled copper wire, and an old tool wallet. There was also a massive ebony desk smothered in blueprints that, even from this distance, looked to have been hand-drawn by someone without much knowledge of mechanics.

They caught Robin's eye immediately, and she broke away from the seneschal the moment she was in the room to investigate them. She squinted at the papers, trying to read the notes in the margins, but they were written in Klonnish. If there were any important folios, any secrets worth stealing among the folders scattered around them, she would never know. But dragging potentially useless documents with her when she escaped wasn't worth her time, especially without being able to read them. She dismissed them from her internal catalogue of things she planned to steal before she went.

Instead, she turned her engineer's mind to the jumble of sketchy lines and fanciful engineering documented by the blueprints and snorted, dragging a finger along an intake hose that would . . . no. That wasn't even remotely how these things worked. Whatever this strange concoction of science and hope was supposed to be, there was no way that anyone would be able to create it. There was no metal strong enough to withstand the sorts of pressures this level of combustion would demand, and even if there was, Robin had no idea how to begin forging it. There were notes in the margins of this design, too, in both Klonnish and Saskwyan, but even with the added text, the little machine was nothing more than a fairy story couched in hard engineering.

Dismissing the flight of fancy for what it was, she moved around the desk, climbed up onto a wooden crate stored against the wall, and peered out the window. She was on the third story, but there seemed to be a heavy growth of ivy climbing up the wall outside. And, just like in her bedroom, and the salon with the chess board, the window was barred. With a sigh, she stepped down off the box.

"Come, Skylark," the Coyote said, and Robin turned to find him hovering over the blueprints. She hadn't even heard him come in—*stupid carpets!* The seneschal was gone, too, and the door was now closed. Probably locked.

"Is this what Queen Diramon gave you? These blueprints?" Robin said, limping back over to join him, careful to protect her ankle—which was nevertheless feeling much improved after some rest and the warm bath. "Do you expect me to make that for you? Because, I'll be honest, I don't even think it's possible. And if it is, then frankly, I don't want to give the Klonn that kind of power."

"You do not have to make it, no," the Coyote assured her. Then he reached below the desk, pulled out a nondescript burlap sack, and placed it on the blueprints. It was heavy, whatever it was, and large, almost the size of Robin's whole torso. "You have to *fix* it."

Robin felt her eyes go wide. "It's real? Omens!" An unbelievable, overpowering curiosity gripped her. "Show me!"

The Coyote smirked and stepped away from the desk, waving graciously to the burlap sack. "Be my guest."

Whatever was within was vaguely cylindrical, like an overlarge bullet. She reached out and laid an abused palm over the sack, wanting to savor this discovery. She had never had an opportunity like this. From the feel of it, the thing inside was metal—that much she'd already seen on the blueprints—but what kind, she had no idea. It was slightly warm to the touch, even though it was off and separated from her own body heat by at least one layer of fabric. Eerie.

When she pulled away the burlap, it took her a moment to form an impression out of the jumble of dials, valves, brass-colored and copper-like metals, wires, and tubes. Eventually, it resolved itself into a sort of small engine. It was formed of twin tubes that tapered to points on one end and had exhaust ports that angled away from the contraption on the other. A glass canister filled with golden aeroship fuel rested just between the points. She couldn't imagine what sort of aircraft could be borne aloft by such a tiny amount of fuel, or by an engine this small, for that matter. She turned it so she could better see the writing on the side of the casing. The words were in some sort of language she didn't know—Frankin, probably—repeated in Klonnish, and then in Saskwyan and what she assumed was likely Telniem's tongue. Underneath that was a script that was completely exotic to Robin's eyes. The inventor's cipher, maybe? If Robin had come up with something this incredible, she might have tried to disguise it, too.

"Weaponized Independent Navigation System," Robin read aloud, returning to the Saskwyan, squinting to make out each small, engraved letter.

She stared in disbelief at the thing, uncertain if she could quite trust the picture her mind was trying to put together. "By the all the gods of all the fools," Robin said, as realization struck her. "Someone's meant to wear this crazy thing?" Thick, heavy leather straps were bolted to the exhaust tubes, padded with insulation against the heat. The fuel canister would sit behind someone's neck, with a hose that led down into the engine. A second hose trailed out the side, attached to what appeared to be a control box with a strap, which, she pieced together belatedly, was likely meant to go around someone's wrist.

Yes, it really did appear as though this was meant to be strapped to a person's back, and then—she balked at the thought. Take off into the sky? No glider, no aeroship, just a person and the endless stretch of blue? Oh, gods, how *glorious*!

Quickly, Robin turned it back around. The fuel gauge and the exhaust ports were angled such that a person's rear end or feet wouldn't get burned off when the pack was worn. It appeared as though it could be steered on the same principle as the gliders, by leaning one's weight to one side or another. Robin found a catch on the casing and flipped it open, cursing the lack of a headlamp as she examined the interior. She had never before seen half the ingenious ways this engine was rigged together, but that didn't mean she didn't recognize that it could actually work. She snapped the casing tightly closed and turned her attention to the control box.

Carefully, she picked up the pack and set it in the center of the room. Then she stood as far away from it as the wire-filled hose allowed. When she pressed one of the control buttons, a twin set of three sword blades popped out of the sides of the device like a switchblade, deadly and sharp. Robin pressed it again, and they retracted.

"I guess that's what they meant by 'weaponized,'" she breathed softly, and carefully pressed more.

Some of the buttons didn't seem to do anything. One made the glass bubble of fuel fill with air to adjust the oxygen mixture, one pressed the air back out of the fuel hose, and one made everything on the pack light up. Another button, the most glorious button, turned the engine on. A pilot light was struck by what appeared to be, from the faint spark that flashed against the inside wall, a tiny flint and steel system placed inside the pack.

The pack shuddered once against the ground. It rose, slightly, and the smell of burning carpet assaulted her nose. The pack hovered in place, neither going higher nor drifting about. Stunned, Robin pressed the next button, and a rumbling roar within the engine warned her what was about to happen. Hastily, she pressed the smaller button again, and the pack stopped making ominous sounds. It returned to simply hovering.

"Holy rudding omens, that's . . . that's actually incredible."

For a brief second, Robin was struck by that same pit-of-her-stomach gravity she had always felt standing under a god's temple. She was in awe. The pack seemed to be staring at her, eyeless and important. Omniscient. *Meaningful.*

Robin shook her head, willed the feeling away—it was just a machine. Amazing, incredible, unlike anything she'd ever seen before, yes. But just a machine, all the same.

Robin shuffled closer and confirmed that she was smelling regular petrol exhaust. She could easily refill the fuel tanks. In the meantime, the pack had filled the room with warmth and the haze of heavy exhaust. Just as she was about to cut the engine, it spluttered, the roar becoming a wet sort of cough. The pack dropped to the charred carpet and went silent. Even the little pilot light had gone out.

She stared at it for a moment. What good was a rocket pack that didn't stay lit?

"And therein lies our dilemma," the Coyote said from the corner. His voice reminded her that he was there, cut through Robin's cocoon of wonder and discovery, sliced straight to the bone, and jolted her rudely back into the real world.

Yes. Right. Of course. She was supposed to repair this thing for the Klonn. For the Coyote. Because she was supposed to *trust* him.

"No other mid-flight managed to repair it," the Coyote said.

"Couldn't?" Robin asked, voice shaking. "Or wouldn't?"

The Coyote grinned, but it was tinged with something other than humor. "Some of the former. Some of the latter. Though, your . . . Woden, I believe he said his name was? He was able to make adjustments enough to make the pack run silently."

Robin narrowed her eyes at him. "Which I assume you then repeated on your own aeroship? *That's* why you're so silent in the air. The fuel conservation?"

"Sergeant Res's work."

Robin screwed her eyes shut, clinging to the edge of the desk.

"They lived," she said softly. She reached up and brushed one finger along the Saskwyan writing on the blueprints. Whose handwriting was this, she wondered. Res's? Woden's? Or some earlier mid-flight, someone so long dead she'd already forgotten their name?

"For a time," the Coyote agreed softly. "For as long as they cooperated. What say you, Miss Skylark? Will you number yourself among the cleverer group, and make the attempt?"

"I'll never be able to replicate it," she blurted. "If that's what you want. I don't know how half of it is even functioning. You can't have a platoon of them."

"I do not want a replica," the Coyote said. "Just make that one work."

Robin stood, forcing herself to take a step back, away from the incredible pack. "Why?"

The smile that split the Coyote's face was not pleasant. "To end the war. Surely, as the pilot in the robin-nosed glider, you know the power one person can wield. All it takes is a few strategic acts, and everyone flees. All it takes is the right *rumor*, stemming from the right act, and you have power untold. Think what that pack can offer a soldier—intimidation on the battlefield, a one-man Aeroforce, an assassin. He could force a surrender by simply showing up."

The word slammed into her like a divine fist. *Surrender*. Robin actually gasped. "And you're going to be that one man?"

His gray eyes glittered, narrowed and focused on her face, as if skimming through her mind and reading her every thought. "Yes."

Robin shook her head, a sort of deep-seated worry crawling up her throat. A childhood fear long forgotten, but suddenly, horrifically tangible: Saskwya could lose. She had said she'd wished for it, flippantly, just to end the conflict. But now that she held the very real possibility that her people could be conquered by the thing in her hands, it was . . . no. Just no.

"Even so," the Coyote added as he took a step forward, crowding her back against the desk. Robin thought he probably meant it to seem collusive and trustworthy, but it just made her feel more trapped. He grasped her hands in his, forcing her to relinquish the control box, his eyes searching hers, pleading almost, begging her to hear the words he couldn't—or wouldn't— say. Not here. Not now. This room, then, was not as observation-free as her bedchamber. Here, the performance, the dance, the game, would need to be preserved. "Imagine the fear, Skylark, on the faces of your soldiers when our king takes to the battlefield with that soldier—with me—at his side. Imagine the fear on the face of your king himself."

"King Auden won't fall for it," Robin insisted, chin thrust forward, defiant. "Some stupid guy with a pack? That's ridiculous. It's incredible, I'll admit, and I've never seen anything like it, but it's just one guy, and one machine."

The Coyote leaned down and whispered into her ear, "What a strange thing to hear from the lips of a Sealie. I thought you would have at least said something about gods and luck, or magic. Do your people not call me a . . . a hobgob?" His breath brushed the exposed part of her throat, and Robin wished suddenly that she had done up the collar of this stupid dress.

"Skill is not the same as luck. And the pack is not magic," she insisted, turning her face away, trying to put space between his mouth and her flesh.

"Then you should have no trouble repairing it," the Coyote said, that same husky growl he'd had in the forest in his voice. He ran both his hands up her arms, terribly intimate. They skimmed over her neck, dry and warm, and cupped her face in his palms, forcing her to meet his eyes. "I trust that you are clever enough to understand what the seneschal will make me do to you if you do not. Skylark, I could not bear it if he did. Please."

Robin couldn't help the convulsive swallow. The way his hooded eyes looked at her, the way his hands held her, tipping her head back so that she was forced to look up at him, to lift her face to him, almost felt like he was about to kiss her. He was warm, even in the pack-heated room, and she was still a bit too relaxed and groggy from her bath. His breath smelled of mint and apples, and his grip was kind, gentle. His thigh, where it brushed against her through her skirts, was strong. For a brief moment, everything he had said made sense. In that moment, she wanted to curl into him, let him protect her, let him end the war and set her free to fly whenever she wanted.

But only for a very brief moment.

She opened her eyes—when had she closed them?—and stepped sideways out of his arms. It was awkward, her skirt got caught on the buckle at the top of his boots, but it didn't change her resolve. "I won't do it," she said.

"Skylark," he warned. His hands flexed at his sides, and she wasn't sure if he was holding back from grabbing her again, or if he was imagining them around her throat, strangling her. Possibly both. "I have been tasked with ensuring your cooperation. Do not make me do something I would not enjoy."

"Kill me, then," Robin hissed, drawing on reserves of courage she normally saved for stupid aerial maneuvers, tinged with what she thought was probably despair. Or desperate stupid loyalty. Al had always warned her that she was liable to get killed for the Air Patrol. "Finish me off like the others, because I won't help you in this."

Misery crawled across his face again, there for a moment and gone in a flash, like lightning, hidden behind a cheap, flimsy-looking grin. He gestured flippantly. "That is very brave of you, Skylark. And very foolish. If I kill you, it only means that I will be sent to shoot down another glider. You do understand this, yes? How many of your friends yet remain in the Air Patrol? How many more would you like to die screaming, like your mid-flight?"

It struck Robin, suddenly, that the reason his smile looked like a rictus parody of the expression was because he was scared. He held his jaw tight, his head upright, and faced what he feared. But he couldn't help the terror that crawled just below his expression. Robin could see it as clearly as if he was signaling it with flags, though she doubted their "hosts" ever got close enough to him to see it for themselves. He didn't want to have to shoot down someone else. He didn't *want* to have to hurt Robin. To kill her. Or anyone else.

He leaned close again, and in a breathy whisper added, "Repair it, and we can use it to escape. Skylark. Please." One of his thumbs brushed against the bottom of her ear, tender. Affectionate in ways that Robin had only seen other men do to other women. In ways that she had never experienced for herself. It made her shiver, made her skin goose pimple and her breath come just that tiny bit faster. It felt good.

Pay attention, Captain! she scolded herself. *The pack. Can you repair the pack? Maybe. Should you? Harder to decide.*

Robin contemplated her possibilities. The pack would never lift two, but it could lift *her.*

She pushed the Coyote aside, made a point of not clocking his expression. His wounded eyes were not going to sway her. She grabbed the tool wallet off the desk and knelt by the pack. It was answer enough for him, she figured. Robin didn't think she actually had the heart to vocalize her defeat. Instead, she turned over the pack and opened the catch on the casing again. Peering intently at the mechanical guts, she pushed aside hoses and cogs, and then sat back, biting down on the urge to laugh.

Oh, clever, clever Sealies! she thought.

She wouldn't be able to tell for sure, not until there was better light and she could decipher what all the strange, archaic components inside the thing did. But it looked as if, instead of repairing the pack, the others had been sabotaging it. It wasn't much—a hose connected wrong here, a cog taken out and reinserted upside down—but it was enough to be obviously incorrect to a flight engineer, yet look completely right to anyone else. The pack would never stay lit, not like this, not with the way the fuel supply was choked by the excess air.

Her brethren had kept the Coyote out of the sky. They were heroes, and no one would ever know. Grief warred with pride, forming a burning lump inside her throat.

Robin scrubbed at her eyes and took a deep breath. She could do this. She could repair it. She could use it. She could rescue the pack, and then rescue herself.

Trust me, the Coyote had said. *Let us end it.*

And Robin wanted to. The poor man, he loathed himself and the things his king made him do so deeply, so intently. But he was also the enemy, and the enemy lied.

No. She had a plan. It felt good to finally have a plan.

"Can you do it?" the Coyote asked again, hovering over her. He laid one hand on her shoulder, careful and respectful. But the pad of his pinkie finger brushed across her skin, shy and possessive, all at once.

What was he thinking? What did he really want from her? Just to repair the pack?

Focus on that, Robin told herself, and then nodded. "Yeah, I can do it."

"And how long do you estimate it will take?"

"About a month, maybe a bit more," Robin lied. The damage wasn't extensive—the pack was a rusty mess, but to make it functional? No more than a week. There were some disintegrating washers, a few wiring bypasses that had clearly been installed a few decades ago, when engineering was less finessed—the wires were more clunky, convoluted, and frankly, prone to sparkage—she would have to update that, bring the components up to spec, replace the naked copper with something insulated, and then, of course, de-sabotage the fuel supply.

It would, however, take a month for her ankle and ribs to be strong enough for her to run, and to use the pack without causing utter agony. If there was as much thrust to this thing as she anticipated, she'd also need time to build up the strength in her shoulders and upper arms to be able to steer the pack—a regimen of push-ups in her luxurious cell would be necessary. A month or more would give her enough time to heal, to regain her strength, and to lure the Coyote into trusting her enough in return to allow her to escape. To convince the seneschal that she had been tamed by the power of the Coyote's charm. To turn their game against them.

Robin shut the access hatch, and latched it securely. "Don't worry, you strange little thing," she told the pack, running her hands across the ruddy casing. The lamplight gilded the edges, gold sparking off the metal as she turned it over. "I'll fix you up."

And then together, you and I, we're going to fly away, she promised.

If that twinged her conscience a little, if she felt ever so slightly guilty for abandoning the Coyote to this awful prison, well, that was between her and the gods.

CHAPTER SIXTEEN

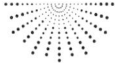

THE NEXT FEW WEEKS PASSED EXACTLY AS ROBIN EXPECTED THEY would. In the mornings she forced herself through push-ups and, when her ribs allowed for it, crunches in order to stay fit enough to actually work the pack when the time came. After, the seneschal always brought in a light breakfast: a very sweet porridge that was simultaneously gritty and gluey, and took some getting used to. He never spoke to her unless it was absolutely necessary. And that was usually when Robin was testing the admittedly limited length of her leash.

After breakfast and ablutions, Robin pulled her strange hair out of her face with Al's goggles, put on the servant's dress—which was always swapped out for another one when she inevitably got it covered with grease and oil, or ripped it into strips to make insulating mittens, or any of the other number of things she did to it in an effort to get them to give her some gods-damned pants. Which they still refused to do, stubborn snobs.

Then she was escorted to the workroom, where she made a show of carefully pulling apart, cleaning, and then putting the Weaponized Individual Navigation System back together. In her mind, she dubbed it "WINGS," and she carefully scrubbed away what appeared to be several centuries' worth of rust and grime, despite the fact it was supposed to be no more than a hundred years old. She polished away tarnish, and banged out dents, focused on cosmetic improvements that masqueraded as mechanical ones. She made the actual repairs it required slowly, stretching them out over many long afternoons while the Coyote watched over her shoulder, eyes glimmering in earnest fascination, but clearly understanding nothing.

"Why did you need a mid-flight for this?" Robin asked, somewhere around the fourth day. She was carefully appearing to file a gear tooth without actually shaving off enough metal to make the gear useless.

"Our engineers did try," the Coyote answered from a large wingback chair near the glowing fireplace. The days had grown chillier, but the windows had to remain open for those times when Robin chose to fire up WINGS. The Coyote spent most of this time sprawled with tight dignity in the chair, polishing his sword or pistol, reviewing stacks of official-looking papers, or reading reports—a guard who was never actually as distracted as he appeared.

And aside from the fact that he actually seemed to enjoy Robin's company, she had no idea why he felt he needed to be here. Possibly they feared she'd damage the pack, rather than repair it, or destroy it, or even choose to burn the place down. Which she had actually considered. She was honest enough with herself to admit that the only reason she hadn't deliberately set her prison ablaze wass because she knew she would end up dying in the fire alongside the enemy stronghold. She was a coward, maybe. Or perhaps she hadn't quite reached the level of despair yet needed to commit suicide-by-sabotage.

She had a plan, after all.

"I can see that," Robin scoffed, in answer to the Coyote's explanation. "'Try' being the imperative concept there. Far as I can see, their so-called repairs have actually made it worse."

The Coyote gave her his full attention then, setting aside his paperwork on the spindly side table and relaxing back into his chair. He liked talking with Robin, that much was clear. And if she were honest, Robin found him interesting to converse with, as well. She knew next to nothing about Klonn culture and beliefs, and it was fascinating to someone as mechanically minded as she to try to understand the deeply rooted *whys* of him. Even when they weren't trying to subtly trick one another into revealing vital plans or secret information. Even when they were just talking about favorite foods, or what the weather was doing today, or who the people in the portraits in the hall were. Nonsense, meaningless conversation meant only to fill the air and the time as Robin tinkered. The kind of comfortable, easy chatter she'd watched her parents indulge in every evening for her entire life.

"When it was clear that the issue was being compounded with each successive attempt, the king opted for a fresh outlook," the Coyote answered.

Before, being called a consumable resource, a "fresh outlook," would have offended. Now, Robin smirked, feeling comfortable enough in their gentle banter to be cheeky and to know that she wouldn't be punished for it. "Maybe she just doesn't like you." She patted the casing of the pack, marveling that even now, when she hadn't turned it on in days, the metal was warmish under her hand.

The Coyote shot her a strange, thoughtful glance. "I thought you said it was not alive."

Robin's hands stilled. There was a trend toward anthropomorphism in the Air Patrol—to call your glider a "she," or a "he," to give it a strapping name. Robin hadn't been aware that she'd been calling WINGS a "she" until just now. It was unsettling, a little, after all the talk of hobgobs when he'd first brought her here.

"It's not," Robin said. "I was trying to be funny. Sorry. Obviously, I wasn't."

"Was not," the Coyote corrected wearily, and Robin felt safe enough to roll her eyes at him.

The fearful tension that Robin had experienced in his presence was fading. The threat of the freezing pantry was always foremost in their interactions, but Robin learned quickly that if she was polite to him, he would return the civility in kind. She had yet to see any of her other "hosts," as he called them (and oh, how she hated that euphemism. She was firmly of the school that you called a thing what it was—their *captors*). But their lack of presence did little to lessen the figurative sword that had been hung over her head. She saw the Coyote and the seneschal, and a rotating cadre of soldiers of every skin tone and gender, in their ominous navy suits, but never any others. Never this mysterious brother. Never this power-mad king. Though, more than once, she had heard the Coyote arguing in Klonnish with unfamiliar voices in the hall.

She had a month to repair the pack for real, to become familiar enough with the layout of the house, hopefully also the grounds, and then their captors would come for their weapon. When that month was up, Robin was determined that it wouldn't be there.

Part of the plan, she realized after the second day, necessitated the need to get the Coyote to lower his defenses around her, to trust her not to take off, to keep any secrets he might impart. She had to—for want of a better term—befriend the bastard who had killed so many of her colleagues. *Trust me*, he had said. But in truth, she needed to get *him* to trust *her*.

He made it easy. Surely he didn't need to spend so much time watching over her; surely an ace pilot with the Klonnish Aeroforce had better things to do than sit in a study-turned-workshop and watch a Sealie fiddle with a rocket pack that honestly shouldn't exist. And yet, he was always there, beside her. He was always in her presence, watching, usually silent, and oozing a sort of proprietary contentment that Robin at first thought was sort of creepy. Now that she knew him a bit better, she realized that much of his childhood happiness had been built upon who was perceived to own what in his Klonnish noble house, and knowing that somehow made his strange content possessiveness . . . less creepy, even a bit . . . endearing? Not so much because Robin wanted to be thought of as a *thing*, but more because she liked the idea of being *wanted*.

Wanted in a way that didn't see her as just a valuable resource, the way the Air Patrol saw her. As a trusty mid-flight, who nonetheless was supposed to be biddable, like Wade did. As a dutiful daughter, like Mama and Papa hoped for in vain each time she came home. Or even, really, like Al, who had seen her as someone convenient, someone closeby, and therefore easy to cling to.

The Coyote saw Robin for all that she was—clever, strong, stubborn—and sought to impress and enchant her with conversation, and inventions, and . . . well, the truth of it was that Robin felt more wholly herself locked up in this prison-palace, trapped under his eye, than she had felt in the entirety of her six years in the Air Patrol. Robin was a whole person here, and what's more, she was allowed to be. Well, except for his determination to make her look, and speak, and dress, and worship like a Klonn noblewoman, that is. But that was all shallow stuff, really, in the end. That was all *cosmetic*. That was for show, and the show was to keep her safe from "hosts," who reported to a king, who had started a war to *free* their "ignorant northern neighbors of their fantasy of deities." A king she didn't need to obey.

The real Coyote, the one she met in whispers and between shadows, he didn't seem to care what she preferred to eat, or how she dressed, or who she prayed to. At least, she didn't think he did. She hoped so, anyway. He appeared to grant her those things, in the same way that she didn't care about how he dressed, or what he ate, or who he idealized.

So Robin answered his questions when he asked them, sure to leave out any identifying details about her home, her life, or where she had grown up, when the conversation turned in that direction. She looked up at him from under her eyelashes, as she had seen the mid-flight girls angling for husbands do. She touched his arm, lightly and in passing, as Mama did to Papa.

It was a good act, Robin thought. He relaxed around her, no longer tense in his wingback chair by the hearth. His gray eyes started to peruse books and paperwork, rather than remain locked on her every movement, every turn of her screwdriver, every bending of wire, every scrape against rust. He grew compliant.

It ate away at her, the guilt and anger, making it hard to sleep. It was a game, that much was obvious. But who was playing it best? Who was winning? And what, exactly, were the stakes?

The agony of knowing that her own dissembling was all that stood between the Coyote and those comrades she had left behind was enough to keep her well-behaved before the seneschal. She couldn't afford to cross him to the point where the Coyote would be forced to retrieve another mid-flight, to kill another pilot.

Though, if Renge was the next on the docket, Robin wasn't sure she'd mind. Only the thought of Renge's mid-flight quashed her desire for the kind of revenge that endangered those close to Renge. No, she'd hash it out with Renge on her own, face-to-face, and preferably with WINGS on, so she could drop the scrubbed up-cow on her head.

After breakfast, and a morning of pretending to fix WINGS, came luncheon. It was taken with the Coyote, and usually consisted of cold, barely cooked meats, strange oozy cheeses, and bread dappled with all manner of small fruit. Robin missed hard cheese, bread that was dark and thick, and the crisp crunch of well-cooked bacon. She missed saying her meal prayers out loud.

The afternoon was passed in study. To fill the long hours of captivity while she waited for parts she claimed needed to be scrounged up by whomever was on the outside, the Coyote gave her a stack of books on the history and culture of the Klonn. There had been something soft, something nice in his eyes as he'd handed them to her, wrapped in a blue ribbon with a flouncing bow. Something almost . . . hopeful.

Like he hadn't just been giving her a book, but a piece of himself. A piece he looked forward to sharing. Robin had looked down, away, at anything but his gaze. She told herself she was imagining what she thought she saw there.

It was a game. Nothing more. They were both playing it. And she could not let him win.

Whether he meant for them to be so or not, the books were not only a gift, but a harsh lesson. The books were written in Saskwyan, and when she looked at the printer's seal on the first book, a shudder nearly made her drop it. It was newly published. Probably with the intent of being used as propaganda for the defeated people of Saskwya when the war was over. The thought of a Klonn-occupied Saskwya froze her to the bones.

"Why Saskwya?" she asked the Coyote one afternoon, when she'd sent some navy-suited soldier to search for a gauge of spanner that didn't actually exist.

"There were a people here, you know, when the Nutvig family came to Klonn." He paused, expectantly, and Robin nodded to show that she was paying attention. "They say the king rousted those who would not come to heel. To those who did, the ones who stayed, he gave civilization. He taught them that the only gods they should be worshipping were their own minds and bodies. Art, my dear Skylark, is the jewel in the crown of civilization. The Art of Song, the Art of Images, the Art of Words, the Art of Nourishment, these are our most respected endeavors.

The Art of Love. And the Art of War. These are the only things that make life bearable. These are the gifts the Klonn give to those we conquer." He smiled expansively, gesturing as if he expected her to fall into his arms and thank him profusely for the wisdom.

Robin shivered, and it wasn't because she was cold.

He was so godsdamned casual about it. That was the worst part. That he believed what he was saying, wholeheartedly and whole-cloth. That he had the easy honesty of someone who knew, without a doubt, that he was unequivocally *right*. Even as he left her to her little prayers and preferences. As if he was an indulgent, clever-er sibling who knew she would eventually grow out of it. Insulting, considering it was this very assumption, which undoubtedly matched that of his king, that was the whole godsdamned reason the war was happening in the first place.

Somehow, he could accept her for who she was—a woman fighting hard to be respected in a position no one had ever expected her to earn, doing work that meant she had to try twice as hard as those around her, Sealie to the bone—and yet still believe, honestly and genuinely, that everything about her would be *better* if she just started to believe exactly what he did. It was contradictory, and insulting, and blindly self-congratulatory. As if her culture and her ways were cute, and quaint, and novel, but not at all a "real" civilization, by the only metric that mattered —*his*.

Robin decided then and there that everything would be just fine if people stopped deciding that someone else was just plain doing life wrong, when for centuries prior, it hadn't seemed to matter to anyone—Sealie or Benne, Saskwyan or Klonn. The problem happened when you tried to tell someone else what they were supposed to believe in: gods, or just one goddess, or some abstract ideal called the Arts. All that really mattered was that people were good to one another.

All the same, she read the books. She read them because she

209

had nothing better to do. Mostly, they were about geography, cuisine, the history of the royal family up to and including the recent king's father, and the Klonnish adoration of the Arts. *No religion in Klonn, my Sealie arse,* Robin thought as she flipped through this last section. *Just because you don't build a temple to it doesn't mean you don't deify it.*

And then, in the evening, there were the obnoxiously ornate dinners, in obnoxiously ornate dresses which somehow all found their way into the wardrobe in her room, and box after box of obnoxiously ornate jewelry that lived inside her vanity. This was followed by a few hours in the salon, where the Coyote coaxed her through the motions of some Klonn dance or another that she was meant to learn, or hovered over her shoulder while she wrestled with drawing pencils for the first time in her life, or brought in an embroidery hoop and an instruction book to teach her the Art of the Needle. Robin proclaimed that she was proficient with a loom and therefore didn't need to know how to embroider, but the Coyote scoffed and made it clear that noblewomen did not weave. Noblewomen were not crude enough to *make* anything. They only improved it, the way they called these little domesticities and cultural accomplishments improving themselves. Robin had scowled at him so hard he'd cringed and never brought up *improvements* again.

As much as she loathed it, Robin had to admit that she had never been so well fed in her life. The food was rich, and she gained muscle that her meager rations in the Air Patrol had prevented. She also gained a few extra curves, the promise of her hips finally coming to fruition with proper feeding up. It was annoying, and threw her off balance enough that she had to make a conscious effort to move with her normal silence.

While she enjoyed their private, personal chats, she knew that when they were in the dining room, the Coyote was performing. She had no doubt that there were eyes behind every portrait, ears behind every tapestry. He called her "my dear," and "Miss

Skylark," and tucked in her chair for her, as if, because she was female and supposedly a Benne noblewoman of some sort—he never quite explained which family she was supposed to belong to—she was no longer capable of doing anything for herself. Every night, she grimaced and minced and played along.

"Why this pantomime?" Robin asked, sometime in the second week. She was savoring the last of a pudding made with sweet rice and figs that she'd never had before in Saskwya, but wasn't too patriotic to admit she rather liked.

"Because this is the one custom of civility I have managed to keep for myself," the Coyote had said, hiding behind his wine glass the way he always did when he was telling a truth he wasn't certain was safe. "I am master still of my estate, and I will act like it."

"*Your* estate," Robin said, and set down her spoon. "Of course it is."

"Where did you think we were, Skylark?" he asked, with that endearingly puppyish head tilt of his.

"I . . . I don't know, really," Robin admitted. "Not a prison camp, of course, but I've seen nothing but forest and lawn out every window. Geographically, where are we?"

By the door, the seneschal cleared his throat in ominous warning. The Coyote wagged his finger at her playfully. "Ah, ah, my dear. You know I cannot tell you that."

"Then, where are we, uh, *not* geographically?"

"My home," the Coyote said, raising his arms to the side like a stage charlatan. "The country home, at least. One of them."

Robin felt something a little deeper, a little more sunken than dread and fear settle into her guts. A clear and certain knowledge that she and the Coyote would never, ever have met had it not been for this stupid war. That he was so far above her in society, in station, that he was wealthy—or at least, his family was wealthy—in a way that Robin could not ever really comprehend. And that, despite that, he was compassionate, tender-hearted, and cared a great deal about the suffering of others. Even if he was an officious, self-important, scrubbed-up ass about it sometimes.

The motivation was flawed, but the concern, she had learned, was real.

If they had met in other circumstances, maybe she could have liked him. Maybe she could have even loved him. She realized now, however, that under those circumstances, he would never have even looked at her sideways. And yet, here she was—sharing his table, being wined and dined, being offered fancy dresses and every creature comfort she could possibly want, except that most basic of all luxuries: freedom.

Omens, Robin realized with a jolt. Laid out like that, it was obvious. So obvious. How could she not have seen? *The books about Klonnish culture, the food, the stupid dancing in the salon after dinner every night, the wine . . . rudding godsdamned hells. He's courting me.*

CHAPTER SEVENTEEN

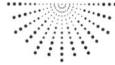

THE REVELATION HUNG OVER ROBIN'S HEAD UNTIL THEY WERE
seated at the chess table in the salon after dinner. *Courting me*, she
thought. *He's actually, truly courting me. Trust me*, he'd said.
Repeatedly. *My dear*, he'd called her. He'd listened when she'd
begged him to let Al have a proper funeral—granted, he'd done so
by simply leaving his corpse to be found—and taken a beating
from his general over it. He hadn't gone back out into the sky
since she'd come here, as far as she knew. And in all the times
they had danced behind their windscreens, all the times he'd had
the opportunity to shoot her down, he hadn't.

Oh, stupid Robin, she thought, chastising herself. *How blind
you've been, Captain Arianhod*. But then, how could she have ever
predicted something as far-fetched as her arch nemesis being
romantic. How could she have anticipated that his intentions
were true, that they were not just part of an elaborate scheme she
had yet to suss out? It was ridiculous.

Their eyes had met over the wing of Wade's glider and . . .
and *what*?

That was it? That was love at first sight for him?

Robin continued to scold herself, even as he laid out the

pieces of the board. He placed the white queen before her, fingers lingering on the ivory crown as he looked up at her from under his lashes, inviting her to play the first piece, like a gentleman.

Her stomach swooped upward, like the feel of doing barrel rolls. Robin was startled by the surge of affection that pressed against the root of her tongue.

By all the gods of the hearth, she thought desperately. *This is dangerous. I can't. I can't let this happen. I have to get out of here.*

Chess was the only place where Robin was his equal in this whole production of noble romance. Everywhere else, the power imbalance was pronounced—Robin followed orders, did as she was told, wore and ate what she was given. But at the chessboard, the Coyote didn't tell her how to play or what to move. He just told her the rules and let her find the pitfalls herself.

That night, she captured his king for the first time. He gave her a glorious, honest smile, and an effusive, "Very well done, my dear!"

He'd surged up from his chair when she declared "checkmate," and for a frightening, disconnected moment, Robin had thought he was going to strike her. Instead, he wrapped his arms around her shoulders, tugged her up out of her seat, and *hugged* her. He was *elated*.

The softness of his shirt, the faint scent of apples and wine, the gentle body heat, these things she remembered from when he'd carried her to her room. What she didn't remember was how *safe* the shelter of his arms made her feel. That was new. Wasn't it?

Even if it wasn't, it was such a strange thing to think about the scourge of the skies. It was terrifying, and wonderful, and for just a few moments, starved for affection and human touch in this terrible place, Robin let herself sink into it. She laid her cheek against his shoulder, closed her eyes, and tentatively relaxed into his touch. The Coyote sucked in a startled breath, one hand sliding up her spine to cradle the back of her head. She still kept her strange hair off her face and pinned back at all times, and he dug his long fingers into the base of her bun. It felt good, loosening the tight pull, and Robin shivered and let him tilt her face up to his.

Careful, careful, she scolded herself. *What are you doing? Why are you . . . ? Hit him. Push him away. He's the bad guy, for gods' sakes!* But his hands were gentle, and the soft spark of hope in his gaze was like a magnet, and if he was honest, if his feelings were genuine, if he really, truly was a captive, like her . . .

Argh! Why is this so hard to figure out? Why can't I get this straight? It should be so easy to—

"Skylark," he murmured, and there was a puff of hot breath against her mouth. He was curling down, his other hand coming up to frame her chin, and—

Al.

She pushed him away. Not hard, but with enough force that he stumbled back a step, clattering into the chess table. The remaining upright pieces skittered and rolled around when they tipped over.

"That's . . ." Robin started, but then didn't know how to go on, so she let the word die in the air between them. "No."

"No?" the Coyote echoed, and in an instant, the mask he always wore when they were in rooms where they could be observed returned, the look of devastation she'd seen splash across his face shuttered behind a wall of feigned indifference.

"This isn't . . . you don't really . . ." She turned away from him, ran her hands through her hair, dislodging the pins and ribbons that held it back. Her face was hot—gods, why was her face flushed? Why was she breathing so hard, and why was something in her stomach twisting and dancing like bees on a honeycomb?

"Of course I—" the Coyote started, reaching for her again, grasping her elbow before Robin yanked herself back a few paces more.

"You *don't*," she insisted. "You can't."

"Because I am the enemy?" he asked, voice level, cool, as he drew himself up, affronted.

"Because you're *holding me prisoner*!" Robin snarled.

The Coyote's jaw dropped open, shock playing across his face, and gods, she almost wished he was wearing that ridiculous helmet. That way, she wouldn't have to see the way he stared at her. The way his expression crumpled, and his eyes shone just a tad too brightly, and— and the way he looked like it was actually *real*. Just for a moment.

"Skylark, we are *both*—"

"So *you* say!" she shouted.

"Please," he said, hand out as he stepped forward, eyes darting toward the closed door to the hall. "A little quieter, please," he pleaded. "Or the seneschal will come inside, and then we will never . . ."

"Never *what*," Robin challenged. "Go on. Tell me how this farce of a romance plays out in your head. I'd really love to know what lines I'm supposed to be memorizing."

"Skylark," he chided miserably. She could see him fighting for control, fighting to keep the mask in place. "Are you saying that you feel nothing?"

Robin opened her mouth to answer, but only a small, hesitant sound escaped the sudden squeeze of her lungs. Gods damn it. Gods *damn* it.

"So, you *do*?" the Coyote said, hope glinting in his eyes before she could get her voice to work properly again.

"It's not about feeling *nothing*," Robin spluttered. "It's about what's happening right here, now, and how this is . . . this is not . . . this is not *right*."

"But if we were elsewhere," he began, in that graveled huskiness he always used to rattle her senses. He was just so persistent. "If this imbalance was not present, if we were simply—"

"You and I will *never* be simply anything."

The Coyote snarled and turned away from her. At first, she

thought it was for a dramatic huff. He set his hands on the chess table, braced himself against it, arms rigid and shoulders locked. But then his shoulders started to shake. Was he laughing? How *dare* he laugh at her here, now, when they—

He picked up a pawn and rolled it between his palms, thoughtfully, his laughter—tense, bitter, angry-sounding —abated.

"When I first laid eyes on you, Skylark, you must understand," he said slowly, low, voice wavering somewhere between genuine emotion and the cool drawl of his performance persona. He set the pawn back on the board and turned to her. "When I first saw you, I was ashamed."

"What?" Robin asked, not expecting this turn of conversation. "Why?"

"Literally out on a wing, and unafraid," he said with a rueful, self-deprecating smirk, his eyes on hers. The bruise over his left one had faded away, leaving him still narrow-faced, but closer to handsome than before. "And there I was, sitting safe in my aeroship, *scavenging* as your people accused me of, too cowardly to do what was right instead of what my king commanded. I saw much of myself in you, as well. Here is one, I told myself, who is skilled, and valued for that skill, and for nothing else. They sent you up after me time and time again, and you bested me. That caught my attention, yes, but your determination . . . and a Sealie, as well. I thought, 'She is like me. She is here because they order her to be.'"

"I could have left," Robin said. "Anytime I wanted, from the day I turned seventeen. I could have left."

"To do what?" the Coyote asked, crossing his arms over his chest and leaning back against the edge of the table. "To be a wife? A mother? When what you really want is the sky?" Robin jumped a bit, startled that he had so perfectly gleaned her own thoughts on the matter from their idle conversations in the workshop. "Oh, do not be so surprised, my dear. I listen when you speak. I understand the call of the world above the war. I tried to balance my orders with my desire to harm no one, and in the end, all I could do was what I was told."

"Soldiers follow orders," Robin said softly. "It's our job. You can't beat yourself up—"

"But ought we to follow the orders we know are *wrong*?" the Coyote interrupted, voice hushed, pitched to be below the threshold of hearing to those more than a few paces from him. "How many deaths, Skylark, before it becomes not just war, but a terrible crime? A genocide? How much blood can one man bathe in and still come out clean?" He dropped his eyes to the board again, and flicked the fallen king with one long finger, glaring at it sullenly. "Why will he not listen to me?"

"Who?"

The Coyote brought his gaze back to Robin's. "The king."

"Why would the king listen to you?"

"We are family," he said flatly, and pushed off the table. He moved around to his customary seat and began to reset the board. "Come, let us play another game."

"What sort of family?" Robin asked, intrigued. She took a few cautious steps toward her own seat at the table.

"Enough that he *ought* to be listening to me. No more, now. I do not wish to speak of him." The glance he sent up at her was shuttered, but she thought she could see pain crinkled in the corners of his eyes, his mouth. "Your move."

"All right," Robin said, settling into her chair and moving her own pawn.

Pawns, she thought. *Going where they're told, doing what they're told to, commanded by a cowardly king who only moves one square at a time . . .* Before she set it down, she ran her thumbnail across the little piece's stylized helmet. *What does this fellow want out of his nightly war? A warm bed, a safe house, a little chess-piece family with the bishop's daughter? Is there a place for romance in the ranks of war?*

She looked up at the Coyote, who met her gaze steadily, gray eyes warm with something Robin felt more and more certain was actually honest. Something that, if she were honest, too, she might just want in return. Something she couldn't *let* herself want.

This trap's becoming too tempting, she scolded herself, before decisively clacking the pawn down into the square of her opening move. *So why not use the bait that's already inside it to get yourself out?*

As the Coyote contemplated his own first play, Robin screwed up her courage and said, "Wanna sweeten the pot?"

He sat back and steepled his fingers under his chin, thoughtful. "What a curious idiom."

"I want to make a bargain," Robin clarified.

"I know what you meant, my dear." He smiled, looking a little lighter, a little freer. "What terms do you propose?"

"If I win, you show me where we are on a map."

The Coyote's face went carefully blank, and Robin bit the inside of her cheek, hoping her own face was equally unreadable. Had she tipped her hand?

"No," he said.

It was too late to back down now. She had to keep on. Sitting around waiting for some happy accident that would lead to her escape wasn't working. All the luck she'd in the sky seemed to have abandoned her on the ground. It was time to be proactive— to chase her freedom instead of letting it come to her. If she didn't, it might not come at all.

Robin sat back and crossed her arms over her chest. "I have no reason to play if I can't get something out of it," she said. Then she stood and walked away from the table, toward the hearth. Her limp had vanished, but her ankle still troubled her at night, when it was cold and damp and she was away from a fire. "You might as well have your—sorry, *our*—warden come take me back to my cell."

The Coyote narrowed his eyes, watching as she crossed to the door and jiggled the knob theatrically.

"What are you playing at? Come back to the table," he said. "Do not turn the only pleasant interaction we have into something else to fight over. Please."

"A bargain, or no game," Robin said, holding firm.

The Coyote sighed. "Very well. If you win, I will give you a clue as to the location of that which is so important to you."

"No, that's not what I said," Robin corrected, kicking back her skirts so she could turn and face him. Damn to all the hells whoever had thought up bustles. "I said . . ."

"I am aware of what you said," he interrupted, watching her intently. "And this is what I offer as a compromise. A clue, nothing more."

The scheme just got a longer tail than Robin had hoped for, but she wasn't completely healed yet, either. She could afford the time to play it out for a while more. "Fine. All right. A clue each time I win?"

"Yes."

"Agreed." Robin didn't do him the courtesy of offering her hand to shake. She just moved back to the table and sat.

The Coyote leveled a calculating gaze at her, something dangerous lingering in the edges of his mouth. "And what do I get if I win?"

The mischievous smile that spread across his face was wolfish, and strangely endearing, all at once.

Hells, she thought. *Didn't think of that, did you, smartass?* Robin felt the color drain from her face, and folded her hands on her lap to keep him from seeing the way they shook. "What do you want?"

The Coyote's smiled shifted, turning warm, inviting, smoldery. "My kiss," he growled softly.

Nervous, disbelieving laughter burst out of Robin before she could suck it back. His eyebrows pulled down in a scowl, as though her laughter at his expense was the height of betrayal. She knew he didn't jest, not about that. Of course he'd *meant* it, but

Robin never thought he'd say it out loud! Never realized just how absurd it would sound.

"Is it so little apparent?" the Coyote murmured, gray eyes flicking up to hers, then dropping to her mouth. "I know my methods might not match those you are used to, but I had hoped . . . am I so very pathetic in my weakness, am I so little respected that even the woman I aim to woo has no kind thought for me? Have all the arguments, the beatings, the mistrust I have engendered with my commanders to keep her in civil lodgings and to a fair work schedule meant nothing? Have I protected her from the interest of the general and his men, from the pressures of their torture, from their indecent attentions, for nothing?"

Robin bristled. "So what, you're saying I have to give in to one kind of unwanted advance to save me from the others? Go throw yourself in a lake, you scrubbed-up asshole." She stomped away from the chess table with as much force as her ankle would allow. She would give anything to have a knife right now. The thought made her all the more furious, because she knew that, even if she'd had one, the Coyote still had the physical advantage. He was taller and stronger, and could wrest it from her with ease. He'd proven that once, already.

"Skylark!" he said sharply, standing, rushing over to her like some pathetic hero in a romance play. "Skylark, wait. Please. I was not . . . that is not what I meant by it. Of course, I do not wish to force you. But you must see it! You must see how I admire you." He reached out and took her hands between his, cradling them tenderly. His gaze, when she met it, was unshuttered, honest, sincere. He was giving her one of the rare windows where she could see him—the real him. And gods *damn* it all to hells—this was not the moment she wanted to see that. Not now that she'd made up her mind about being proactive.

"Well, in case the stupid ghost hair has made you forget, I'm a Sealie," Robin hissed, keeping her voice as low as possible. "This won't work. Doesn't matter about any idiotic crush you might have."

The Coyote's posture changed—he rocked forward slightly, shoulders curled in, eyebrows drawn together, as though her words had caused him physical pain. "No longer a Sealie. " His normally smooth voice was suddenly low and ragged. Wrecked. "Not if you wish to stay safe."

"You told them I'm Benne."

"And you would be safer still if you were Klonn." He shifted, stepped forward, pulled her toward him until she was nearly flush against him. Then he leaned in and whispered, "It is not so much to ask, is it? Just one kiss?"

"I . . ." Robin hesitated. "But will it be just a kiss to you?"

"I will make it be so," he growled, breath warm against her skin. "That is my deal."

The clues, she chided herself. *Do it for clues. It's just a kiss. Just one. Don't lose this opportunity over something so small, so stupid. Doesn't matter if it may mean more to him. Just don't let it mean more to you. And for the love of all the gods, don't let him know it'd be your first.*

"Okay. Okay, yes, I agree," she rasped out.

The Coyote's whole countenance transformed for a second time in as many minutes. He released her, stood straight again, chest thrust out, shoulders back. He grinned, and it was like the sun emerging from behind a storm cloud. He held out his hand, all gentlemanly manners once more, and escorted her back to the chess table. He sat and righted the pieces that were knocked over when Robin stomped away.

Adrenaline pumped under her skin, though she couldn't say if it was in anticipation of kissing the Coyote, or in fear of it. Robin clutched the arms of her chair hard, distracting herself by cataloguing the scratch of the damask against her nails, the fall of the Coyote's dark hair in the lamplight, the details of the lupine faces carved onto the chess pieces—wolf kings and snarling foot soldiers. Robin took a deep breath, calming, centering herself the way she'd been taught. She turned her palms upward under the table to remind the gods of their own bargain with her, and reached out to move her first piece.

The Coyote moved his. Robin narrowed the whole of her focus on the board, eyes darting from piece to piece, calculating, concentrating. In response, the Coyote too leaned forward, attention intent. A sort of manic gravity fell between them. The only sound was the tick of the clock on the mantel and the soft *thock* of the pieces being placed. The game was intense, and Robin was concentrating so hard on trying to anticipate each move the Coyote could possibly make, that very soon a headache clanged behind her skull. She pinched the bridge of her nose, and then, miraculously, as if divine light shone upon the board, she saw it.

She bit the inside of her lips to keep from gasping in delight and held her breath. *Don't see it, don't see it*, she prayed.

The Coyote reached out and, in all his usual arrogant confidence, played exactly as she hoped he would. He had barely released his knight when she slid her rook forward and crowed, "Checkmate!"

The Coyote froze. His gaze skipped over the board, retracing the last few minutes of play, and then he looked up at her, a gasp of shock on his lips. "How did you . . . ?"

"Just good luck, I guess," Robin said.

Then his expression soured, returning once more to the cruel mask of indifference he always wore when he held his emotions secret and close. He crossed his arms, slumping back into his chair. Then he stood, walked over to the mantle, grabbed a crystal decanter of something very green, and poured a finger's width of the liquor into a delicate glass of a matching design. He sipped it slowly. Then he turned to face Robin, his expression once more placid, his hands steady.

"We made a deal," Robin reminded him softly.

He nodded. Once. "That we did. Very well. Your first clue is south."

Robin rolled the clue around in her mind, savored it, peered at it from every angle,

but no matter how she contemplated it, it still made no rudding sense. "What the hells kind of clue is that supposed to be?" she complained.

"The only one you will receive."

"Tonight," Robin reminded him. "There's always tomorrow."

The Coyote's eyes dropped to her mouth again. "Yes. Yes, there is."

A delicious shiver crawled up Robin's spine, and she wasn't sure if it was fear, or desire. *Maybe it could be both?* she asked herself.

The little porcelain clock on the mantelpiece struck ten, and as the last chime died away, the seneschal unlocked the door and stood there in the threshold, waiting. Robin gathered up the confection of her skirts and marched over to take his crooked arm, head high.

South, she repeated to herself, all the way back to her room. Once she was locked inside and alone, she retrieved the red lip paint from the vanity drawer and, on the back side of the mirror, wrote down the clue in very small letters.

Hopefully, the Coyote was vain enough that the hint was real and, if her luck was returning, he would give her more the next time she won. Eventually, she hoped, they would all make sense. But she would have to win every night to find out.

CHAPTER EIGHTEEN

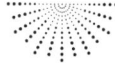

THE NEXT DAY, ROBIN SPENT SIX HOURS REPLACING A SINGLE rusted screw in WINGS, and figuring out how to calibrate the fuel hose so less sat at the head of the rocket pack, making the pilot nose-heavy and liable to tip into the dirt the moment they were horizontal. After, Robin sat down to a dinner so charged she feared the energy between her and the Coyote might wither the potted fern that protected their privacy. The seneschal kept appearing with new dishes, stopping to whisper things to the Coyote in Klonnish, things that sounded encouraging, like he was trying to convince the Coyote of something. His pale eyes kept cutting to Robin when he spoke, and she didn't like it one bit. Whatever he was advising the Coyote to do, Robin wasn't sure she wanted his . . . tacit approval. It made her question if she was doing something right by their counts, and therefore wrong by her plans.

When they finally sat down to chess, Robin won. She won again the next two nights, as well, and the Coyote grew more and more agitated with each passing bout. As a result, he started . . . "punishing" wasn't the right word. But there was a penalty. He lost, and he behaved differently, so maybe it was like he was trying to give her incentive to lose.

He began to lean into the soft touches Robin laid on his arms in the study, reaching out to reciprocate. Robin was torn between the ease of the habit, the ease of touching him in passing, every time she could, the comfort that grounding herself in his presence provided, the ruse that she was cultivating that she did indeed trust him now—and stopping for fear that she would lead him to think that his affections could ever be returned.

They couldn't. Not ever.

Could they?

Ugh!

And then there was the way he looked at her, the way his whole body swayed toward her when she entered the gravity of his orbit, the way he tucked her hand against his inner elbow, knuckles warm against his ribs, the way she caught his eyes on her mouth, as if he was thinking of nothing but the kiss that was to come . . . all of it spoke of genuine admiration, of affection, of adoration, and Robin couldn't, she simply *couldn't* afford to let it sway her. Not if she was going to betray him. Not if she was going to escape.

Since when, she chided herself, *is escaping from an enemy prison "betraying" them? You have to trust and be loyal to someone before you can betray them. I don't trust him. I don't. Do I?* She honestly didn't know anymore.

And for his part, the Coyote, when he lost their nightly game, offered up useless, one-word clues. Robin continued to write them on the back of her vanity mirror, where no one, she hoped, would find them. As the week wore on and his losses piled up, the Coyote's conversation in the workshop, once easy and meaningless, became quiet, confrontational, and brief. His conversation at dinner became barbed with innuendo that Robin had never had the court training to unravel. Across the chess table, he became alternately smoldering and petulant. When he took her hand, his fingers were hot and possessive, and when he looked at her, his eyes blazed with something she thought might be anger, while secretly wondering if it might be lust. Whenever they had occasion to touch or make eye contact, he made sure that both lingered on her skin, like drying honey had stuck them together. And yet he never pushed himself at her, never demanded, never behaved entitled, never whined. When she said no, he stopped. When she ducked away, he didn't pursue.

He *respected* her, she realized, and it was something she had never in a thousand beehives would have thought she'd have as a captive. He was trying, Robin realized, to tell her of his feelings without having to say it aloud. To convey his desires without allowing it to be overheard by their mutual captors. It was a dangerous, dangerous game he was playing, and Robin was slowly losing the battle against admiring him for his daring.

I've gone completely daft, she thought, every night when she returned to her bedchamber cell. *Shuffling through the opening steps of a courtship dance with the Coyote? He's the enemy. I'm mad to even consider it. And yet . . . and yet . . .*

She'd been on the receiving end of affection before, had seen it enough on Al's face, among some of the other mid-flights; she'd caught Papa watching Mama with a lazy, contented smile. She had seen want on other people's faces, too, but she had never been the target of such naked and desperate *want* before. It made something inside her get warm and quivery, anticipatory and flattered. Then she would remember that it was the Coyote who was looking at her like that, and all the warmth turned to nausea, the anticipation to paranoia, the flattery to fear. She couldn't even put a locked door between them. She had no control over where she was, for how long, or if he was even there with her. The juxtaposition between potential lover and potential murderer was tearing at her. It was distracting, and what's more, it was dangerous.

Maybe that was part of his game, as well.

For on the fifth night after they'd struck their bargain, Robin lost.

"Oh," she whispered, sitting back, watching as the Coyote slowly knocked over her king with one long, purposeful finger, his signature haughty, smug smirk curled into the corner of his mouth.

"Checkmate," he growled softly, voice low and ragged in that way that made her insides clench and her heart accelerate. He stood, and held out his hand with all the grave cordiality of a monarch. *"Finally."*

Robin swallowed hard and thrust out her chin.

Just a kiss, she reminded herself. *It doesn't mean anything. Just make good on your bargain, and be done with it. There's nothing to be scared of, because it doesn't* mean *anything.*

Swallowing hard a second time, she wondered why now, here, it was so much more difficult to calm her breathing and screw in her courage than it ever was in a midair dance. *Far more personal,* she thought, and then wished she hadn't. Spine cold and knees shaking, she stood and took his proffered hand.

The Coyote stepped around the table, so they were side-by-side. He reached up, ran the tips of his fingers over the skin of her bare neck. Robin shivered again, and told herself it was only because his hands were so warm and her skin felt so cold. Her flesh contracted with anticipation. He smiled, softly, and for a second, Robin was startled by the beatific honesty that shone from the expression, such a match for his mother's above the mantel. Such genuine pleasure. Then she wondered how she could have ever forgotten that he was handsome beneath that ill-kempt beard.

He cupped her face gently in his hands. He ran his fingers through her terrible white hair and pressed her head back, so she had to look up into his face. He twined a lock from behind her ear around his finger, teasing. He played at being the tender lover well, that's for sure.Robin resisted the urge to squeeze her eyes shut, to revel in the feel of his fingers undoing the pins that held her braid in place, to stay blind to what was coming, and willed her body to remember that it was possible he was just pretending, too. That she was only leaning into him because she was starved for affection, weary with worry, and that what was happening didn't matter. Her heart thumped harder, and she twisted her hands into her skirts more viciously, this time to keep from reaching out and carding her own hands through the short, dark hair at the nape of his neck.

Instead of getting on with what he so obviously so wanted badly, he paused, her ghost hair twisted up in a gentle chignon, held tight in his grip. Then, from his belt, he pulled out a long, thin hairpin. Like every other gift he'd bequeathed, it was elaborately jeweled, carved of ivory and spattered with sapphires, a soft-eyed wolf peering out of the cameo-style topper.

"This was my mother's," he said softly, as he slid it into place, securing the bun gently.

"You're determined to take this farce of a romance at face value then, are you?" Robin whispered, one last parting shot before she was forced to . . . to . . .

"Yes, Skylark," he whispered, and he was so close that she could feel his breath puffing against her mouth. "I am. But it is not a farce to me, and I will not take what you are not willing to give." He pulled her closer, leaned in until his lips brushed her earlobe, his breath hot on her skin. "I will have a kiss from you because you wish to give me one, or not at all."

Then he dropped his hands to hers, lifted them both, and pressed his mouth gently to her knuckles—first one hand, then the other. Then he turned them over and kissed the scars on her palms, left and right, as well.

"Wait, but—I don't—what? That's it?" Robin blurted, feeling strangely robbed as she sagged without his support.

The Coyote laughed and raised one brow, watching her with that godsdamned smirk. "Would you like more?"

Gods yes, Robin's body said. But he was still her captor, her enemy, and he had given her an out. So she forced her mouth to say, "No."

The Coyote chuckled and turned, going to the door to signal for the seneschal. Robin departed without meeting his searching gaze, and went back to her bedroom gladly. She sat in front of the vanity and stared at her face. Her cheeks were flushed, her pupils large, her hair a mess. And he hadn't actually kissed her!

"Godsdammit," she whispered. "What's wrong with me?"

Trust me, the Coyote in her memory begged. *Be mine*. Though he had never said the words out loud, the possessive nature of his affection had left little room for imagination about his ultimate goal. And Robin had twisted that, used it. She had preyed on his good heart, on his desire to end the war, and she was going to leave him. Did that make her any better than his braggart brother, or his mad king?

I can't stay, she reminded herself. *I can't stay, and I can't tell him what I'm planning, or I'll never get out. I don't know if he'll tell them, but I can't take that chance. I can't—*

The skin on her hands, where his lips had touched, burned, and she clenched her fingers into fists. *What if it isn't true? What if really is all just a game?* But her heart denied that possibility, even as it ignited with the pain of guilt, of shame, of sorrow.

Oh gods, what was she doing? Sitting here, agonizing over flirting with the man who had shot her down. The man who had stolen the sky from her. Robin took a deep, shuddering breath and covered her eyes with her hands. She wanted to scrub at them, but feared she'd get the stupid Klonn cosmetics all over her cheeks.

Vicious and sudden nausea clawed at her guts. She felt the heat drain from her face. Robin shot to her feet, toppling the vanity stool behind her, and fell to her knees, arms wrapped around her midsection as though she could use them to hold the remnants of her dinner where they belonged.

She had to leave. She couldn't stay here any longer. For all that the Coyote was her enemy, she knew she felt something for him. Not love, not yet at least, but . . . affection, perhaps, the first faint buzz of something that, if she let it, if she wasn't *careful*, might grow into the very thing he desired from her. And guilt, because she knew she couldn't trust him. Couldn't trust herself with him.

What if it was wonderful? What if it was perfect? What if it was *right* to kiss him? Because that was a prison, too, of a kind. Wasn't it? He could make her want to stay if he could make her love him.

The room lurched a little, suddenly too hot. Stuffy, close, suffocating for all its grandeur.

No, she told herself as she leaned forward and rested her forehead on the plush carpet, cool against her heated skin. *No, he doesn't mean it. Doesn't mean any of it.*

She wanted to scream, to flail, to sob with the uncertainty that tore at her with vicious canine claws. Instead, she stayed curled around herself, head on the carpet, and breathed, slowly, in and out, until the panic and pain and guilt ebbed away. She decided that she had to keep playing the part, at least for now—until he slipped up and offered her a chance at escape. And then she sat back, resting her hands on her thighs through too many layers of skirts, and took a deep, steadying breath.

If she stayed here, she would never be allowed to *fly* again. Ever.

And that was unacceptable. No matter what else her heart might feel, the arguments her brain tried to levy at her, that was the only thing that mattered. She would leave, and soon. As soon as the opportunity presented itself.

With the panic abating and nothing else to occupy her thoughts, she let her mind wander back toward the mystery of the clues. *South, bird, three, flight—damn, and double-damn*, she thought. *These are rudding awful clues. Bird . . . feathers? Fly? Wings?*

As the bird flies? Ugh, I can't remember the whole list. Her brain spun in circles, trying to match the twisted logic of the way the Coyote played chess with the clues he had spun out like a spider's web. She pushed to her feet and turned, intending to go back to the mirror and the list of random words that refused to turn into anything solid. Exhausted and annoyed with herself, Robin paced in the only tight, small circle the furniture allowed. She stared at the darkness of the ceiling, hands on her hips, thinking, head tilted back. *Next move, Captain. What's the next move in this chess game? A key. Get something to jimmy the lock, something they won't miss. Something thin, long. Something like . . . something like . . .*

Robin stopped, going utterly still. Though she was alone, and the Coyote had promised her that this room, this cell, was free from prying eyes and ears, Robin schooled her expression to utter blankness, and tried very hard not to look like she was assessing whether or not the hairpin resting ever so gently against her nape was thin enough to slide inside a keyhole.

CHAPTER NINETEEN

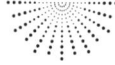

ROBIN BRUSHED HER SHOULDER WITH CROSSED FINGERS. WHY would the Coyote give this to her now? Surely he must know what she'd use it for; surely he hadn't been so blinded by his desire as to be lulled this far into complacency. Surely it wasn't a mistake—all that claptrap about his mother; what did it mean?

Stop it. Don't overthink, she scolded herself. *This is your chance. Take it. Worry about the rest later.* She shoved the hairpin into her bodice, hiding it amid the layers of lace and silk. Then she turned the mirror around and scanned the red words written on the back, muttering to herself as she tried to build connections between the clues and what little she knew of the building she was in. She committed them all to memory, and then smudged the lip paint into illegibility in case anyone tried to use it to follow her.

A glance at the window confirmed that her room was on the western side, the sun setting across the wide grass lawn behind the border of the forest. *Okay, so south, three, bird, league. Every stupid word is about shapes and distances. Not helpful if I have no reference! How far is a league compared to a Saskwyan kilometer? We're south of Pyria, definitely, but where is Lylon in relation to . . .*

She thought of the map she'd seen, the day she'd first had to fly on her own. The forests of Klonn were densest north of the city, so that meant Lylon was . . .

South of here, has to be. South, bird, three . . . three . . . we're three days walk from the city? Three something as the bird flies? That puts us in the forest between Lylon and the southern ports, doesn't it? Gods-dammit, I wish I had a map!

She closed her eyes, tried to visualize where their location might be based on past sojourns over this part of the forest. There was a low hill to the east, and Lylon below them, and—

"Rudding hells," Robin muttered, both amazed and appalled at her own thick-headedness. An estate in the woods. A private airstrip. A target drawn in red concentric circles on a topo-graphic map pinned to the floor between her feet. "The bloody fingerprint. Idiot."

Now, she thought. *That was the sign you've been waiting for. It's time. Now.*

She made sure her hair was secure, her boots were laced tight, that Al's goggles were around her neck, and that she was wearing as much of the disgustingly ornate jewelry as she could manage. If she was getting out of there, she was taking as much of the Coyote's wealth as possible. There was no telling how much she might need to pay to keep people quiet, or to garner enough supplies to make it home.

She only wished she had a pair of trousers—she didn't relish the thought of traipsing through the forest in skirts—and a bit more time to change. As it was, she was stuck in the sapphire-blue, brocade gown she'd worn to dinner. Even her usual servant's dress would have been a better choice, but she'd ruined her last one, and the replacement hadn't yet arrived. Stuck with the cumbersome pile of silk and lace, she rolled up her sleeves and removed most of the petticoats to free up her feet; she kept the bottommost layer to protect her bare knees from the stiff, scratchy underside of the silk.

WINGS wasn't ready yet, but she couldn't dawdle now. There was no telling when the Coyote would take the hairpin back. Maybe it was test, a ploy. Maybe she was about to walk right into a trap. Maybe—*no. Stop*, Robin told herself sharply and shoved the worry aside. Just like in a glider, she had to shut all other concerns away, and focus. *Beak to the sky, Skylark. Time we bloody well got the hells out of here.*

Trust me, her memory whispered at her. *I will win us our freedom.* But she couldn't bring herself to picture the face that went with that echoed voice, *did not* allow herself to think of what that face might look like when the Coyote found her gone. How betrayed he might feel.

And what they might do to him because of it.

She couldn't afford to think like that. If she did, if she thought about him and what he was starting to mean to her, she would stay. And that would be that. She would have committed herself to the Klonn cause, to never returning to Pyria, to never seeing her parents again. To being a Klonn nobleman's lover until she died of confinement. Used. Tamed.

And Sealies were never meant to be caged.

Screwing up her courage, Robin pulled the hairpin from her bodice, crossed to the door, and picked the lock. The ivory stick was not as agile as she preferred, but with the help of the straightened back of one of the dozens of pairs of earrings Robin had refused to wear, she managed to jimmy it open. Her breath caught in her throat as the internal mechanism clicked. She waited for the sound of boots, for the Coyote, or the seneschal, or one of their "hosts" to come around a corner. But none came.

But what about him? her heart screamed, her mind circling back and back to the thought of him, to the memory of the mark on his face that first night. Something in her chest twisted, and she stamped down on it, hard. *No, there's no time to convince him to come with me. I am a soldier of Saskwya, and I have a duty. I am not some husband-hunting, wealth-poaching flirt.*

Robin firmed her resolve. She clutched the hairpin in her hand, ready to wield it as a weapon if need be. It would be inelegant, and would force her to get much closer than she'd prefer, but on the other hand, the possibility of stabbing out one of the seneschal's eyes loomed large. She would be doing the Coyote a favor, too, if she did manage to blind him.

Folding the pin into her voluminous skirts, she crouched further and listened at the keyhole. The hallway seemed genuinely empty, but Robin's heart still thumped hard in the base of her throat. She took a steadying breath, and, pushing down to keep the hinges from creaking, just as she did at her parents' house, slowly turned the knob. It gave all the way, and the door barely whispered as she pulled it inward. Pin brandished once more, she stepped around the door, flattened herself against the wall on the opposite side, and peered out into the hall. Her caution, it seemed, was unnecessary—no one waited for her in the hallway, weapons drawn and ambush ready.

This might actually be too good to be true, she thought, but it was too late to turn back now. She was already out of her room—the lock was already broken. The seneschal would know she had tried to escape the minute he put his key to the door.

Robin swore and picked up her skirts. She slinked down the hall, toward the first turn, as quickly as she dared, thankful for all the practice she'd had thieving from the factory fields. She turned left at the hallway that branched off behind the little taxidermy dog. Heading what she hoped was south, she tried to keep her sense of direction straight amid all the twists and turns of the corridors. Objects d'art acted as her path markers, and she prayed that she remembered the way to the study. She'd rarely been taken the same way twice.

It would be embarrassing indeed to pick the lock to the study-workshop, only to find herself somewhere else entirely—like the Coyote's personal bedchambers. A sudden and ridiculous image of the Coyote waiting at her final destination, grinning at her from the middle of a large wedding bower, made her pause. She took several deep breaths to stave off the panic, and readjusted her grip on the pin, reassured and ready. *Stop it!* she scolded herself. *You know that's not who he is.*

But the image did give her an idea—surely they hadn't put bars on *every* window, had they? What if there were others, rooms with windows that were clear? Windows she could slip out of silently? She tested all the doors on the way to the study. Some were locked; some opened, but led only to empty rooms with no windows at all. Each time she opened one, she feared she'd see the Coyote smirking at her from the other side. She never did, but that just served to increase her anxiety. Her back teeth ached from pressing them together so tightly.

The study, when she got to it, was exactly as she had left it that morning. WINGS was safely tucked away in her burlap sack, the tool wallet conveniently tidied up and closed beside it. Robin glanced around, making sure there was no one hiding in the shadows, and then closed the door behind her. She crossed the room quickly, stuffing the hairpin into her hair for safekeeping and easy access, and freed WINGS from the burlap.

Crouching low over the rocket pack so she could see more clearly in the gathering darkness—she didn't dare turn up a lamp —Robin was grateful that the last few weeks had afforded her more than enough time to become familiar with its inner workings. Swiftly, she painstakingly undid every clever mistake she had rigged into its guts. The biggest problem was the primary fuel feed line. In an utter stroke of genius, some mid-flight before her had redirected its flow, cycling it into the air mixture valve, ensuring that no matter what else was done to repair it, the pack would literally drown itself if it was ever turned on. She had figured out this fix a while back, but had left it intentionally for last.

It should have been simple enough to unscrew the cap, switch the feed line over one port, and screw it back into place, but her fingers kept slipping, her hands shaking from the excess of adrenaline.

Stop it! she scolded herself. *Focus! Don't screw this up!* Her heart was pounding so loudly all she could hear was the ragged *whoosh-thump* of her own breaths and pulse jamming her ears. *Calm down, Captain, or you'll never hear anyone coming!*

With a quick, wrenching twist, the fuel line was put back in its proper port. Robin lowered the access hatch, latched it, and then slipped WINGS back into the burlap bag. She rolled up the tool wallet and shoved it in her bodice, then grabbed another flat screwdriver off the desk and slipped it into the knife holster in her boot. Tugging the drawstrings of the burlap bag tight, she looped them over her head and around one arm. She'd much rather have just put the pack on, but the metal might cast reflections, and she couldn't take the chance that a glint at the wrong time might give her away.

I've done it, Al! she thought, and the relief that flooded through her made her pause, scrubbing at her eyes. She refused to let herself cry, though, because if she started, if she let even one tear fall, she knew she wouldn't be able to stop. The Coyote would find her there, a sobbing, sopping heap, and he would finally be able to keep her because she wouldn't be strong enough to resist anymore. She had fought so hard. She had played the game for so long. She was tired. She was angry, and she was *tired.*

Rage, Robin said to herself. *Focus on the rage. Use it. Get out of here and get your revenge. For Al. For Wade. For all of them.*

As she turned to go, planning to find a room where the windows weren't barred, the blueprints heaped on the desk caught her eye. She didn't dare leave them behind, not when there was a chance that the Coyote could use them to force another mid-flight to try to build a replica of the pack. She couldn't take them with her, though, either. An untimely rustle of paper might be the undoing of this endeavor just as surely as a glint of moonlight on metal might.

Plan of action decided, she picked up the blueprints and, quiet as possible, laid them in the cold grate of the fireplace. Tinder was already stacked and ready for tomorrow, so it was simple to take a match from the box on the mantle and light the corner of the paper. Robin waited until all the pages were curled and burned beyond saving, and then snuck back out to the hall, ears open. She held her breath. Nothing.

Pressing herself flat against the wall, she moved as silently as she could over the carpet, wincing at every squishing footfall. *Cold, calm, collected*, she told herself, breathing steadily and trying to focus on getting out, getting away, getting free. Not wanting to waste time searching for windows on an upper story that would make her have to jump down, she decided to try the rooms on the way to the kitchen. It was riskier—if there wasn't an escape before that room with the nightmarish pantry, then there was no guarantee that the kitchen had a delivery door, or that it would be empty of anyone doing dishes or preparing bread for the next day. But it was the only other access point she could guess may be there in this otherwise labyrinthine house.

Back on the ground floor, she sent a quick prayer up to the gods of luck, brushed her shoulder with crossed fingers to guard against ill omens, and picked the lock of the first unfamiliar door she found. When she slipped inside, closing the door silently behind her, and crossed to the window, she found it miraculously unbarred. Though it was mullioned into little rigid squares. She studied the window and angled her head against the glass so she could peer at the latch outside that would release the casement and allow her to remove the pane of glass and slip out. The matching latch on the inside was gone, so no one could open it from here.

Casting around the room, she realized this one was a proper library. The shelves were littered with curios, and among the detritus, she found a paperweight large enough to serve her purpose. Carefully, she tore a strip from the bottom hem of her gown and wrapped her hand. Then she picked up the paperweight and slammed it against the bottommost square of glass.

It shattered on the fourth try, and Robin stilled, holding her breath. No sounds beyond her own harsh breathing broke the silence of the night.

She knocked the broken glass away with care, then squeezed her arm through to the pulley on the outside. Her hand met only air. "Omens!" she hissed. "Not rudding close enough."

She shoved hard against the mullion with her shoulder, wincing at the bruise it would cause, at the way the few remaining fragments of glass snagged on her sleeve. She took a deep breath, trying to force her thudding heart back into a rhythm that reminded her a little less of a terrified jackrabbit. The adrenaline floating through her blood made her shaky and impatient. She forced herself to take a deep breath and go still. She had to stay calm, or she would make some sort of horrible mistake that would put an end to this little adventure faster than a stray dog falling on a scrap of abandoned bone.

Patient. Slow. Calm, she reminded herself, while the rest of her screamed: *Let's go, let's go, let's go!* All up her arm, her skin tightened into prickling goose pimples, sweat drying rapidly in the chill evening air.

She stretched her hand out again, imagining for a brief second that somehow, the air could get between her joints, as if that could make her fingers go just that little bit further. Dust and paint flakes pressed against the cheek she had smooshed against on the wall; they stuck to the sweat there, giving her a smattering of what she was sure were strangely shaded new freckles.

So . . . close!

Her fingers slipped over the roughened handle of the window's outer latch, the pockmarked surface scraping teasingly at the tips of her nails. Another hard shove against the mullion, and she managed to close her hand around the whole thing. Taking a deep breath, she pulled back inside.

She forced herself to go still again, and took another deep breath to forestall the urge to just yank at the pulley. Impatience and recklessness brought down gliders; it could bring down this venture just as well. Feeling more sure, she eased her arm soundlessly back through the glass, and then pulled the whole frame out of the window. It came away easily, in one piece, and she set it aside to lean against the wall.

The only sound that split the still night air was her soft hiss. She stepped back and eased the pressure off her burning shoulder muscles. When she peered out the window, she realized it was several feet up off the ground. Absolutely climbable. There was even some of that convenient, wall-covering vegetation, the thick and twisting ivy she had taken note of before. Once the ache in her shoulder had eased, she managed to wriggle out head first, and then swung her legs around so she was pointed the right way 'round. Carefully avoiding any other windows, she began her downward descent. The ivy creaked ominously in the cool air, but Robin made it to the ground in one piece, her heart pounding like a trip hammer, her feet crunching on the frost-rimed grass.

Her fingers were already growing red and numb in the chill, and she wound them into her skirts for protection. Skimming along the wall, staying low, she paused in the deep shadow of a corner, where a wing met the main building. She looked up and gasped.

The Coyote hadn't been exactly honest with her. It wasn't just a country manor or a forest estate, after all. The place was a godsdamned *palace*.

The scope of the grounds was large enough that the garden wall was a vague white line in the distance, broken up with a highly sculpted view of groomed hedges and roses strangling a rigid trellis. Beyond that, the untempered wilds of the forest were held at bay by the landscaping. Behind her, the wall was cold white marble shot through with veins of silver and shadings of a pale bluish-gray. Robin resented the further proof that the seneschal seemed to be dressing her as a matched accessory to the Coyote's household, and pushed away from the wall to make a break for a hedge.

A sharp tug on the hem of her dress brought an aborted scream to her throat, fear surging upward to suffocate her larynx.

No! I won't go back! she thought, as she yanked the hairpin out of her hair and whirled around to stab at whatever hand clung to her. The pin met not flesh, but the hard surface of the wall, and was turned aside easily. It skittered out of her hand, spinning into the gravel with a clatter that sounded overly loud to her strained ears. Her gown was snagged on a broken ivy branch. Robin bit down hard on her cheeks to keep from screaming in frustration. Being on edge for so long was starting to make her imagination run wild. She tugged on the gown and didn't suppress the gleeful smile that spread across her face at the sound of the fabric ripping free. The pin she gave up for lost. It had skittered into a shadow, and Robin didn't have the time to crawl around searching for it.

Taking a deep breath, she craned her head back and stared up into the night to check for any aeroships that might spot her escape across the lawn. Stars winked welcomingly in the open sky above the house.

How Robin had missed the clean, free air of the sky. The fresh air sang in her lungs like the siren's call of a god of fortune. *Soon*, she promised herself.

Satisfied that she wouldn't be spotted from the air, she bent and crept across the lawn, toward the nearest pool of shadow. By the time she was at the edge of the garden her arms throbbed from holding the burlap bag away from her side, and her shoulder burned where the rope of the drawstring dug in. Panting, Robin stopped only when she was fully concealed by the shadow of the ornamental garden wall. She squatted and rested against the white marble, measuring the distance she would have to climb, finding the holes in the gullies between the great slabs with her eyes before she would have to test them with her finger-nails and boots. Robin cracked her neck, rolled her shoulders, flexed feeling back into her fingers, counted backward from one hundred in order to calm her breathing, and then pushed away. She didn't dare to stop for long.

Her absence would be discovered—that was certain. The question was whether it would be in the morning, when the seneschal brought her breakfast and found her room empty, or whether it would be sooner, if there was a patrol who inspected the windows for—

Shouts in Klonnish. A siren wailed. Robin swore and brushed her shoulder with fingers crossed.

Behind her, the windows of the huge building blazed to life, and the sharp retort of dogs barking played across the wind. There was no time to find a stealthier exit, so she brushed the bad luck off her shoulder a second time and scrambled up to the low ledge. The trip over the wall was brief, but Robin's arms complained bitterly by pricking the tips of her fingers with pins and needles. When she was finally perched on the top, she hauled the bag up to her level.

"*Deh!*" someone in the distance shouted, and immediately a circle of light swept across Robin's body. It was too low to cast illumination on her face, so she ducked her chin down, hoping her brown skin would at least keep her face from reflecting back. She wished her strange new hair was as easy to cover. She should have stolen some sort of cap.

She scrambled around and swung her legs over the other side of the wall, peering into the thick shadows to find a safe place to land.

"Turds," she snarled into the night. "Godsdamned, ill-omened, stinking frozen coal-bags of turds!"

The vicious barking was getting closer. A wrenching heave and a thundering *boom* filled Robin's ears as the piece of wall she was clinging to shuddered violently, gravity yanking her—and most of the wall around her—down into the bracken.

A small scream escaped her throat before she could rein it in. *They shot at me! They actually shot at me!*

CHAPTER TWENTY

ROBIN HIT THE GROUND. THE CRUMBLED CORNERS OF MARBLE bricks drove up into the palm of the hand she threw out to brace herself, her teeth clacking together hard enough to make lights spark behind her eyes. The bag clattered onto the crumbled stone beside her, and she didn't dare spare the few seconds it would take to check that WINGS was unharmed. She just hauled herself upright, and dove for the trees. More flat, rapid pistol cracks filled the air, and she zigzagged from shadow to shadow, trying to remain a difficult target.

When she was far enough ahead that she could no longer hear the dogs, she ducked down into the cover of a natural hollow to rest, ears wide open for any other clues of where she might be. She wrapped herself around WINGS to take advantage of the ever-present heat in the metal, and gulped at the air. A dry rustling caught her attention, and Robin stilled in the shadows.

"I know you are there, my dear," called a voice, and Robin's throat closed up in panic.

Instinct told her to hold still, but surprise jerked her upright. His back was to her when she finally caught sight of him, so she used the time it took for him to turn and face her to get her hand on the flat screwdriver in her boot. She set WINGS down carefully, quietly, to keep her arms free enough to fight.

Oh gods, she didn't want to have to fight him.

"My dear Skylark," the Coyote said when he saw her, and his voice was soft. He could have called to the soldiers, could have shouted her position to the world. Instead, he crept forward, cautious as a cat, purring into the night. The moon was at his back, so his face was shrouded in shadow as he scanned the forest around them, head swiveling slowly from side to side. She wasn't sure if this was a gift from the gods, or a curse.

If she saw his face, she would know what he was thinking. She would know which version of the Coyote she was speaking to— the ruthless aeroship pilot or the besotted boy? The charming man? The captured noble? The scheming villain? Depending on which one it was, she might not have the resolve to use the screwdriver, to plunge it into his chest or stomach, to fight for her freedom, to get *away*.

"Would it not be more comfortable back inside the house? It would be warmer, at least."

"I won't go," she hissed back, and he paused, head turning toward her.

Gave yourself away, Robin scolded herself. *He didn't actually know you were here. He hadn't seen you, after all. Rudding hells.* She crouched, rolling up onto the balls of her feet, but her hand was stiff on the hilt of the screwdriver, the cold seeping into her bones.

"Yes, Skylark, you will," he said. His voice was strange, muffled and ragged. Hollow. "Let us not have any trouble, now."

"I'm nothing but trouble," Robin said, and saw that he meant to lunge seconds before he did it. She rolled to the side, straightening to keep him in her sights and danced away, screwdriver up. She got the moon at her back. He disentangled himself from the forest floor and stood, revealing his face in the cold light.

He was wearing his wolf mask again. The fearsome countenance with which he had first faced her glimmered with menace. All warm memories of him dissipated immediately. *Enemy*, her brain howled.

"Think about it, my dear," the Coyote said, righting himself cautiously, knees bent, ready to spring again if Robin allowed him an opening. "I have a gun, and a sword. You have only a knife."

"Screwdriver, actually," Robin corrected with an ironic head dip, mocking the manners he had tried to drill into her.

"Please, Skylark," the Coyote said, voice jumping and cracking, and there was the man back again, the tender heart behind the hobgob face. "I have orders to return you, and the pack, at all costs. The things they will do to you if you do not come of your own volition . . . please, allow me to help you."

"Then I won't go. Seems simple enough."

"The things they will do to *me*, then," he said. And though he had threatened gun and sword, both were still strapped at his hips. His hands, when he held them out before her, were empty, palms up, begging, *praying*.

Robin *wanted* to take them. Wanted to trust that he wouldn't use that grip to hold her, to get close enough to knock her out, to hurt her. She wanted to grasp his hands and wrap her arms around his waist and comfort him, but she couldn't. She *couldn't*.

"No," she whispered. "I won't go back. I can't. I can't live like that anymore. I'm Sealie. I won't allow you to turn me into some scrubbed-up Benne."

"It was a lie," the Coyote said. "Meant to keep you safe."

"How can I be sure?" Robin challenged. "How can I know whose side you're really on? Who you're really playing?"

"Them!" he snarled.

"Then prove it! Come with me. Rob them of their greatest weapon and help me get home."

The Coyote hesitated, his fingers flexing just once, as though he wanted to make a fist and didn't dare. "I cannot."

"You can. You *can*, just . . . please, please, just don't go back there and—"

"Oh, but you are clever, my dear." He took a step forward. "Clever enough to know that we can try another day."

"I'm not clever," Robin said with a headshake. "Just desperate."

"Clever enough to work out my clues," he insisted, jerking his chin southward, in the direction where she'd been heading. "Clever enough to pretend to be repairing the pack while you were actually sabotaging it. Clever enough to string your ruse along for weeks."

Robin felt the blood drain from her face. The night suddenly became darker, chill and claustrophobic. "You knew?"

"Yes, you are clever, my dear Skylark," the Coyote said, his voice low, a sorrowful song in their small, silent patch of the forest. He sounded like a dove. "For you did exactly what I set you up to do—you escaped with the pack."

Confusion warred with fury. If he'd known all along, then why had he let her? Why hadn't he just left the doors unlocked that first night? Why the game with the chess boards, and the bargains, and the ruddy stinking hairpin—or was it that he knew she would never take the pack if he'd let her at the start, that he'd been giving her not only the time and space to repair it, but also the resources. Robin hadn't had to scavenge a thing for the repairs. She'd just asked for them, and they'd appeared.

"So, what . . . you just . . . let me go?" Her voice shook, and her lips were parched, and the tension spiraling between them, always there, always slightly lazy and curling, began to tighten like a pulley chain.

He shrugged one shoulder, a surprisingly unpolished gesture for him. "I set certain things in motion. However, you forgot one thing."

"What's that?"

He spread his arms wide, the parody of an invitation to dance. "Me."

"*You?*"

The Coyote reached toward his belt. Robin paused, waiting to see if it was his pistol or his sword he drew first. Instead, he held up something small, thin—*the hairpin.* "Oh, Skylark, you were supposed to *save* me."

"What?" Robin said, not accepting it. They were dancing again. Not the kind they did in their aircraft, soaring and ducking between the clouds, not the raucous jigs of the Sealies or the sedate ballroom figures the Coyote had tried to teach her. No, they were waltzing now, tiptoeing between loyalties, and lies, and truths too honest to bear. Dodging, weaving, following, being followed, only to turn on a heel and change the dynamic, to chase instead. And all to the steadily increasing tempo of the dogs and the soldiers coming closer. "No, no, you can't expect me to . . . not when you never told me . . ."

"Together, Skylark. We were always meant to escape together," the Coyote whispered, low and husky in that way that always made her insides squirm.

Robin frowned. "Well, you're out here now. What's the problem?"

"Ah, but I am being followed. " He gestured behind him. "I am not free! I was sent after you, and if I return alone . . ." He trailed off and his free hand balled into a black-gloved fist.

"Don't return!" Robin begged, taking a desperate step toward him. "You're out! We're both away. Come with me, now, before they realize we've run off together!"

"I cannot," the Coyote said, eyes darting around the darkness of the forest. "My brother . . ."

"What does he matter?" Robin challenged. "He locked you away and forced you to be a pawn for your king. Please, come with me!" She held out her hand, palm up, begging him to take it with the curl of her fingers, the fire in her eyes.

"He will know. He will know I went with you, and we do not have the luxury of the head start we might have had otherwise.

We do not have the supplies to hide in the forest, as I had planned. Already, he will have the word out to watch for me. If I go with you now, we will be hunted in every city, across every field." He tucked the pin back into his belt, wrapped his hand around the hilt of his sword and jiggled it furiously. "You made your move too soon, Skylark. This is not how it was supposed to go!"

"But it's the way it's happening now. C'mon. Learn a thing or two from a Sealie and improvise!"

"To go with you now would ensure your death," the Coyote said. "And I will not have that. But neither can I bear to see your wings clipped. I cannot. . ." He swallowed hard, voice gruff with a depth of emotion, of despair, he had never shown her before, and pushed off his helmet. It thumped into the deadfall, grotesque and silent. His face was pale, worn, his hair a sweaty mess, his mouth a miserable curve matched by the slump of his shoulders, his scruff out of control.

Robin didn't think about it. Didn't debate it with herself. Didn't even let herself pause long enough to question why. She just stepped up into his space, screwdriver still held loosely in her fist, and *kissed* him.

Her free hand fisted in the silver frogging that marched down the front of his ice-blue jacket, and she yanked him downward, even as she surged up onto her toes to be able to reach his mouth. His lips were slack, startled, but so very soft and . . . and *warm* in a way she hadn't expected. Their noses bumped, and their teeth clacked, and his beard was uncomfortably prickly.

It was awful, really. It was a terrible first kiss.

But then the Coyote's hands were on the back of her head, his fingers in her hair, and something changed, something *shifted*, an angle, an exhale, and . . .

Instead of a sweet, gentle kiss, the Coyote prised open her mouth with his tongue and made a thorough job of it. The desperate, growling sounds he pressed into her mouth reached down into her chest and squeezed her heart. He only let her up for air when she was flushed and panting. He grinned down at her, pressing their foreheads together sweetly, triumph making his eyes glitter in the moonlight. Her tongue was still thick with the taste of him: wine and apples and comfort.

All the things she couldn't have. Couldn't afford to let herself *want.*

The Coyote's fingers traced the necklace around her throat— the heavy diamond and sapphire thing from their very first night. "Oh. Now you wear it," he muttered with a chuckle.

Her lips tingled, as though he were still kissing her. Robin wallowed in the phantom sensations of his kiss. Then, deciding it wasn't enough, Robin craned her neck, tilted her chin up, and kissed him again. This time, the Coyote kissed like he was searching for something—first along her top lip, then her bottom lip, the corner, her chin.

Deciding it was her turn in the pilot's seat, Robin mimicked him, echoing the things he had done, taking his two brief lessons to heart. The Coyote moaned against her lips, and Robin felt a swell of possessive, selfish victory in her breast to have made him lose some of his well-polished control so quickly. His hands had moved to the small of her back, and she let go of his jacket to run her own hands through his damp, messy hair, reveling in the way the slick softness of it licked at her skin.

She had heard kisses could be powerful, addictive, and comforting. What she hadn't known is that they were also a language all their own. And his were saying, with every sigh, every shift of his body, every glance: I admire you. I want you.

I love you, Robin thought.

And that was startling enough to yank her back, away from the dreamscape of fantasy and physicality, back to the winter-cold forest. To what she was supposed to be doing. And who she was *not supposed* to love. From the way he stared down at her— eyes wide, pupils huge dark pools, cheeks flushed, mouth red and chapped, wonder and awe slackening his features—Robin wondered if her kiss had given her away, too.

"I . . . we . . . can't just stand here and do this," Robin panted, letting go of his head. "We can't *stay*."

"We are from two different sides of a war," the Coyote said, mournful and resigned. Something tickled the back of her head, and she realized he'd slipped the hairpin back into her bun while they were kissing. Possessive bastard. "And we both have too much to lose to join the other one."

"Screw the war!" Robin snarled. "There's Frankin! There's Telniem! There's the islands I've only ever seen in maps, whose names I don't even know. We could—"

"And would you be content with that? You, who values hive and community so much? A Sealie? Could you live apart from them, from your parents, your people, for all your days, with only me? With *me*? Could you trust me enough for that?"

Robin hesitated before taking in a breath to answer. It was a small one. But for the Coyote, it was enough.

"I see," he said, misery creeping into the gravel of his voice. "I cannot give up *my* people, *my* family, *my* culture so easily, either, Skylark. Especially knowing that there would be no welcome for me in your country."

"You don't know that," Robin protested.

"Oh, but I do," he said with a bitter half-nod. "I know that very well indeed. And yet . . ." He held out his free hand, palm up, fingers beckoning. Begging. "Do not leave me, Skylark. As captives, we can be together. As captives, we owe no one allegiance but one another. We can have that, at least."

"I can't do that." Robin took a small step back, just to see if he would let her. He did, and she took several more, quickly, putting as much space as she could between them without knowing the forest floor, without tangling or toppling herself because she wasn't looking where she was going.

"Then . . . then I will . . ." The Coyote hesitated, licking his kiss-raw lips, and then squared his shoulders. *"Minn abin votch!* Then I will come with you. We will make a hash of it, I am sure, but we—"

The small crack of a twig snapping yanked Robin's attention to a dark pool of shadow just behind the Coyote's shoulder. Moonlight flashed on metal and—

"Get down!" Robin shouted. Panic drowned out caution. She lunged back toward the wall, to where she'd left WINGS.

There was the sharp report of a pistol just beside her, and she rolled to the side as dirt and twigs sprayed upward. She had the sinking feeling that whoever was shooting at her had missed on purpose. As she slung the string of the burlap sack over her shoulder, she spared a glance at the Coyote, sprawled on the ground to the side, but still breathing, still whole, *thank the gods.* But he was staring up in horror at the soldier with the pistol—the seneschal.

And his weapon wasn't aimed at Robin.

CHAPTER TWENTY-ONE

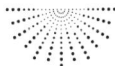

Robin stared down at the screwdriver in her hand and swallowed hard. She had been living on edge for so long that she had forgotten what it meant to really feel that surge of fear, to really believe that it was possible you were about to die.

It felt just like being strapped into a glider again. It felt fantastic! It felt like freedom. And if she only had her glider now, she could . . .

Daring to take her eyes off the Coyote, Robin put her screwdriver back in her boot sheath and brushed her crossed fingers over her shoulder. Slowly, as soundlessly as possible, she reached inside the burlap sack, getting her hand on the control box, and then froze when she heard a soft click beside her ear. The round tip of the barrel tickled through the hair on her temple.

"You give this? To *her*?" the seneschal sneered, and Robin felt the mouth of the pistol nudge the cameo at the top of hair pin. "And yet, this too is useful. You give her that, and you give us the key to your cooperation. Understand what is at stake if you move against me, boy. I will not hesitate."

The Coyote nodded, once, his features battling against the mask of his control, barely containing the snarl on his lips. He rose to his knees, and crossed his hands behind his head demonstratively.

The seneschal scoffed, and then poked the back of Robin's head twice with the pistol. "Up. Up."

Desperate horror bloomed on the Coyote's face as Robin stood at the bidding of the pistol. Robin withdrew her hand, the one closest to the seneschal, slowly from the bag, raising it above her head, trusting the shadow cast by both their bodies to keep her other arm hidden.

"Do not do this," the Coyote pleaded. "Please, she is not like the others, I swear to you. Spare her, and we—"

"Silence, *Dei*," the seneschal snarled. His grip shifted on the butt of the pistol. "Your brother is most disappointed in you."

The Coyote swallowed hard, the fear on his face ratcheting up. Robin had never seen him be so open, so *himself*, while in the presence of others. That, more than anything, sent terror shivering up her spine.

"You, girl," the seneschal ordered. "Come."

"No," Robin said.

The seneschal hesitated, clearly not expecting her defiance. "*Nema?*"

"*Nema*," she agreed, and then repeated it again, "No." The more she said it, the more powerful she felt. The more she knew it was the right choice.

"Very well." The tip of the gun brushed her cheek, and then pointed downward, toward her knee. "The general only needs you alive and able to fix the pack. I shall leave your hands as they are. However, you cannot run from us if you cannot walk."

"Wait! Just wait," Robin said, stalling. One arm still buried inside the sack, she deftly wriggled her fingers to get her wrist through the strap of the control box. "Please, just wait. I, uh, you . . . you're not really going to shoot me!"

"No? And what makes you think so? You are the one who has brought us to this impasse, after all," the seneschal sniffed.

"Okay, okay!" Robin said, playacting cowardice. "I'll come. I swear I'll come. Just point that somewhere else." Unseen, her hand slipped through the leather loop. Her fingers found the buttons. She met the Coyote's eyes across the darkness separating them. They were wide, and sad, and scared, but *proud*, too —proud of her, she realized, and Robin clutched that close, jammed it into her heart.

"*I am sorry,*" she mouthed. A small, sad half-smile quirked in the corner of his lips, acknowledging what she'd finally ceded to him—no contractions. He nodded back, grim, and final in a way that made Robin's guts twist. *Oh, gods,* she thought suddenly. *This might kill him, too. This might . . . no, go, go, he's given you his blessing, you just need to . . . omens, don't be a coward. Do it!*

"I just . . . I have a question," Robin asked, shifting backward subtly so that the tail of WINGS was aimed in the seneschal's direction, desperately thinking, *please, please let this work.*

"And that is?"

"What makes you think I haven't already fixed it?" She shook the sack lightly, indicating what she meant, but also to get the straps over her shoulders. WINGS wasn't designed to be worn on the front of a body, but right now, Robin was willing to take that risk.

"It works?" the seneschal asked, taking a step forward, trying to get a good look at the sack through the shadows. She couldn't see his eyes, but his surprise was written all over his posture.

"I sure hope so!" Robin said as she slapped the button that ignited the engine.

WINGS rumbled, and the exhaust ports flared to life—and the seneschal *screamed.*

Robin shot backward, the angle of her ascent taking her up over the forest canopy and halfway across the forest itself before the spurt of inertia sputtered out and the engine went silent. For a brief, glorious second, she sailed through the night. Then she landed heavily on her back amid the dried, dead husks of a field of autumn grain, all breath wuffing out of her as her stomach was driven up against her spine and the ivory hairpin jammed against her neck. She slapped at the pack controls, and the engine spluttered to a stop.

"Holy rudding omens!" she blurted as she saw the dark swatch through the dried soil she'd cut with her back. She was bent awkwardly against a stalk, and she gave herself to the count of ten to catch her breath and clear her head of vertigo before she tried to move. A flare of pain in her ribs told her that she'd probably aggravated the old injury, but she breathed through it, and it faded soon enough.

Then she sat up, pulled what remained of the smoldering burlap off of WINGS, and inspected the pack. It looked just fine. She turned it around and strapped herself in properly, control box on her wrist, straps across her collarbones, fit snug around her waist and between her legs.

In the distance, someone screamed again, but she was too far away to know which of them it was. A chorus of flat cracks, like a cacophony of gunshots, filled the air. The seneschal's pistol had probably been caught in the wash of fire, making the ammunition go up like Gods' Day fireworks. The seneschal could hang, for all she cared, but the Coyote . . . *I can't let him burn to death! Not like Al.*

Her feet were already leading her back toward him before she'd even realized she had taken a step. But it was already too late. If she went to him, she'd be caught.

And he might not even be alive anymore. The thought slammed into her guts like a fist. To have had him, for just a moment, or to have thought she had him, and then . . . then . . .

No, she told herself. *No. There's nothing you can do.*

You killed him. Bile filled her throat, noxious and horrible. She swallowed hard against the sudden rush of nausea. *You kissed him, and then you killed him. That horrific screeching, that's the sound of him screaming, the sound of him dying, and you—you just—*Robin bent double and emptied her stomach onto the ground. It was awful, acidic, and she heaved and sobbed at the same time, guts churning and heart cracking, even as she jammed her palms against her ears.

As soon as she was able to get herself back under control, she stumbled backward, away from the puddle of puke. She spat hard, over and over again, trying to get the sour taste out of her mouth, trying to remember, to chase the phantom memory of the wine and apples that had been the Coyote's kiss.

His last kiss.

She ran the back of her hand across her mouth, then scrubbed at her cheeks with her sleeve. *Get it together*, she shouted at herself. *If you keep standing here like a stupid duck, they'll catch you! Don't . . . don't waste his sacrifice like that. Don't waste Al's sacrifice like that.*

A faint orange glow bled between the trees in the distance. A plume of black smoke had begun to blot out the stars. The sound of the soldiers and dogs was becoming audible again, along with the crackle of winter-dry timber.

Go! The least you can do is trust him now. Follow the clues, and hope they lead to some sort of civilization.

All around her, there was nothing. No one. Just open air.

It didn't feel like the victory it should have.

Joy warred with grief and regret. Shoving aside the tangle of feelings, she planted her feet and looked at the sky she'd so desperately missed. Feeling for the button with her free hand, she depressed the ignition slowly. WINGS made an enthusiastic chugging sound. The thick leather pad against her back warmed slightly as the two cylinders began to bottle up their exhaust. Pressing the second button, Robin pushed off with a jump, and couldn't help but whoop with elation, though it was a sodden, wet cry of triumph, as the thrust from the pack kept her aloft.

She pushed the second button again, and the output increased. WINGS thrust her high above the treetops. Knowing herself to be practically invisible in the night, save for the glimmer of flame at the base of the exhaust ports, Robin angled her body horizontal. A faint orange glow rose just above the tree-tops. With a glance at the stars to verify her direction, Robin deduced that it must be Lylon, or some other large town. The city, whichever one it was, was far enough south of the front lines that it probably wasn't an Air Patrol bombing target, or else it wouldn't have been so lit up. *I can lose myself in a city*, she thought.

Grit was in her eyes as the wind whipped the last of the tears off her face. She pulled the goggles up from around her neck so she could see where she was going, though they darkened every-thing considerably. Then she raised her scarred palms to the sky. Flying without a glider was even better than she'd thought it would be. It was a shame that she'd had no time to experiment, no time to learn the intricacies of flight, no time to play. A shame that she couldn't share this with . . . with . . .

A shame that all she could do was run.

Unless . . .

Unless she stopped running altogether. Unless she used WINGS as the Coyote had meant it to be used: to strike terror into the hearts of the enemy, to make them flee, to make them *lose*.

"No more running," Robin decided, shouting over the roar of the wind. "You hear that, gods? You hear me, WINGS? We're not going to run! And we're not going home. Not until the job is done. The only way I'm getting home is if this war is over. And if Saskwya can't end it"—she looked over her shoulder at WINGS —"and if he can't be here to do it with me, then I will rudding well do it myself!"

Curious of what would happen, Robin deployed the blades of the pack. Her flight stabilized slightly, but even more fantastic, the vibration of the air as it passed over the steel made the blades hum. It was a sweet, clear, and cyclical chord, like birdsong.

Pumped up on the elation of escape and the affirmation of a choice well made, Robin hummed along with WINGS as she flew.

"And bees shall follow me home," they sang together. One voice pure and clean, the other crackled with a grief she wouldn't allow herself to feel, not until she was safe.

Together, it was almost loud enough to cover the sound of her heart breaking.

A SEALIE DRINKING SONG

(TRADITIONAL PUB CALL-AND-RESPONSE SONG; TO A RHYTHM)

Drink up ye lads,
And drink up lasses!
Quickly now,
For life soon passes!

Tilt the glass,
And open your throat,
And pour it in,
Until ye float!

So drink up lads,
And drink up lasses!
Quickly now,
For life soon passes!

Our feet are nailed
To cobbled stone,
And we've been forced
To call this home!

So drink up lads,
And drink up lasses!
Quickly now,
For life soon passes!

But our hearts,
Still with the gods,
Are freer than
They'll give in odds!

So drink up lads,
And drink up lasses!
Quickly now,
For life soon passes!

So drink your wine,
So down your mead,
So guzzle your beer,
And thank the bees.

Yes, drink up lads,
And drink up lasses!
Quickly now,
For life soon passes!

Finish your whiskey,
Finish your gin,
Finish your rum,
For what might have been.

Aye, drink up lads,
And drink up lasses!
Quickly now,
For life soon passes!

A thumb at Benne,
A thumb at Klonn,
A thumb for oppressors,
All dead and gone.

Quick, drink up lads,
And drink up lasses!
Quickly now,
For life soon passes!

But we are alive,
And we are in love,
And here we drink
Thank gods above!

So drink up lads,
And drink up lasses!
Quickly now,
For life soon passes!

Oh, drink up ye lads,
And drink up lasses!
Quickly now,
For life soon passes!

ACKNOWLEDGMENTS

The Skylark's journey from concept to published page has been a harrowing one. The third full novel I ever completed, and the first one I ever wrote specifically with the intention of showing to my agent for publication, this novel has left me crying on a street corner in New York City, laughing and dancing in a white wig at a steampunk festival, filled with me with hope for my career, and filled me with despair. There are about seventy labeled drafts of this book on my hard drive. In the time that I've been working on this novel, steampunk has seen a resurgence, and an ebbing away again. The novel inspired a beautiful song of the same name by french band *Victor Sierra*, which ended up coming out *years* before the novel. So, needless to say, this piece of work has been a real . . . piece of work.

Maybe I should have given up.

Maybe I should have trunked it and moved on to the next thing. (I half-did, many times). But then we wouldn't be here, would we, in a time when discussions around religious freedom are so important in the real world, and the themes and aims of this novel have finally crystalized for me.

This novel was conceived at the first—and though we didn't

know it then, only—Canadian National Steampunk Exhibition, which was, to date, one of the most fun cons I've ever been to. Two wonderful things came out of that weekend for me. (Well, three, if you count Professor Elemental taking a nap on my shoulder in the Green Room, which was pretty cool, in and of itself).

First, I was put on a panel with Dr. Mike "The Steampunk Scholar" Perschon, where we sassed and snipped and laughed together as if we'd known each other for years, when we'd actually known each other mere moments. Mike's friendship has lasted beyond that weekend, and I treasure it daily.

Secondly, I accepted a drunken dare.

The thing you have to understand about a bunch of theatre majors getting together to put on costumes and drink for a weekend is that, eventually, somebody's gonna start making up *stories*. Or dare someone else to do it. And somebody is gonna be stupid enough to accept.

Steampunk costumes come in stereotypes, and what we had sitting in the circle that night was this: a biomechanical assassin, a devious airship piratess, an aviator in a white wig (me), and a wily spy-mistress-cum-madam and her secretly clever mountain of a bodyguard-slash-lover.

The first incarnation of *The Skylark's Song* was born that night, as I pointed to each character in turn and declared how our backstories were connected, conjuring the Saskwyan-Klonnish war out of the wine fumes.

Through edits and revisions, the biomechanical assassin eventually became an enemy aeroship ace. The piratess became a devious friend of the cause. And everyone swapped skin tones because, even if all of us were (mostly) white, there was no inherent reason why the protagonists of a book set in a pseudo-fantasy land had to be.

The Skylark's Song was the first (and only) complete novel I presented to my first agent, and the one that taught me that there is such a thing as the right fit in this industry. It was the first novel I presented to my current agent, as well, but we put it to the side because by then, it had been so worked over that we had to take it back about twenty-five drafts and figure out where it had all gone wrong. In the meantime, I had written *The Untold Tale*, which ended up ballooning (in a good way) into a series.

And in that time, the Skylark circled in my brain, coasting on the updraft, waiting her turn.

What followed after was five years of realigning, recasting, changing the motivations, the appearance, the beliefs, and the core traits of the characters. One character was removed entirely, only to return as the love interest when my first agent demanded that there be one—a love interest who has switched sides so many times that I don't think even he remembers who he's loyal to, and has switched names so often that I barely remember what it was to begin with. The poor man flip-flopped between being Robin's Wickham and being Robin's Darcy so many times that I think he wishes I would never watch another Jane Austen film adaptation ever again.

But here it is.

Finally.

From drunken dare to the book you now hold, it's been a heck of a journey. And it's only half done.

And, like most journeys, this one would have stalled out long before it really got going without the love and support of the following:

Stephanie Lalonde, who is, as ever, the best cheerleader a writer could ask for. Steph is a critical and experienced secondary reader whose squeals of glee often reach supersonic levels, and whose emotional reactions are genuine. When she cries and calls me bad names, that's when I know she likes it. She is also the one person who always knows exactly how the story is supposed to go before she ever picks it up, because she lets me recite the whole plot to her so I can find the holes. And yet, somehow, she still seems surprised and moved by the tale. She is a rare and wonderful friend, and I am lucky to have her in my life.

Adrienne Kress, who helped guide me through the new territory that was YA. When I had to gut the plot and start afresh, she was there to help me through the crippling self-doubt, the shakes, the excesses of tea, and to challenge me to make my characters behave in realistic, emotional ways.

I also want to thank the following people for courteously allowing me the use of their characters, gadgets, costumes, and ideas as the building blocks of the world: Kenneth Shelley, Stephanie Lalonde, Joshua Boycott, and Ashley Regimbal-Kung.

Gabrielle Harbowy, who edited the book in a record amount of time when I needed a second pair of eyes, way back when this all started, and who always takes my panicked phone calls and helps me tease out the strongest way to tell my stories.

Karen Wood, for loving everything I write, even when we both know it's not that good yet and what she's really loving is just the potential.

Ruthanne Reid, another marvelous beta reader and fellow author who taught me the importance of "tweak, tweak, tweak."

Brienne Wright, who keeps my feet on the ground, but my dreams in the air, and calls me the most vicious names when I thwart her hopes in-book.

Laurie McLean, my agent at Fuse Literary, who read this back before she was ever my agent, and who became a great pilot on this then-rudderless project.

Kisa Whipkey, the editor who finally helped me find what this book is *about*.

The REUTS Publications team—Voule, Kisa, and Ashley—who took on this book and dealt elegantly with an extremely shortened deadline when it was sprung upon us.

Also, a big thanks to the members of the Toronto Steampunk Society for letting me lurk among their ranks, and to all the guests, organizers, and attendees of the Canadian National Steampunk Expo for being the best research petri dish a girl could ask for. I must especially highlight Liana K., Adam Smith, Amanda Stock, Countess Leonora, Steampunk Canada, Mike "The Steampunk Scholar" Perschon, Doctor Terrawatt, Professor Elemental, and Jaymee Goh/Silver Goggles, for being willing to chat with me about what steampunk means to them, and why it's a vital SF/F cultural, performative, and literary aesthetic.

ABOUT THE AUTHOR

J.M. is a voice actor, SF/F author, professionally trained music theatre performer, not-so-trained but nonetheless enthusiastic screenwriter and webseries-ist, and a fanthropologist and pop culture scholar. She's appeared in podcasts, documentaries, radio programs, and on television to discuss all things geeky through the lens of academia. J.M. lives near Toronto, loves tea, scarves, and Doctor Who (all of which may or may not be related), and her epic dream is to one day sing a duet with John Barrowman.

Her debut novel *Triptych* was nominated for two Lambda Literary Awards, nominated for the CBC Bookie Award, was named one of Publishers Weekly's Best Books of 2011, was on The Advocate's Best Overlooked Books of 2011 list, received an honorable mention at the London Book Festival in Science Fiction, and won the San Francisco Book Festival for Science Fiction.

Connect with J.M.
jmfrey.net